My Life

Without

You

Adrienne L. Edwards

My Life

Without

You

Adrienne L. Edwards

Published by
Discovering Beautiful Minds
P. O. Box 380391
Clinton Township, MI 48038

Discovering Beautiful Minds

P. O. Box 380391

Clinton Township, MI 48038

My Life Without You

Library of Congress Control Number

Identifiers: LCCN 2021900366

ISBN: 978-1-7352064-0-0

For more information contact:

Discovering Beautiful Minds, LLC

Email: info@Discoveringbeautifulminds.com

Website: www.discoveringbeautifulminds.com

Printed in the United States of America

Dedication

To all who have been hurt, don't let your past keep you from living. Love yourself. Forgive yourself. Forgive those who hurt you, and live in peace.

Spread your wings and fly freely.

Prologue

March 2, 2015

After waiting fifteen minutes in the exam room, there was a light tap at the door.

"Come in, Valerie said softly." She closes her diary and places it beside her.

"Hello, Ms. Augustine. How are you today?" Dr. Elliot is tall and slender. His silver hair is trimmed low.

While shaking his hand, Valerie replies, "I'm pretty good Doctor Elliot, thanks for asking."

"So, what brings you in today, Ms. Augustine?"

She tosses her braids over her shoulder. "Well, for one, I keep having sharp, cramping feelings in my stomach. I'm not on my cycle, but cramping is the only way that I can describe the pain that I feel sometimes."

"Where is the pain located?"

Placing her hand on her stomach— "Right here on my lower right side."

"When was your last menses?" Dr. Elliot questions, his pen moving as he writes her responses down.

"It was about a month ago. I don't remember the exact date cause I forgot to put it in my calendar." Val stares blankly upwards, then shrugs her shoulders.

Dr. Elliot takes some notes in his chart. "And is there anything else?"

"Yeah, I've been feeling nauseous, but I think it's the iron pills you put me on. And I don't wanna keep taking 'em cause they make me sick to my stomach."

Dr. Elliot takes no time completing a physical on Valerie and then leaves the room.

Shortly later, Dr. Elliot is back in with Valerie's test results.

"Well, I don't think it's the iron pills that are making you sick. And I don't think it's a wise choice for you to stop taking them either."

Her eyebrows arched. Valerie feels her palms begin to sweat as her body grew warmer with anxiety.

"Why not?" she finally replies.

"To answer your question frankly, Ms. Augustine, your blood is already too low, and you're going to need higher levels of iron, especially right now.

Valerie's face is flushed pink as she stares at the doctor waiting for him to finish.

"You're pregnant Ms. Augustine," the doctor said calmly. "About six weeks along, and you're going to need to keep taking the pills to supply healthy amounts of iron to you and your baby."

Immediately, Valerie's world seems to come to a screeching halt. Shocked, Valerie drops her head down to look at her stomach. She touches her belly lightly—her mind racing with unnerving thoughts of being a mother. How could I be so absent-minded? I'm such an idiot. Tears begin to fall down her cheeks slowly. Valerie is overwhelmed with emotions, and she knows she has to tell Romelle soon. Somehow, she will have to break the news tonight.

"When you're ready Ms. Augustine, you can put your clothes back on. I want to schedule you for some more tests," the doctor said cautiously. "I want to make sure that you don't have any complications concerning the pregnancy since you mentioned the pain that you were having."

Wiping away the streaks of tear stains from her face, "What do you mean? Is everything okay? Is the baby going to be ok?" Her eyes are wide with concern.

"No need to worry right now. I'm sure everything's alright. We just need to run some precautionary tests. We will give you some referrals to an OBGYN, and I will leave these pamphlets for you on becoming a mom, and what to expect when you're expecting."

Valerie nods her head. Emotions start to rush in, and she can't help but think...

What if he's up to no good? I wonder what he's been doing lately? After I forgave him for letting some random chic feel all on him at a party last year—he bet not be doing some stupid shit!

He's always busy lately. And some random number keeps calling him, that he never answers whenever I'm around. I swear... If he's cheating on me, I'm smashing every last window in his car, and pouring bleach on all his clothes!

Thoughts fill her mind as she leaves the clinic with referrals and pamphlets on becoming a mom.

I'm really pregnant... Having this baby is going to change everything. Is Ro gonna be happy that we're having a baby? We should be fine. I can get a full-time job after my classes to pull my weight. Ro doesn't need to worry about anything because I'm still going to get my degree and I'll have a job in my field soon.

She sits in her car. The parking lot is half empty. She glances out the car window, and her mind begins to fill with hope. I did forgive him for the incident last year. So won't he forgive me for missing my birth control pill just one time?

It was evening time, and Romelle was driving Val out for a dinner date. Valerie didn't say much to Ro on their way to Olive Garden. All she can think about is how she is going to tell him they were having a baby. The anxiety is overwhelming. He will be happy, she thought. He always said that one day he wanted a little boy or girl to raise. I don't know how we are going to do this, but it'll all work out. Maybe we can start looking for a place together—A cozy two-bedroom apartment. We have a great relationship, so what can go wrong?

Romelle pulls up in the parking spot closest to the door. Looking over at Val, Ro asks, "So do you know if you're working on my birthday yet babe?"

Snapping back from daydreaming, Valerie looks at Ro and simply responds, "Yes. Wait. No, I meant my time off request was approved earlier this week, so I'm off."

Working for the biggest electronic store in Detroit was always fun and kept Valerie busy. But how could she work full time, go to school full time, and raise a baby? That question has been running in Vale's mind since she'd left the doctor's office.

The evening air was brisk and wet. Snow has just fallen, and it looks like a white Christmas all over again. Winter has come in with a blazing furry. Snowstorms after snowstorms nearly left the city of Detroit buried in their homes. Yet, there are still more heavy snowstorms to come. Valerie is used to the cold winters in Michigan. Salt trucks always line the major streets, ready to plow at any given notice. Winter this year is brutal, harsh, and unforgiving. However, spring is just around the corner.

As the Italian restaurant became increasingly closer, Val takes in the picturesque scenery—city lights, people hustling to get out of the blistering cold, city buses going by, and sounds of horns blaring in the distance as cars hustle about.

Grabbing Valerie's hand as she climbs out the car, Romelle shut the car door of his 2014 black Magnum behind her. He pushes his broad shoulders up against her as he wraps his long arms around her slender waist. "You know I love you, right?"

Her heart fluttering, she hardly notices the spine-shivering cold in the evening air. "Yes," she replies warmly. She follows alongside Ro as he leads her by the hand to the restaurant.

"Good evening, how many tonight?" the hostess asks, as they both walk in.

Valerie and Romelle step up to the counter. "Two please," Ro replies.

"Right this way please." As the hostess leads them to their table, she lays down two menus.

"It's a slow night tonight," Romelle said, shifting in his seat across from Val after she sits down.

Val doesn't respond, She, instead looks down at the menu, turning the pages back and forth.

"What's up with you tonight Val? You seem distant. Is everything okay? Did everything go okay at the doctor's?"

Before Valerie could have a chance to respond, the waitress appears to introduce herself and take their orders. They both ordered two strawberry lemonades with light ice.

Ro glances back at Val after the waitress left. Pulling his shoulder-length dreads back into a ponytail, "So, what's the word? What did you have to tell me?"

With her stomach turning and twisting into knots, Val feels her throat becomes restricted—lumps forming in her throat. She swallows hard, wishing she had a glass of water. She doesn't know how her boyfriend is going to take the news. She barely understands how she's dealing with it herself. Deciding to tell him the lighter news first. She clears her throat...

"Well, as I said, I do have your birthday off, and I know you wanted to go to Miami for your birthday. But I have a surprise."

"Okay, what is it? Spit it out, Val!"

"Well... The surprise is, I booked us a seven-day Caribbean cruise babe!"

"Wait, what? Really?!" He shifts his body upright. His eyes are intent.

"Really!" Val replies. "On the Oasis of The Seas."

That's awesome Val! When did you do that? What day do we leave?"

"I booked the trip earlier this week, and we leave on your birthday."

Ro leans over the table to give Val a kiss.

Valerie feels a warm sensation trickle down her body as the heat from Ro's kiss envelopes her.

"Thanks, baby! I can't wait until we get there!"

As the waiter approaches, she sits the drinks down on the table. Valerie writes something down on a napkin with her pen. She knew that Romelle was not paying attention. Ro is busy ordering their food.

Romelle turns and looks at Val, "You still haven't said anything about the doctor's visit today."

Val's wipes her palms across her pants, trying to dry the sweat from them. With her right leg bouncing up and down, Val tries to get out the other news. She takes a sip from her glass." "Ro, it's something else I need to tell you," she finally responds. "It's about the doctor's visit."

"Are you okay? Did you find out why you've been in so much pain?"

"Yes, babe, I did."

"Well,... What did they say?"

She saw the concerned look in Ro's eyes, so she just slid him the napkin that she'd handwritten a message on.

Staring at her, he grabs it and opens it up.

"We're pregnant Ro," he reads out loud. Ro just stares at the napkin without a word. His eyes remain fixed on the words.

She couldn't read his facial response. "Ro, please say something."

Finally, looking back up at Val, Ro broke his silence. "I leave for basic training at the end of next month," he blurts out.

Her eyes narrow sternly across at Romelle; her eyes burn. Angry, Valerie yells, "Wait! What do you mean you're leaving for basic training next month?" Her blood boils over and up through her veins like a knight thrusting his lance through his opponent. Val's demeanor changes drastically. She sits straight up, and her lips press together tightly.

"I didn't want to tell you like this."

Her dark brown eyes become wet as she fights back the tears. She draws her hands back as she feels Romelle's hands clasp hers.

"Val, I met with a Navy recruiter a month ago. I didn't want anyone to change my mind, so when I spoke with my dad, he told me to follow my dreams. I promise I was gonna tell you."

"When Romelle?! The day you were gonna leave?"

"No, I just found out today that I passed my test when you were at your appointment." Ro reaches for her hands and plants them in the palm of his. "The recruiter told me this afternoon, I swear Val. I didn't want to say anything until I knew for sure that I was eligible to go."

Val looks at him intently. She yanks her hands away from him as her hands start to become numb. Her breath elevates as she pants with anger. The banging in her head makes her feel as if she has just got run over by a Mack truck. "What about school Ro? Aren't you going to stay in school to become a Marine Biologist? Are you really just gonna drop out, after all your hard work?"

His tone changes rapidly, "Going to the military is the best decision for me right now. How could I be so stupid and believe that you would be supportive of my decision? I'm not changing my mind. I'm going whether you like it or not!"

Valerie's drenched cheeks was soaked with tears rolling down like a steady stream of rain falling off a rooftop. Thoughts of abandonment start to fill her mind. Feelings of heartbreak and pain cover her entire body. Her anger for Ro intensifies—"I can't believe this!" She couldn't understand why Romelle was going to leave her. Feelings of betrayal, discouragement, and anguish flood her mind.

"What about you and me Ro? We were planning our life together, and now it seems you have planned it without me. And what am I supposed to do now that I'm pregnant, raise our baby by myself?"

"Baby look, I know that this is untimely news right now—"

She abruptly cuts him off, "Untimely news! No, this is crazy! Are you seriously going to go?" Pounding her fists on the table—her voice is stern. "You can't go now. We're having a baby. Can't you change your mind or something?"

"Val, first, lower your voice! Second, no, I can't just change my mind."

"Why not Ro?" she said, slamming her right hand on the table. "Don't you love me?"

People are staring at them and whispering. The waiter comes over with their food and places it on the table. "Will there be anything else?" she asked.

Ro shakes his head. "I signed my papers today Val!" Romelle responds. His tone is strong but lower this time. "The recruiter asked me to stop by his office, and I swore-in already. I'm not staying here. Like I said before, I'm not changing my mind, not for school, not for you, and not for anyone else either! I told you this was for me. You always want to do things your way," Ro continues. "Why do I have to stay here? Why can't you just let me do this one thing? I'll come back for you, I promise," he said, as his deep hazel eyes gaze into hers. I mean, I'm not thrilled your pregnant right now, but that doesn't mean we can't make this work even with me in the military.

"No, that's not how it's going to work. If you leave, we're done. Cause if you go, you're going to leave, and you'll find someone else to love. I'm not stupid Ro. You won't come back," she said. Her slumped shoulders gave way to the embarrassment that she feels, the heartache and the disappointment.

"You really think the sun rises and sets on your ass every day. You're always trying to tell me what to do! And you think that I have to listen to you!"

"No, I don't!" she cried.

His voice rises gradually. "See Val, that's the problem. This has always been the problem with you and me. You never want to listen, and you never want to hear my side. You're Selfish! So damn selfish Valerie!"

Valerie gasps as she sits back in her chair. His tone is harsh and unforgiving. Sitting and soaking in embarrassment, Valerie clasps her hands tight, and before she could say another word, she notices the eyes of people staring. The restaurant seems to have paused in time. The couple next to them was staring and listening to their every word. She covers her face with both palms of her hands. "I thought you said it's you and me forever?

I thought you said you would always be there. You lied Ro. You lied," she cried. Her tone is strong, "I hate you, Ro!"""

After that day at the restaurant, Valerie hasn't spoken a word to Romelle. She reluctantly cancels their cruise, and she continues to go to school with no sign of Ro anywhere around. She cries herself to sleep every night. She feels empty and lost. She can't bring herself to pick up the phone to call him. *Why should I call him? He doesn't want the baby or me. Ro has always been stubborn. Why do I love him so much? Why can't I just let him go?*

He is more than just her boyfriend. More than just the father of her child. He is her best friend. The only one who knew her secrets, and the only one she trusts to the end of time. Val loves Ro unconditionally, and nothing was going to change that.

Val sits in her bedroom, the dim lights reflect off of her desk. Soft music plays in the background. The air in her room is frigid, and one lamp dims the vastly dark room. She strolls over opposite her bed and takes her journal and pen out her desk.

Dear Romelle,

This is very hard to say. Nothing could have prepared me for this moment. I don't know where to begin. Please understand that I'm not angry with you. I want you to know that I'm at peace with you leaving. At first, I was furious and could not understand why you would choose to enlist in the military. With a baby on the way, I wanted us to become even closer. I was looking forward to our future and starting a family together, yet

I want you to live your life the way you wanted. I see now that I was stopping you from doing what you felt was best for you. I also want you to know that I have decided to terminate the pregnancy as of three days ago. I didn't want to tell you in person, and I didn't want you to change my mind, so I decided to tell you in this letter. I didn't want it to be like this. It hurts me incredibly, but I know this was best. You will always be my world and my best friend—and I will always love you.

I Love you beyond forever,

~Val.

With a firm grip, Valerie nestles her nose up to her scented red teddy bear she sleeps with every night. The smell of his cologne lingers on it— reminding her of him and the moments they shared together. The sound of their favorite song by Maxwell plays on her speaker. The sight of their picture on her nightstand all grieved Valerie to no end. She drifts off to sleep, her tears soaking into her satin pillowcase.

Valerie's phone blares and wakes her out of her sleep. It's five o'clock in the morning. Four new text messages. She opens the new messages that lit-up across her screen, blaring Ro's name with a heart emoji's behind it.

Ro

I'm here at MEPS. I really hope you come see me off.

I miss you!

I apologize for our fight.

Why are you not returning my text and calls?

How many times do I have to say I'm sorry.

I need to see you before I leave babe. The bus pulls off for the airport at 10:00.

Please come Val. I love you.

It was a new enlistees ship-out day, and Valerie was still so upset with Romelle that she couldn't stand to see him off. She takes her phone and snaps a picture of her letter she wrote last night. She sends a text message out to Romelle... Read on the plane—NOT A MINUTE BEFORE!

Chapter 1

Sunday, August 02, 2019

It's been four years since Valerie saw or heard anything from her best friend. After one year of crying and depression, Valerie learns to live and move on with her life. Although moving on came with a lot of lonely nights, feelings of abandonment, and new responsibilities, Valerie was not going to let her decisions in life define her, nor stop her from finishing her business degree at Wayne State University.

Now twenty-four, she reminisces on how she walked proudly across the stage with two-year-old Nairobi by her side. I remember just like it was yesterday when I had my daughter. My little girl is turning four in one week. Wow! She's growing so fast, Valerie thought as she stared at her daughter while she was sleeping in her pink princess-themed canopy bed.

"Hey babe."

Turning around to face her husband, "Yes, Rick?"

"Are you going to stand there all night watching our little girl, or you gonna come to bed?"

"Sorry honey," Valerie responds quickly. "I must've lost track of time after I put her to bed. Let me go into Noah's room real quick and kiss him goodnight. I'll be right there."

Valerie walks into six-year-old Noah's room—kissing him goodnight. She pulls the covers up over his chest and turns his Spiderman lamp off before she leaves out.

Noah is from Rick's previous marriage. His skin complexion is brown and a mix between cocoa brown and dark brown. Rick's former wife passed away shortly after delivering Noah, just two years of marriage; Rick had to adjust to being a single parent.

Walking into their bedroom at the end of the hallway, Val comes up behind her husband, wrapping her arms around his stocky build. Planting her head upon his back, she leans in and embraces the firmness of his body.

Rick turns around, leans down, and kisses his wife. Rick strokes her neck as he softly kisses her lips, her left cheek, and then her right. Finally, after kissing her forehead, he gazes into her deep dark eyes. His smooth-warm skin envelops his wife with comport.

"Meeting you is like waking up to a fresh new morning of ocean waves rushing upon the shoreline," Rick said smoothly. His voice is deep and tranquilizing.

Valerie loves how he always reminds her of his affection for her often. She didn't imagine ever falling-in-love again, especially with a professor. She met him at a business seminar that was held at the university. There he stood at the podium talking, his voice soothing and handsome. After the two-hour seminar ended, Rick stayed around for a meet and greet. Valerie stood listening nearby and found him very interesting and easy on the eyes. Approaching Val, Rick reaches his hand out to shake hers. "Hi, I'm Rick Finway, and who might you be?" he said. His deep-raspy voice catches her by surprise. Val would later find out that he had been eyeing her the whole time and made it his business to make it over to her. Something about him piqued her interest, as she would later agree to meet Rick the next day for coffee.

Wasting no time proposing to Valerie—Rick bent down on one knee after dinner one Sunday afternoon. After six months of dating, he had told her he knew she was the one and needed her in his life—six months later, she was married--but kept her last name. The wedding was quick and simple—Rick announced to her that it was love at first sight. Rick confessed how much he adores her smile, laughter, and the joy she brought to him and Noah.

As they both stood at the Alter, she would watch her husband say to his friends and family... "Valerie you were not hard to fall in love with—I loved you from the moment we met. You clicked with Noah and me seamlessly, as we did with you and Nairobi. You make me live again... I will love you forever until forever doesn't exist anymore—and even then, you will still have my heart."

Rick built a home from the ground shortly after marrying Valerie. Living in Chesterfield—enjoying their three bedrooms with an office, a third-floor balcony overlooking the pool in the back of their home, a natural fireplace, which they use in the winter months. The finished basement was complete with a half bath, an office room, and an arcade room.

Just five days away from Nairobi's birthday, Valerie's anxious to see the Cinderella-themed birthday party next week.

"Honey!"

"Yes, Val?" Rick replies. "I'm finishing up with fixing the drain in the kitchen."

Walking into the kitchen, Val grabs a glass out of the cabinet. "I'm about to make some lemonade, would you like some?"

"No thanks, love. I just had a beer."

Val sighs under her breath. She stares at her husband who's head is buried underneath the sink. "Just one right?" she said finally.

Rick slides from under the sink. His eyes are fixed on his wife. "Yeah, just one Valerie." he responds. "What are you? My mother?" he asks with a firm look.

Val smiles and brushes off his question. "Well, I wanted to talk to you about the party."

"Yeah? What's up?" He brushes his pants in a sweeping motion as he slowly raises himself off the floor.

"Well, I know I told you that the princess bounce house, the pony ride, and the castle cake was going to be $650, but I wanted to add a Cinderella visit with the princess party company."

"What's that?"

"Cinderella comes to visit for an hour—she brings with her the horse and carriage for the girls to ride in for about fifteen mins.

And she also brings the tea and crackers for tea time with Cindy! It would top off the party, don't you think honey?"

"Right? But how much is this going to cost us, Val?"

"Well... As I said, it would top off the party, and I know Nairobi would love to have a visit from Cinderella!"

"Right! But how much is it Valerie?"

"$500."

"What the hell! Why is it so much?" Rick says sharply. He stands with his arms crossed over his chest.

"I know honey. I just want the party to be perfect for our little princess."

"It will be perfect V, without you having to add more expenses to it. She's already going to love her party," Rick snaps sternly.

The weather is warm and muggy. The stifling air sticks heavily in the kitchen. The ceiling fan twirls around fast, admitting a small breeze past Val. The sprinklers spray back and forth on the grass, and a squirrel scurries across the lawn as the water sprays upon his back.

Noticing his annoyance, Val choose her words carefully. "I know that, but I know she would also love a visit from Cinderella—all girls would, so why not let our daughter have this experience, babe?"

"Because I've already paid over $500 for her party, the decorations, and her costume," Rick snaps back. "You want me to spend over a thousand dollars for our daughter's fourth birthday party! I guess next year you gonna want me to spend over two thousand dollars!"

"Why does this have to be such a big fuss over something that is for our daughter? That's okay Rick! You don't have to do it. I'm sorry I even brought it up," Valerie shouts. She grabs her glass of lemonade as she storms out the kitchen, slinging the patio door open.

Valerie was standing on the patio deck outside, pursing her lips together. The thick air sticks to the back of her neck. She wipes the sweat dripping down her face. She stares at two robins flying over her bird feeder when Rick approaches her from the back with a hug. His firm peck pushes up against her back with intensity.

"We can do it baby," he whispers softly in her ear. I'm sorry I got upset with you. I'm supposed to get my mom's roof redone and put in the new hot-water tank next month. Thinking about financing that on my credit card, I must've thrown my frustration off onto you. I'm sorry V. Don't be angry with me, alright? Take our checkbook and go book the Cinderella visit."

Gazing up at her husband as she turns around, his dark eyes penetrate through her heart with love. "Honey, I just want her to feel like a princess," she replies. She lifts herself up on her toes and kisses his lips softly. "I can never stay mad at you too long. You know you have a way of making me forgive you."

Reaching down to pick his wife up, Valerie wraps her legs around his waist and wraps her arms around his neck. "I love you V. You and the children are all I have, and you mean the world to me. Everything I do is to keep you happy."

Kissing his soft-thick lips, "I know dear... I love you for that, and nothing can take my love away from you."

Rick carries his wife as they walk back into the house and pulls the patio sliding-glass doors shut. His arms are wrapped around her firm-curvy butt. As he walks into the living room, he smirks as his wife feels the firmness in his strong-hardened pecks. He glances into her almond-shaped eyes, "Your eyes seem to speak to my whole body," he taunts, as he lowers her onto the couch.

With Noah and Nairobi sleep upstairs, Valerie gives in to her husband's advances. She closes her eyes as he lifts her tennis skirt up and glides his fingers up her pearls. The erotic sensation of lust flows through her body, sending warm vibrations as her heart beats faster and harder. Her pearls are wet as she awaits what he has in store for her. She enjoys the feeling of being his wife, having security, and being in love again. She is deeply in love with Rick, but there is an emptiness that she feels inside— a secret pain that won't go away.

Chapter 2

It was Thursday, one day away from little Nairobi's birthday party. Everything is set for the next day, and Valerie has to make just a few more stops to pick up some things before tomorrow's party. As she heads for the exit door of the bank, she puts her wallet back into her purse. Approaching the exit door, she notices a gentleman standing holding the door open for her. As she looks up to say thank you, she eyes the military officer's uniform.

"Val! Is that you?" the gentleman says.

Glancing up at his handsome, hazel-brown eyes, there is no mistaken what her eyes see standing before her. She can hardly believe it. "Ro?!" He's still very easy on the eyes. She smiles at his clean-shaven face. With his attractive good looks, athletic build, and charismatic tone, Val's whole body goes numb. Her body feels light off the ground as Romelle's long arms wrap around her firmly—twirling her around affectionately. She feels his gaze penetrating through her dark almond eyes...

Still holding Valerie by her waist, as he puts her down, Ro finally broke his silence. "What have you been up to? How have you been?" His smile radiant as he stares at Valerie.

Standing on her tiptoes, arms stretching around his neck, Val delights in the touch of his warm embrace. Taking in her view, she was in awe at his well-defined manly stature and how well he looks in his Navy uniform. Still shocked to see Romelle standing before her, Valerie's cheeks are flushed. Stepping back a pace, eyes bulging, "I'm good. How long have you been back?"

"Two weeks now," Romelle replies.

"What? Really!" She wonders why she's just now running into him. Because... He's not her man— it's probably best. There's no reason for her to have seen him any sooner. Switching topics, she takes in his new appearance. "I see you cut your hair off! No more dreads huh?"

"Yeah, I had to for the military. The only reason I would ever cut it. You like?" He takes his hat off and holds it in his hands.

Her deep-almond-shaped eyes dance in delight. She hesitates, "Yes," she replies.

"You look good Val. Really good," he said, with a boyish grin.

Grinning from ear to ear, she says nothing in response.

"Well, did you finish your degree?" Ro asked.

"Yes, I did finish," she nods. I have my Bachelor of Arts degree in business.

"Really? Wow, I'm so proud of you! I knew you would finish. You've always been a smart student. By the way, how's your mom and dad? Have you spoken to them?

"Yeah," she responds. She steps back for a moment. Her head hangs low.

"Is everything okay?"

"Well, my dad is sick, and he can barely walk anymore." She tosses her braids over her shoulders. Customers walk in and out of the bank as they talk. Val watches as cars pull in and out of the parking lot. The air is warm, and a cool breeze teases the air with a hint of relief.

"Wow, is he going to get better Val?"

"Apparently not," she shrugs. The doctors say he has stage three lung cancer."

"But he never smoked a day in his life! Are they sure?"

"Yes, he has refused any type of medicine or treatment. He's living out his days happily, and he says when it's time for him to go, then it's time for him to go."

With a downcast look, Ro shakes his head. "Wow Val, I'm sorry to hear that. I'm truly sorry that I wasn't here for you."

"It's okay Ro. I know he's ready to go. It's nothing you could've done to make things different."

"No... It's not ok Val. We're best friends, and we always will be. I should've been here for you."

"Well, enough about me Ro, what about you? How was basic training, Mr. Navy man? You got some stories to tell I bet," she smiles.

"Yea, I definitely got plenty of stories to tell. But I want to tell you over dinner or something. I want to meet up with you and talk all night long like we use to when we were kids. You remember how we use to stay up all night talking about life and what we wanted to do?"

Valerie couldn't help but notice the way Romelle's smile lit up. His dimples hung deep. Val's emotions for Ro comes rushing back as she gets a whiff of the familiar smell lingering off in the cool breeze off Romelle's body. She knew he was wearing Cool Water cologne, taking her breath away. As she closes her eyes quickly, she starts to reminisce about the love they once shared. But she knew her thoughts were dangerous, so she opens her eyes quickly and cuts the conversation short.

"Yeah, well, I better get going now. I don't wanna hold you up anymore."

Romelle grabs Valerie's hand as she tries to walk off to her truck, which was just two parking spaces over. Her heart is pulsating as she looks over at him. His hand feels gentle. He has the same look he used to have whenever he didn't want her to go. She remembers how he used to ask her to stay just a little longer with his seductive eyes. His eyes gaze into her eyes as she tries to pull away from his hand.

"Don't go, Val," he said softly. You're not holding me up from anything baby."

Her breath panting faster with nervousness, she takes in a deep breath. She didn't want him to call her that. She's married, and she no longer belongs to Romelle. But who was she fooling? She didn't want to leave. She didn't want him to walk back out of her life.

Chapter 3

August 14, 2019

*Let him who is without sin cast the first stone... Or something
like that— If you knew my story, you wouldn't judge me. Whether I turn out to be a Victim or if I turn out to be a survivor, that
won't define who I am— For I am neither.*

~Val

Valerie fills the pages of her journal up with words she
has not said or written since before her wedding day.
Seeing Romelle sent shock waves down her spine. She
feels overwhelmed with emotions and confused. Why did she
have to see him last week?

Why did he have to look and smell so damn good? That cool,
strong smell of sexy— she was paralyzed the moment she
caught a whiff. Cool Water Cologne—a scent that always peeks
her arousal. It smells clean, refreshingly light with a hint of
masculinity that she'll never forget. That's Ro's scent, and she
will forever be emotionally cuffed to it.

I'm married, why am I feeling this way? Valerie closes her notebook and puts it away. *But who am I kidding? I'll always love him...*

Seeing Romelle was a surprise. She had always had thoughts of him, wondering where he was at? And what was he doing? Thoughts of him never went away. After having Nairobi, thinking of him was overwhelming. Thoughts of him lingering in her mind, seems like forever, as she thought of his scent, the way he always comforted her when she was sad, his funny way of making her laugh through difficult moments, the way his gentle hands caressed her body, and the way they use to kiss so passionately.

Too much came rushing back in all at once. How can I tell him about our daughter? How would he feel knowing that I didn't get an abortion? I never could go through with it... Her head feels like heavy bricks. The pounding headache won't go away. Too many thoughts—too many emotions. She shares something special with Romelle.

Later on that day, Val retreats to the backyard with her family. The afternoon air feels hot and muggy. Early rain showers left the air thick and humid. The sun gleams upon the tall apple tree she has in her back yard that stands adjacent to her flower bed. The flower bed is full of rose-pink tulips that are fully blossomed—yellow and white gardenias and red roses make her yard colorful. The hunter-green grass and flowers sprinkle with vibrant colors and look like a picture right out of the Better Homes & Garden magazine. Valerie takes pride in her yard. She has a lawn company come once a month to manicure it and pull the weeds up. She gazes at the purple and yellow-tinged butterfly as it lands on her rose-pink tulips. The strong-fragrant scent of tulips and gardenias always attracts such beautiful butterflies.

Val sits on her patio deck, staring at her kids playing in the swimming pool with their dad. Rick is splashing Noah and Nairobi with the water as they swim with their inflatable swim ring, tossing their beach ball back and forth across the water.

"Throw me the ball dad," Noah yells out.

Throwing the beach ball at Noah, Rick sends a wave of splashing water with it.

"Daddy, stop! Why you do that?" Noah cries.

"Do what?" Rick begins laughing at his son.

"Splash me with so much water daddy. Now I can't see! You got water in my eyes," Noah says, whimpering.

"Ohhh, poor baby, Nairobi remarks laughing at her brother."

"Shut up, daddy's girl!" Noah snaps with a thrust of water towards his sister.

"You shut up. You cry baby!" With a wave of water, they both begin to have a water fight. "Noah's a cry baby!" Nairobi says, teasing him over and over.

Tossing the beach ball back and forth, splashing water at each other, and paddling from one part of the pool to another gives way to the sounds of summer-time fun.

The children are laughing and screaming like children often do in their neighborhoods on hot summer days. The sound of a lawnmower distracts Valerie for a brief moment as her next-door neighbor, Mr. Rogers starts mowing his backyard. A low-wooden picket fence separates them. Low enough to allow Val to see him wave at her as he passes by her patio. On the left of her, Mrs. Brewster isn't home, but her water sprinklers are set to come on at 5:30 pm. Ahh. And there it goes. Like clockwork, she says softly, as Mrs. Brewster's sprinkles spray across her newly cut lawn.

Val takes a sip of her cool glass of lemonade. The taste is light and trickles down her throat with ease. She looks down at her vibrating phone. New Message notification blares across the screen. Romelle's number pops up. Smiling bashfully, she hesitates opening it. I wonder what he wants? Valerie can't help but wonder how good it feels to see his name come across her screen. They had exchanged numbers before leaving the bank parking lot. They have been texting back and forth, catching up. She keeps her phone on silent and often away in her purse when her husband is around. Rick finding out about her running into Ro hasn't exactly come up in their conversations. Feeling antsy, Valerie opens her unread message.

Romelle

What's up? Thinking about you...

"Mommy, look!"

Valerie looks up quickly as she hears her daughter yell out her name. "Yes, baby. I'm looking." She puts her phone down without answering Romelle back.

Shouting across to her mom, "I can swim on my back!"

"Aww, that's wonderful Nairobi. Did daddy teach you that?"

"Yup. It only took me two weeks," she replies.

"I'm so proud of you baby! You're doing so good."

"You should jump in with us mommy," her husband calls out playfully.

"Then who would make sure the house didn't burn down honey?" Her funny sarcasm leaves her husband bursting with laughter. Valerie has dinner on, and it's almost ready. The smell of baked lemon-pepper chicken, spinach, and white rice fill the air. The cornbread has its delightful aroma that could lift anyone's down spirit. Ten more minutes on the timer. She continues to watch her little daughter.

As she watches her daughter back-stroke in the pool, she smiles with intent. She pictures her as a swan. Her strokes were so smooth and in a dance-like formation. Nairobi's ballet lessons seem to be coming in hand for swimming too. Val glances back down at her phone as it buzzes for a second time. **New Message.**

The screen illuminates again. Ro sends her another message. Her facial expression lights up like fireworks as she reads it. The message is simple, but it makes her feel like she has butterflies flying around in her stomach.

Romelle

Wanna meet?

Of course, she wants to meet up with him. She's been thinking about him since she woke up this morning. She thought about him when she put a pot of coffee on. She thought of him when she took her shower. She even thought about him when she hugged her daughter good morning earlier. Wondering what he's doing. Where he's staying? If he sleeps in just his boxers like he did when they were together. She wonders if he's thinking of her. She can't stop thinking of him and hasn't been able to lay her head on her pillow at night without wondering if he still thinks of her like she still thinks of him. She knows it will be risky, but she wants to see him.

Valerie

Sure

It's 7:45 pm by the time she reaches the canal. She sees him as she approaches the lighthouse at the end of the pier. Slamming the door shut to her red 2018 Ford Durango, she takes in a deep breath—noticing the royal-blue Chevrolet Camaro SS that Romelle drove. It's the only vehicle parked in a small but secluded area. Not many people knew about the canal just off Lake Superior. However, Ro had brought Valerie to the canal when they were just fifteen— Val needed to talk and needed to get away from home. She instantly reflects on the first time Ro brought her here the moment she drove up. As she walks closer to the end of the pier, Valerie can't help but feel melancholy. What drew them here a long time ago engraved in her mind. Everything looks the same except the boardwalk. The boardwalk seems much longer then. It once had a feeling of being treacherous, cold, and void of life. The walk along the pier takes her right smack-dead in the middle of the lake that autumn day in 2015. Maybe it was because Valerie needed to feel like she was a part of the water then— so desperately wanting to jump in and end her life.

A sense of newness rushes in like a flood. Val can't help it, but feelings of anticipation enclose her. Her heart beats faster as she plants her eyes on Romelle. The sun rays feel warm against her brown skin. Her hair is half-pulled up attractively arranged in goddess braids. Her long sundress flows and scraps the ground as she walks-- accentuating her soft curves. Her heavy breast bounces up and down in her bra as she glides towards Ro.

Valerie's eyes are fixed on Ro. He looks so good in his white tee-shirt and fiery red shorts. His black and red gym shoes look brand new— No creases or spots in them anywhere.

"Hey Val," Romelle calls out as he turns around and sees her walking down the boardwalk.

"Hey."

"I see you finally made it. I was beginning to think you stood me up," he jokes.

"Boy! First off, ain't nobody stood you up!" she scoffs. "I had to finish something before I left out."

Valerie doesn't tell the whole truth—she did have to finish something. But what she didn't say was how she had to get her children ready for their baths and set the table up for dinner before she rushed out. Her husband had gotten the children out of the pool while Valerie set the table up for dinner. Valerie was so nervous telling her husband she was going to step out. After she spoke with Rick, she rushed upstairs to bath her daughter first. Then she told her to get to the table to eat. When the bathwater for Noah was running, she told her son to jump in and don't take forever getting out, or his skin would wrinkle. She told her husband his dinner was on the table and if he didn't want it to get cold, then he should stop playing with the TV remote.

"Well... I'm glad you made it." He grabs Valerie by her slim waistline and gazes into Valerie's eyes. "Did you miss me?" he asks with a confident smile upon his face.

He must know I missed him. Why else would he be smiling at me like this? Wanting to say absolutely yes, she thinks better of it. Instead, she settles for a joke. "With every bullet so far."

Laughing at her joke, "Ok. So you got jokes I see. Same ol' irritating Val."

"Same ol' full of himself Ro!" Valerie missed making jokes at his expense. She missed his charismatic smile, and the sound of his deep voice—his voice is like rolling thunder on a stormy night. She missed his deep dimple on the right side of his cheek. And she missed looking into his mesmerizing eyes. She missed everything about him. Why did they have to part? It's never what Valerie wanted. Romelle leaving for the military was not easy for her at all. She was vexed with him for a long time— she never thought she could forgive him for leaving her and the baby that he knew nothing about today, but here they were.

"I have something for you." Ro pulls a small box out of his back pocket.

"What is it?"

"Look in it and see for yourself," Romelle replies as he hands her the box.

Opening the black box, Val finds a dog tag inside. Raising her eyebrows, her face is set. "You still have the tag I gave you after all these years?" It was her cap and gown picture from high school.

Looking at Valerie in her eyes, no hesitation in his voice, he simply replies, "Yes. Now look on the other side."

She turns it over and sees that it's engraved—I'm going to marry you, it read. Val is stomped and can't believe her eyes. She clasps the chain in her hands tightly. "I... I... Don't know what to say"," Valerie states at Romelle in silence.

Romelle pulls something out of his pocket and places it around her neck. "Now, this is what I actually got you. That dog tag of you is mines and I won't part from it," he exclaims as he takes the dog chain from Valerie's hands. "Baby, read the one around your neck."

She flips the dog tag around her neck over. Tears fill her eyes as she reads it, finding it extremely hard to hold them back. She looks up at him with endearment, then back down again at the dog tag. It's a picture of Romelle in his military uniform, the back of it reading... Forever yours.

Valerie is at a loss for words. Her throat feels constricted— She finds it hard to swallow.

"Do you like it Val?" Ro asks with intent.

"No... I love it!" Valerie can't hide her love for what he has given her. She stares at the picture of him. *Why did he wait all this time to tell me he still wants me? Why hadn't he written me or tried to reach me by phone in four years?* Confused, she gazes across the lake. The same Lake that held her gaze many years ago. The same lake that ushered her in. This time, the lake has done much more. The lake endows her with love and affection. The lake seems to give her life instead of trying to take it away.

Romelle holds Valerie close in his arms. Holding her close to his body. He updates Val of his life since he left Detroit.

"Baby. I know when you wrote the letter to me four years ago, you were angry with me. I left to make something of myself. I left to accomplish what I wanted for my future. I wanted to stay with you, but I couldn't. I didn't want to leave you nor our baby. I thought of you and our baby every day in basic training. I wondered what we would've had. I wondered if the baby would've looked like me. I wondered what our lives could've been like if you had kept the baby."

Valerie listens in silence. Hearing him speak on that night at the restaurant brings a flood of unwanted feelings crashing back into her mind.

"See, there was no easy way out for me. I had already signed the contract, so I couldn't drop everything and stay. But I realized..."

Ro looks across the water for a moment. He lets out a deep sigh.

"There was no me without you Val," he continues. "I loved you. I loved you beyond the moon and the stars. I loved you beyond eternity. And I love you still. You are my first love... My only love Val," he sighs. "I wanted you then, and I want you now. And I'm not leaving anywhere without you by my side this time. You belong to me, and I belong to you. We are made for each other because I know you're my soulmate," he affirms.

His words hang in the air as her head rests gently upon his chiseled chest. The sun is setting on the distant horizon—The water is calm. The faint smell of nature peeks into her nostrils as she takes in everything around her. She wants to cry on his shoulder. The heavyweights of Romelle's confession feels all too much for her to process in one night. She begins to feel her heart pound faster and faster beneath her yellow and white sundress. Her mind was unsure of what to say or do. But she was sure of one thing—She knows that it feels good to hear Ro tell his truth.

The sunset is beautiful. Dusk has set over Lake Superior— It's now after ten o'clock. Valerie looks around and realizes the lateness of the hour. She feels a longing to stay in every breath she takes in. But she knows it's time to get home. Besides, how is she going to explain herself to her husband?

Her heart and mind are saying two different things. She doesn't want the night to end. Romelle is holding her in his arms just like in years past. It feels comfortable--relaxing. And even endearing. Time passes by so fast, but in Ro's arms, time is standing still. The cool night breeze is flowing through her hair, and she gazes upon the Lake, crippling Val's will-power to say her goodbye.

She hasn't mentioned that she is married to him all night. She has taken her ring to the shop for re-sizing a week before running into Ro at the bank. But now, she doesn't want to bring attention to her situation. Situation? Her marriage to Rick isn't a situation. It is more than that. He is her husband. She loves him dearly. She doesn't want to damage her family. She is not a recluse. She has never cheated on Rick, nor has she ever wanted to. Besides, the grief of losing his wife six years ago is enough hurt to last a lifetime. Balancing her responsibilities as a wife and as a mother is challenging at times. But she never complains. She loves being married, and she loves her children more than life itself.

There is silence between them. Both sitting on the pier with their feet dangling over the water—the moonlight bright above them. The stars twinkle in the clear dark sky, and the chill of night has given way to the sensations of shivering arms and chattering teeth.

"Your cold Val, let's go sit in my car." Ro glides his hands across her arms vigorously, like a boy scout trying to start a fire.

Valerie doesn't want to keep her husband waiting for her-- she feels compelled to break away from Ro and end their nightcap of shared emotions. "No, I really must be going."

"Stay. Just for a little while. I don't want you to go, baby."

"I can't," Valerie replies. "It's late."

"Why not? Do you have someplace to be in the morning? If so, you can just come to my place, and I'll be sure to wake you up in the morning before I go for my morning jog."

"No, I just can't."

Ro grabs Val's waist closer to his. Gazing into her eyes. "I'm still in love with you." He turns Val's face towards his with a simple touch of his hand. "I can't be without you any longer. Kissing her passionately, he cups her face in the palm of his right hand.

The warmth of his soft lips, and the gentleness of his touch, Valerie can't help but fall into him, kissing his soft lips in return. The sensation of his lips on hers is powerful. She begins to feel his hands follow her neckline and down to her smooth-rounded breast. Her breast was firmly in his palms. Touching her ever so gently, she begins to feel warm. She feels his well-defined pecks moving slightly as she places the palm of her right hand on him.

The intensity of an undying love arouses her tremendously. His kisses press her mouth deeply. She feels the heat of his tongue pressing firmly to reach the inside of her mouth. He begins to lay her down gently on the deck as he presses his body firmly against hers. Her eyes closed shut. She feels the pulsing sensation between them. His moans captivate her as she struggles to remain quiet. Forcing herself to bear it all without a word.

He grabs her by the waist, picking her up off the boardwalk. His strength is fascinating. She feels him grab the rails of the pier and slightly move her dress up. Her eyes open, and she sees him intently looking at her. His gaze fixed upon hers. He grabs her round-plumped butt—feeling every curve of her hips while her smooth butt bounces in his hands. Her pearls are moist and throb with pleasure. He rubs his hands gradually all over her soft butt...

His hands feel so good on me. Her thoughts pierce her with infatuation. The touch of his fingers between her legs sends her body jolting upwards. She catches his gaze still upon her—his eyes asking for permission to do what they both want so desperately to do.

She slowly leans her head backwards, and she moves slightly upwards to allow him access to her pink-laced satin panties. She feels his hands navigating up her inner thighs, enticing her even more—He pulls her panties to the side as he reaches her moist pearls with his fingers. His tongue glides up and down her neck with wet suctions of kisses. His warm breath tickles her skin with hot vibrations. She stares upwards toward the sky. The stars radiate brightly under the clear sky. The sounds of crickets call in the distance.

Tilting her head forward, she kisses him in small-gentle motions--Kissing his cheeks, his neck, then his chest. She's thirsty for his affection.

She wants him with every breath in her lungs. This is what she used to dream of years ago—Getting Romelle back in her life. The love of her life. The father of her daughter. Nothing matters at this moment. Only the two of them. She feels love in this very moment--Her first love returning to her again...

The fast beating of his heart lays upon her breast as she grabs him closer to hers. She kisses him intensely and allows herself to be free. Free in that very moment. She gradually leans back slightly as he kisses her breast and subtly begins moving his tongue down her cleavage— her nipples arouse in heat. Next, she feels what has pleasantly been waiting for her. Her moans echo loudly from the back of her throat in the cool darkness of the night.

Chapter 4

August 15, 2019

Today I woke up thinking about him. I can't help it. Last night was so crazy. If you were to tell me that I would not only run into my first love but make love to him on the pier, I would say you were lying. This is insane! I can't believe it. He's back. Back in my life. I thought this would never happen. After dealing with our break-up and dealing with him leaving for the military, I didn't think this day was even possible.

As I sit here on my window ledge in my bedroom looking out the window, I see Rick washing his truck. He has no idea that I've been unfaithful or broken our wedding vows. He has no idea that Ro is even back in town. We never speak about him. We've never even entertained the thought of him coming home from the military. Why is that? Why hadn't we talked about him one day eventually meeting Nairobi? She is his daughter. Why hadn't Rick asked me to reach out to him to let Ro know that we have a daughter? So many thoughts cloud my mind... I don't even want to think about it. A blue Jay has landed on my bird feeder just outside my window. Must be nice to be a bird. Nothing to worry about. No stress— No judgment— No sins.

~Val

C losing her journal, Valerie lays it down in the usual spot—In her desk drawer in her room. She trusts her husband not to go through her personal things and feels sure that he would never violate her trust. Val walks down to Nairobi's bedroom, where she finds her taking her baby doll's hair down. She gazes at her with envy. Remembering when life use to be so simple as a little girl, imagining herself playing on the floor with her favorite doll. The doll was soft, had big brown eyes, and her hair was black. Val admires her daughter's playful nature as she knows that one day she will be all grown up— not playing with dolls, but involved with a boy who will tell her he loves her and wants to marry her. If life was only that simple!

"Hi sweetheart," Valerie said, walking into her daughter's room. Nairobi Jumps up. "Look, mommy. You like my baby's hair?" She shows off the new hairstyle she's given her baby doll.

"Ohhh, she looks wonderful! I love her hair sweetie." Val exclaimed.

"I did it all by myself."

"You did?"

"Yea, do you wanna play with me, mommy?"

Valerie takes the top off the toy chest and removes the baby doctor play-set and the bakery chef doll set. Turning around from the toy chest, "Well, of course, I do sweetheart."

"Ok, mommy. Grab that chair in the corner." She points to her small pink chair at her play table.

"That's ok. I'll sit on the floor with your pumpkin."

"But mommy."

Her eyebrows arched. "What?"

"You're too big. You can't sit on the floor."

"Hahaha. Very funny Nairobi."

"But you are momma," Nairobi said, smirkingly at her mom.

"Girl! I ain't big! You got me messed up. I can play wherever I want to." Val said with a smirk. Now shut up and grab me that pink doll car." Val shook her head from side to side as she rolls her eyes and smiles at her daughter.

Forty minutes pass before Valerie realizes it. Her daughter was having so much fun that Val's daydreaming became frequent. Should I let her meet her dad? How would she take it? Ro would be shocked to see he has a little girl. At least my daughter knows that her father exists and has a picture of him that my mom took years ago when we were going to the high school prom.

"Mommy!" Noticing Nairobi at the bay window pointing at something, Valerie slowly lifting herself up off the floor. "Yes, what you see out there, sweetie?"

"It's daddy. He's home!" She said, bouncing up and down.

"Oh really?" That's strange. Looking down at her watch, she notices it's a little after 11:30.

What is he doing home so soon? He said he was going to catch up with some friends after he washed the truck. I wonder what he must've forgotten.

Little Nairobi dashes out her room, barely missing and knocking over the plant sitting on the hallway stand, and bolts down the stairs.

"Daddy, daddy!" She calls out while running down the stairs.

Valerie's mind is filled with thoughts of Ro with every waking second. She thought of him when she tossed and turned last night— thoughts of their sexual encounter. In the shower, her thoughts intensified with every move across her body as the soap caressed her soft wet skin. Playing dolls with her little girl, thinking if he would love their daughter unconditionally. She thought of how overprotective he would be as a father when she poured herself a second cup of coffee. Her thoughts of his initial reaction of having a daughter frightened her—wondering thoughts if he wants a child at all made her dizzy. Her headache teased her with guilt, which ceased just moments earlier after she swallowed two pain pills.

Valarie paces herself as she walks down the stairs. She readies herself with a smile to greet her husband at the door.

"What did you forget babe?" as she meets him at the bottom of the stairs.

"Hey, I left my phone on the kitchen island charging." He hugs his daughter and sends her upstairs to play. "Where's Noah?"

"Oh, he's playing with Jason in Mrs. Hubert's yard across the street. Jason got some new toys and wanted to play with Noah, so I let him go."

"Ok."

"Oh. Bae, how long you think you're going to be gone?"

"Maybe two or three hours. The boys wanna get some drinks this evening, so I may be longer."

"I thought we were taking the children to the movies later."

"I'm not going." His eyebrows frown, and his face is rigid. Rick moves towards the kitchen.

Seeing the annoyance on his face, Val's eyebrows arch. "Why not?" she questions.

Grabbing his phone off of the kitchen island, Rick strolls past his wife without hesitation. "What does it matter to you?"

Valerie's eyes widen. "What the heck is that supposed to mean?"

"Don't worry about it, he says calmly," without a glance in her direction.

"What's wrong with you?" She's flailing her arms, trying to get his attention as he continues to walk.

Rick glides his phone in his back pocket.

"Don't ignore me. I know you hear me talking to you!" Val exclaims.

"So what! I don't have to answer shit." Rick reaches the front door.

Valerie is caught off guard at her husband's response. Feeling her head swell with anger the more he refuses to admit what's wrong. Valerie slams the door closed as Rick tries to open it. Standing in front of the door, blocking him from trying to reach the knob, Valerie crosses her arms and waits silently for a response.

"Move out my way Val," he said, as he shoves her to the side.

Moving her body back in front of the door, Val rolls her eyes. "No! Tell me what the heck is your problem." She throws her arms across the door to block Rick from leaving. "You ain't going nowhere until you talk to me, and tell me what the hell is going on? You leave out one way, but come back another..."

"Left out one way!" He glares at his wife. "You must be blind and clearly don't know shit. I never left out one way and came back another."

"Yes, you did Rick!" Her voice matching his, echoing through the house loudly. She crosses her arms in front of her.

"That's really what you think, huh? You must be blind. You really wanna know what the issue is Valerie?"

Valerie sees the intense look in her husband's eyes. She wonders if her husband knows anything. Pondering... I did get in late last night. Did he catch the time I came home? Naw, he was asleep. OMG! What if he saw Ro's messages he sent me last night or earlier this morning. She begins to settle herself down. "Yes, I really wanna know," she finally replies.

"The real question is, what's wrong with you?" His cheeks flushed and nostrils flaring. "You come in late last night like nothing was wrong. I never got a text or call from you telling me anything. No, I'm running late. I'm making another errand or nothing! Then you took a shower and climbed into bed like nothing was wrong. When I go to put my arm around you, you move over as if you didn't wanna be touched." Rick's facial expression is tight. "So again, I ask you... What's wrong with you?"

"Baby, I didn't wanna wake you," she lies. She moves in closer to him--she gently rubs his bearded face. I knew it was late and I didn't want to bother you. I went to the store and grabbed what I needed, but then my cousin from Arizona called me. Remember I told you the other day she was having some problems with Brittney?

"Yeah." His jawline flinches.

"Well... Her fifteen-year-old butt got caught stealing from the store again, and this time the police were called. I stayed on the phone with my cousin for hours. I would've called you, but I couldn't believe what her crazy butt did. And I'm shocked honestly that she didn't learn from the last incident when she was caught but let go with a warning."

His face was expressionless. "So, you couldn't drive home and talk to her in the house?"

"Rick... I was just sitting in the store's parking lot. I was try-ing to be there for my cousin. Darlene doesn't deserve this.

She's a good mom." Val's arms wrap around her husband, and she slowly pulls him closer to her. Valerie stared into his eyes. "Baby, you know I would never leave you worried like that. It's just my cousin needed me. And I can't imagine being a single mother going through this by myself." Kissing him on his lips softly, "I'm so sorry babe." Kissing him on his lips over and over again, she asked, "Can you forgive me?"

"Yeah, I guess so." His face is more relaxed.

"Thank you, baby," she said, smiling with relief.

"But don't do that shit anymore."

"I won't babe," she said, hiding her guilt.

"I gotta go. The boys are waiting on me."

"Okay dear, have a good time."

"And by the way... I'll probably still go out later on with them tonight. But I'll let you know a little later."

Valerie waves goodbye as she shuts the door and stands there with her back up against the door with relief. Her guilt-ridden emotions force her to collapse to the floor. The shame... Feelings of remorse amplify her thoughts. Crouching herself over, she hides her face in her knees, wondering if she can ever forgive herself. She has to think of something quickly. She never had intentions of telling her husband a lie at all... She hadn't thought that far. She hadn't thought of much, besides her uncontrollable desires towards Romelle—the euphoric feelings of falling back in love all over again with her best friend, her first love--is paralyzing.

Chapter 5

Dear Diary,

Last Night I had a dream about him... He was lying beside me on my pillow, staring me in my eyes. We were face-to-face, his gaze was so intent. We lay under the sheets naked, as we had just made passionate love. He was kissing me tenderly on my shoulders as he lay behind me —holding me firm in his warm arms, he said nothing. Strange though--Somehow, the dream switched from us lying next to each other to us being at a park. Nairobi was there. She was meeting her dad for the first time. Romelle couldn't stop smiling, as Nairobi asked him one question after another. He pushed her on the swings—her four ponytails flying in the wind. She told him about her dance lessons, her backstrokes in the pool, and about her brother Noah. They played Mr. Fox, Mr. Fox, what time is it until they heard the ice-cream truck. Ro brought a banana boat ice cream sundae for them to split. As I woke, I remember their laughs. So vivid. So real.

My daughter knows Ro is her biological dad—there's a picture of us on the nightstand in her room. She always knew he was a soldier but never thought she would get the chance to meet him. I never let my daughter believe that her dad did not love her. I told her that he loved her more than she could ever imagine. Even if he doesn't know about her, I would never make Nairobi think her father didn't know her or want her.

In the dream, Ro was so happy to have a daughter and even happier that it was with me. I have to tell him. I can't let this go on. I want my daughter to know her father & visa versa. Will he be mad at me for keeping this a secret for so long? I hope that he won't be upset that I couldn't go through with the abortion. I hope he truly understands. Besides, It's my body. It was my choice. No one else's but mines. Surely, he has to understand that.

On another note, I feel so horrible! I have not only lied to my husband, but I had an affair. I've never lied to him before and never thought about cheating on him. I'm such a terrible person. How can I ever forgive myself? What if he finds out? I would be so hurt knowing the pain I caused upon him and our children. Yes, they are still young, but that doesn't matter. I feel like such a failure. I'm such a damn fool!

~Val

Valerie closes her journal and continues sipping hot hazelnut coffee. The aroma of freshly brewed coffee fills the air. Her black coffee mug clanks on the glass table as she sits it down. Her eyes are fixed on the scenery outside. The incandescent sun gleams down without a trace of rain in the sky. No cloudy skies anywhere. Her neighbors are out mowing their grass. Joggers fleet past in the streets, and a couple walks by briskly with their dogs.

Sitting on a barstool in the kitchen, Val circles a group of letters on a crossword puzzle she's working on. Buzzzz... Val glances over and looks at her phone. A new text message from her husband appears across her screen.

Rick

Don't forget to get the paintbrushes babe.

Rick text's his wife from work. He promised Val that he would give the family room a fresh coat of paint today after work.

Valerie

I won't baby

Valerie stares out her kitchen patio doors. Two birds feed on her bird feeder outside. She loves to watch the birds in the morning fly to the birdhouse. Maybe she'll spot a Blue Jay or a Red robin.

It's Tuesday, and the children are off to day camp —the house is void of noise. Val takes another sip of her coffee. As she places her mug back on the table, she lets out a deep sigh and closes her eyes. Lord, help me get over him. I can't keep going like this. I'm thinking about Ro night and day. Her heart is riddled with guilt.

She slowly gets up from the barstool. Her eyes trace over the crystal vase that sits on the center table. With her right hand, Valerie selects a pink tulip and brings it close to her nose. Her eyelids close as she inhales deeply and smells the strong, sweetest aroma that is sent down her nostrils.

Val heads toward the family room and turns the CD player on. She selects something soft and soulful. One of her favorite artist, Anita Baker, mezzo-soprano voice range fills the air.

Music blares through the house. Valerie sings and hums to the lyrics of Body and Soul— She feels every lyric of the song. No matter how much she wants to get the thoughts of Romelle out of her mind, she finds it nearly impossible. She knows it's wrong, but how can she let go of him when all she can do is think of him?

Valerie turns off the rushing water that pours out of the showerhead. She grabs a towel and puts it around her body as she steps out of the shower. She wipes the steam from her foggy mirror with a swipe of her hand. She then steps towards her closet. Valerie slides open the walk-in closet doors. She searches for something light to wear. With Anita still playing in the distance, she feels refreshed from her shower as it clears her mind and relaxes her tense body.

It's 86 degrees today. What shall I wear? She throws on her royal blue sundress that falls to the floor. She adjusts her bra straps to hide under the spaghetti straps of her dress. Her rounded breasts sit just right in the low-cut dress. The dress hugs her hour-glass figure. The dress accentuates her curves with every move of her body—It fills out nicely around her curvaceous butt. The dress flows and sweeps across the floor with every step as she walks towards her vanity. Val places her diamond stud earring in her right ear. She stands in the vanity mirror, applying lotion to her skin. Her cocoa brown skin is flawless, smooth, and clear. She attractively arranges her goddess braids over to the left side and adds gold hair accessories sparingly.

She smiles at her reflection in the mirror. Then she walks into the midst of Warm Vanilla Sugar as she sprays it into the air. She puts the spray down on her bathroom vanity and continues humming to the sounds of Anita Baker that is still playing. Valerie always looks and smells divine. That's the part she loved about being a little girl... Playing dress-up. She grabs her cotton candy lip gloss and glosses over her full-size lips. She snatches her purse and keys off the bench at the foot of her King-size bed.

"Okay, so where did I put my phone?" Valerie asks herself. She rambles through her purse-- Noting. She walks downstairs to see if she left it somewhere else. She looks everywhere as she tries to retrace her steps. She slams the books around on the dining room table— knocking over the small woman figurine as she searches about.

"I could've sworn I left it on this table," she mummers. "Where the heck did I put it?" She hears a faint sound in the distance. She quickly walks towards the family room as she follows the sound.

"Found it!" she says exhaustedly. She grabs the phone off the CD stand. She had placed it down to turn on her CD player earlier.

Valerie notices she has two missed calls and one new message. She realizes that one call was from her best friend Alley, and the second call is from the pharmacist. Noah's prescription must be ready.

Ro

Hey beautiful!

Wanna see you. Can we meet?

Romelle's message was sent 25 minutes ago. Val's eyes widen, her cheeks growing warm without warning—butterflies in her stomach, she begins to walk towards the front door. She stops short of the door, slides her phone in her purse, then opens the front door. Valerie walks to her two-car garage and hit the remote button on her key fob. As the garage door opens, she unlocks her truck door. As Val sits in the driver seat of her truck, she pushes the start button, and the ignition roars. Not able to fight the temptation any longer, she glances over at her purse and grabs her phone. The message unlocks with her face recognition. She gives in to the urge and sends a message to Romelle.

Valerie

Meet me at Lowe's on Shelby rd. In 45 mins.

Valerie puts her phone on the middle tray and begins to pull out her driveway. Coming to the end of the block, Val stops at the stop sign and hears her phone beep. Her eyes lower towards her counsel— Her phone lights up across the screen with a new notification...

Ro

OMW

Valerie wasn't in the store long before Romelle had texted he was waiting outside. Approaching the sliding glass doors, Val notices he has gotten out of his car and is waiting for her —his right arm on top of his sports car and his left hand holding a bouquet of tulips. His Detroit Pistons hat fits snug around his oval head, and his bent-in brim casts a dark shadow just above his eyes.

Her cheeks are flushed as she walks up to him. "Hey!"

"Hey, beautiful!" Holding the flowers out for Val to grab.

Her smile illuminates the atmosphere as Valerie grabs the flowers out of his hands. She closes her eyes as she brings them up to her nose—she inhales deeply. She bats her eyelids and smiles with delight as she catches Ro's gaze upon her.

"You didn't have to get me anything," she said softly.

"I know. Just say thank you," Romelle replies. His plain dark blue tee-shirt is close-fitting around his athletic build. His muscles bulge slightly through his shirt, outlining his chiseled pecs.

"Thank you." Sniffing the flowers, a scent of sweet fragrance fills her nostrils. She delights in the fact that Ro remembers that tulips are her favorite flower.

"Hop in," he says.

Not wanting to give in to the temptation of being alone with him, she stands paralyzed at his driver side door.

Ro grabs her and leads her by her hand. He opens the passenger side door ushering her into his car. His white air max 97 gym shoes look new. He shuts the door for her. He then walks over to the driver's side and hops in.

"Where are you taking me, Ro?" Her mind recalls her careless actions with him on the pier.

"It's a surprise. I've been thinking of this since the other night."

Valerie looks at the time on the dashboard--11:05 the dashboard illuminates. "Okay," she says cautiously. I don't have to get the kids until 3:30... I guess I have time for a quick run, she thought.

"So what' cha been up to?" Romelle asked.

"Nothing really."

"Well... I've been thinking about you constantly. I don't know about you, but I can't seem to get the thought of you outta my mind."

The air was thick, but the cool breeze made the air bearable. The sound of a train going by is in the distance. Horns blare the alerts of its presence loudly. People walk about busily in the streets, and city busses stop to pick up and drop off passengers. It's the middle of August, and the weather is still warm and beautiful.

Valerie doesn't say much in the car. She enjoys the scenery around her. The new leather smell inside Romelle's car is a compliment to his vehicle. She admires how nice he keeps his car. The car looks just waxed on the outside and never sat in on the inside. The new car smell gives off a pleasant feeling that she is reminded of when they were freshmen in college. His 2011 Chevy Malibu was always kept clean inside and out. Valerie is not surprised that he still takes good care of his car. She knows that Ro's love for sports cars is his hidden addiction.

"You okay Val?"

"Yeah, I'm good," she responds, turning to look at him.

"You just seem quiet," Romelle said.

"I'm enjoying the ride. And taking in the scenery."

"Good," he replies.

Valerie notices Romelle taking a right-hand turn onto the 26-mile road. People were walking their dogs and jogging along the sidewalks. Manicured lawns and shady trees line the street. Val is familiar with the area; she's been in this area plenty of times.

The twenty-one-minute drive to Stoney Creek Metropark was quick. Pulling up to a parking spot adjacent to the picnic area, Valerie takes in the view of people relaxing under the sun, and people swimming in the crystal blue lake. The birds flew overhead in search of food while people cooked food on the grills.

Romelle turns his engine off and steps outside the car. Walking over to Val's side, he opens the door and reaches for her hand to help her out the car.

"Thanks," she says, as she steps outside of the car. The sun rays warm upon her face.

Romelle closes the gap in-between them as he grabs her slender waistline. He cups her chin with one finger and softly whispers, "Your welcome."

Valerie's heart drops as she feels his breath upon her lips. His eyes trigger her body without warning, and she feels warmth in areas she shouldn't.

He gently pulls her closer, and his lips are a mere inch away from hers. Val's knees begin to weaken.

Romelle smiles at her and begins walking towards a tree that has no-one near it. "Come on," he said. He leads her to a nice shady area away from other people.

Val tries to gain her composure. Her body has a mind of its own and won't let her have normal reactions around Romelle. I *would've melted right into his arms if we had kissed*, she thought.

"Oh wait! I forgot something."

Val watches Ro stroll back to his car. His confident stride makes him even more handsome. Val uses to think the way he walked was so sexy. Hell... All the girls did! Her reminiscing thoughts captivate her as she stands motionless, staring at his body.

Ro hits the button on his key fob and lifts a black and white blanket and a basket from the trunk.

"What are we doing here Ro?" Valerie asked inquisitively.

"I wanted to be with you. I remembered how much you love the water and thought this would be a nice place to meet up."

Romelle lays the blanket down under a big black gum tree. He places the picnic basket from under his arm and lays it on top of the blanket.

"Lay down baby," he said. He takes a bottle of red wine out of the basket first. Two wine glasses follow. He reaches in and takes out two turkey sandwiches, a small container of strawberries, and a bag of plain ruffles potato chips.

"I remembered everything you liked," Romelle said softly.

"But how did you have time to put this all together? You met me at Home Depo so quickly."

He shrugs his shoulders, "Wishful thinking, I guess. I packed it up and was waiting for you to text me back. And why is your voicemail always full?" he said scornfully.

"Yeah. I'm still terrible at clearing my voicemails. I must have over fifty of them," she chuckles.

"You still doing the same thing, and it's four years later. Clear your damn voicemails girl. Can't anybody ever reach you cause it's always full?"

She laughs, "Okay, Okay! I'll do it today. Anyways. She continues on... "How did you know I would say yes?"

"Because I felt you wanted to meet me just as bad as I wanted to meet you."

Her eyes are set on Romelle. Deep down inside, she knows he's right. She couldn't lie to herself. Nothing but thoughts of him fills her mind since that night, she wanted his mind, body, and soul.

"You too confident for me!" she remarks. Quick way to avoid a suicidal response is to be sarcastic. She doesn't want Ro to know how she really feels. She's just as much in love with Ro as she was before he left for the Navy...

Popping the top of the wine, Romelle opens the bottle and pours the wine into the glasses. He then reaches for the strawberries and pulls one out of the container. He gestures towards her mouth as he drew the strawberry closer to her, "Open."Valerie opens her mouth and Ro places the strawberry in her mouth, allowing her to bite some of it off. "Drink your wine baby. I want to feed you the strawberries, so just relax and let me feed you, he taunts."

Valerie smiles as she picks her wine glass up and takes a sip of the chilled drink. It clinches the inside of her jaw as she feels the smoothness of the wine going down her throat. She feels at ease, wishing this moment could last forever; she enjoys every minute of it. She allows him to finish feeding her the strawberries.

Next, she grabs the turkey sandwich and chips. They both eat and talk, laugh, and drink their wine. Val listens with curiosity as Ro tells his stories about being in the military—his tour in Germany, telling how he enjoyed every minute of it. Noting the fondness in his eyes and the excitement in his deep voice as he speaks with pride. In her heart, she knows that he had made the right choice. She couldn't dismiss the pride in his eyes as he tells her story after story.

Two hours passed by quickly. The stories they shared between them is like a time capsule--moments stuck in time. After eating lunch and finishing up their wine, Valerie lays down on the blanket. Listening to Ro puts her in a trance... Not thinking of anything else, she enjoys his conversation, the tone of his voice, and the content in his eyes. Looking up at the sky, she feels free. Free as a bird. Enjoying the cool shade, she listens to Ro reminisce about when they were teens.

Ro lays beside Val and gently places her head on his chest. "You know, I brought you out here because I wanted to talk to you."

"About what? What's on your mind." Valerie is a little nervous about his response--she braces herself, turning herself to face him.

Gazing down into her dark brown eyes, he glides the backside of his hand across her face. Stroking her face gently, he finally breaks his silence.

"I want you back in my life Val. I want my best friend back. I want all of you because there is no one else for me. I know leaving you and coming back after all these years feels different. I still feel the same way about you as I did yesterday. And I don't think you have a boyfriend. You would've told me by now. Besides..." He hesitates. He sighs as he tucks one arm behind his head and looks upwards towards the sky. "I trust you," he continues. "I know you are the one for me. I know you wouldn't lie to me. If you told me you had someone, then who am I to interfere? I would let you go. It would hurt tremendously, but I would let you go..." He takes a minute before he continues.

Valerie listens intently. How could he say that? He had no idea what was going on in her life. I'm married, she says to herself. My ring is in the shop, getting resized. But that didn't matter. She has already broken her vows...

"Baby."

Her heart jumps every time he calls her that.

"Yeah?" She looks up at him.

"I'm sorry I left you. But I needed to do something for myself. I wanted the baby, you know. I wanted us too. I wish you hadn't aborted our baby..." His chest rises slowly as he takes a deep breath. "Shoot," he says abruptly. "I didn't know how or when to bring this up. I know for women, it's a difficult issue to talk about. But I want to talk to you about it—that's if you don't mind. This is why I brought you out here today. I needed to get some stuff off my chest. About the baby. About you. And about us. I want us to start over—I want us to have a family. A real family this time. I want you to have my baby. I want you in my life all the way," he said confidently. "Are you still my baby?" he questions.

Thoughts of what Romelle has just said fill Valerie's mind. What should I say? Is he serious? He doesn't even know about Nairobi nor Rick. I was going to tell him. But I didn't expect this... Valerie hadn't expected Ro to express his love for her. Biting her lips, Valerie looks the other way and sees a red robin land on the ground next to the tree adjacent to them.

"Ro," She finally responds." Without taking her gaze off the red robin in the tree in front of them, she hesitates, biting her lower lip.

"Yea?"

"There's a lot about me that has changed," she finally admits.

"Like what?" Romelle replies without hesitation.

"Well... Like everything."

"I'm listening Val."

Sitting up, Valerie brings her bent knees up to her chest. She lightly brushes off the crumbs from her dress. She looks him in his hazel eyes nervously. Not knowing just where to begin. She begins with one statement...

"We already have a four-year-old daughter— and her name is Nairobi..."

Chapter 6

Romelle jumps up—his eyes sharpen and are fixed on Valerie. "What the hell did you just say?" His tone is demanding.

Valerie feels Ro's tone roll like thunder, and it pierces her soul. She's riddled with guilt. There is a lump in her throat. She begins to rub her chest back and forth across her heart as she begins to feel tightness. She stands up cautiously. She winces as the tightness grows, and a wave of nausea forms in the pit of her stomach as she searches for the right words. All she can do is wonder how to explain not having that abortion four years ago. She knew that this day would eventually come—she knows this is the right thing to do. Her breath is calculated as her head becomes lighter— built-up anxiety finally releases. The cat is out of the bag now; there is no turning back. "I can explain," she says finally.

Romelle closes the gap between them. The veins in his neck are flinching as his jaws clutch together tightly. "What do you mean we have a daughter, and her name is Nairobi?"

"Well, remember four years ago, you were leaving for the Navy?" she begins.

Romelle's expression tightens. He stands with wide legs, folding his arms across his chest. "Yeah!" One brow is arched up as he continues to stare at Val.

The air is thick. Val notes Ro's nostrils are flaring, and his lips are curled. "Did you read the message I sent you?"

"Yeah, on the plane—you basically broke up with me. Never allowing me to say anything back to you..." He hesitates for a moment. He clasps the palms of his hands down his face and exhales out deeply through his nose, "You blocked me remember!" he exclaims with frustration.

"I know I had to. After I received the messages you sent the day you shipped out, it was the only way I could deal with the pain of you leaving. I couldn't keep seeing your messages. I know I was wrong for that.

"Damn right, you were wrong. I practically begged you to come see me off, but you just left me on read. Not a word..."

Romelle's face is reddened. He wipes the sweat off of his forehead with the back of his right hand.

"I know Ro, but... um, remember what I said about the baby?"

"Of course, I do! You said you were aborting the baby, and I should move on with my life." He throws his hands up in the air. "Like you never asked me what I wanted." The muscles in his jawline begin to flitch rapidly.

Valerie feels guilty inside—he was right. She never asked him, nor did she meet up with him when he asked her. It was too painful. She couldn't bear the thought of him leaving her. "Well, I never got rid of the baby. I couldn't go through with it." Her eyes begin to burn as water wells up in her eyes.

"Valerie! Why didn't you tell me this before? Why are you telling me all this now?" Romelle scorns.

"I tried," she yells through her shaky voice. Tears stream down her face—her voice sounds hoarse as it cracks under pressure.

"When? When did you try?" Romelle said with his fist repeatedly pounding in the palm of the opposite hand. "You've waited all this time, and I'm just hearing about our daughter now!" His inquisition continues. "Does she at least know about me, know who I am—that I'm her father?" he said, as his eyes squint low with confusion.

"Yes, she knows all about you. She has a pic of you I keep on her nightstand. She knows you love her and that you're away in the Navy. I tell her all the time how much you love her."

He stands still for a moment, looking down at the floor, then backs up towards Val. "Does she look like me? Is my daughter smart?" he asked in a low tone.

"Yes, she looks exactly like you. Every time I look at her, I see you. Her hair hangs down to her shoulders, and it's naturally curly. She's bright, learns quickly, and full of life. She can hold a conversation with you that makes you want to put her on TV commercials." Val exclaims. "Everyone says she's very smart for her age."

Val pauses to allow Ro to take it all in. She notices he puts his hands in his pockets—his stance is less frigid now. *I shouldn't have just let him walk away. I should've been stronger, less prideful—but now it's too late. I started a whole life without him. How could I've been so stupid?* "Ugh, I feel so bad! All I ever wanted was for you to know about our daughter." She moves closer to him, "Seriously, it's been on my mind constantly." Her throat feels constricted. Her mascara tears away from her eyes—as tears begin running down her cheeks. "I thought I'd never see you again. I--I didn't know how or even when to tell you."

"How about you could've told me when we ran into each other at the bank. Or how about when we made love to each other on the pier. I can't believe you kept this from me all this time. You kept her a secret—but told me you were aborting the baby. Did you ever think of what I wanted?" He slowly lets out a deep sigh as he wipes away the sweat that accumulated on his head. "I was hurt, devastated. I was crushed when you broke things off with me and broken when you said you wanted to get rid of the baby. I had no way of reaching out to you. I wanted the baby... I wanted..."

He walks away from Val, shaking his head. He stands off to the side as he puts a small distance between them. He stares blankly ahead as the children play in the park nearby. He reaches in his pocket and pulls out the picture of the two of them he keeps in his wallet.

Valerie retracts her steps and stands back. She tries to keep her distance as she gives Ro space. She understands why he's avoiding eye contact with her. She rubs her temples—her head throbs, giving way to the tension she feels from Ro. *So, he did want our baby all along. But I assumed he didn't, assumed he wanted to be free—assumed free from me...*

"After I got off the plane, the Navy Sergeants were standing right there. They rushed the other guys and me off to the arrival gate where all the other soldiers were waiting at attention," Romelle begins. "Everything happened so fast. I was in basic training the whole time thinking about you and our baby. Wondering how you were. Wondering why you didn't keep our baby." He looks away. "I really had a hard time Val. I even got sent back once because I couldn't pass my PT test. I know it was because I was missing you and upset with you all at the same time. My Drill sergeant had to talk to me. He told me to get my shit together and get my head in the game, or else he would fail my ass. I told him what happened before I left home, and he helped me to focus. I knew I had to get myself together quick-ly." He turns back to look at Val, his eyes wet and his voice softer. "I wasn't in the states long after I finished. I ranked high in my class and was one of the few chosen for a special mission in Africa after graduation."

Val sees the hurt in his eyes. Everything is all her fault. He did want a life with her and Nairobi—he loved her still. How can I be so insecure? Why didn't I think? Why didn't I wait? Her thoughts carried on—her mind succumb to guilt. "I'm so sorry Ro." She steps up towards him. "I never meant to hurt you. I swear." she cries.

Romelle looks away. He tips his head back to look heaven-ward, and he places his hands onto his head, "MAN!" he blows.

Next, he hangs his head forward, letting it hang low. He glides his hands into his pockets.

The conversation has taken its toll on both of them. Valerie hears the hurt in his voice and sees the pain in his eyes. She needs a moment to find the right words to say to him. The sun is hot on her face. The deep-crystal blue lake is calm. She stares at the families jumping in and out of the lake. The park begins to crowd with more people since their arrival. Val notes the couple swimming with their two children and immediately thinks of Noah and Nairobi. Her gaze suddenly shifts— looking down at her watch, 1:46 pm— Still time to talk. She still has time to finish their talk before she picks her children up.

Romelle turns and walks up to Val, "Look, I know you felt you were doing the right thing when you texted me that letter you wrote me years ago. But, you're selfish," he scuffs. I told you that the last time we had a fight. You never think about anyone else but your damn self! You didn't want me to go to the military. You said you were aborting the baby—you lied! I trusted you." He steps away from her as he throws his hands up in the air. "You never answered my texts or calls before I left, and you never answered my calls when I was in Germany—."

"Wait, what?" Valerie cuts him off. Her blood rushes to her head quickly. What did he just say? She can't believe what she just heard. "What do you mean, you called me?" she questions, with a high-pitched voice.

"I called you a couple of times, but you never answered. You were that mad at me that you refused my calls."

"No, I didn't!" she replies. Her eyeballs bulge out as her eyebrows raise. "I never knew you called me." Her voice is shaky, and she feels her heartbeat pounding through her chest. "I never got any calls from you, I swear!" she continues. That was the truth. Val never received one call...

"Wait!" she shouts. I did drop my phone in the toilet at school. That's the only time I was without a phone for a minute, I swear!" she said, with her hands stretched out in front of her. "I had to buy another phone because I couldn't receive or make any calls, I could only text out—before the whole screen went out. Or wait! Maybe it was those, scam likely calls. "She's mortified by the thought of missing his calls.

His eyes are glued to hers. "I called you as soon as I was able to dial out. I called you over and over again, and you never picked up," Romelle said.

Val begins to cry hysterically—her heart feels as if it stops beating. She gasps for air. "I didn't know. I knew I got some weird calls, but it said scam likely, so I never answered. I get those calls all the time." Her chest is rising and falling in rapid spurts. "Remember, you did too. I didn't know that was you—I promise! I... I promise. I didn't know. I would've answered if I knew it was you." She turns her palms over in front of her face and asks, "Why didn't you leave a voicemail saying it was you?"

"I tried," he says, his face solid. "I tried every time I called. But of course, I've always told you that you needed to clean out your voicemail. I couldn't leave a message because your voicemail was always so freakin full. So, I stopped trying—I figured you were still mad at me for leaving."

~ 71 ~

"I wasn't mad. I was hurt. I thought we would start our family a little sooner than we'd hoped. I wanted to graduate with you and spend my life with you—."

"See, that's just it," he responds, cutting her off—his head shakes from side-to-side.

"What, she replies?" The hits just keep coming. What can it be? What now...

"My dad had a talk with me, back when we were sophomores in college."

Valerie respects Ro's parents. His mom and dad were like second parents to her years ago. Especially his mom—forming a bond when she was fifteen that would forever change her life.

"What about," she asks?

"He talked to me about my life. He asked if I had given any thought about what I really wanted to do."

"Well, I thought you were doing what you really wanted to do," she says, with one eyebrow raised.

"That's what you assumed," he responds. "My father knew I wanted to go to the military, just like granddad and just like him. I never wanted to go off to college—I did that for you."

"Wait, what are you talking about?" Valerie's brows knit together. She always thought he wanted to go to college, and when they both got accepted into Wayne State University, she thought he was happy. Dammit, I had no clue. She studies him closely. "I don't understand. I always thought you were happy we got into the same college."

"Babe, I was happy because you were happy. Whatever you wanted, I did it—no questions asked. I never wanted to hurt you. Not like you had been hurt before. The look on your face, the hurt I felt for you—the anger I felt inside that night at the lake when we were fifteen..." Ro cracks his knuckles as he lowers his head. He wipes the sweat off his head. He lifts his eyes to meet Val's. "That night on the pier, you told me every-thing—you were only fifteen..." He balls his fists up and continues. "What happened to you made me sick to my stom-ach, and I carried the weight of that night on my shoulders every day." His eyes meet the ground again.

A cool breeze flows past them. Valerie knows it is hard for him to look at her. She can sense the hurt— still real in his voice.

He's the only friend I ever told what happened to me. He's the only person I trusted. How could I be so blind? We were both kids then. "Go ahead, I'm listening," she said softly.

He kneels and plays with the grass—plucking it up out the ground. He tosses it to the side, hand after hand—he pulls, and he tosses. "I cared for you so much. Too much!" he continues. I never wanted to see you hurt again, so for years, I just did whatever made you happy—no fuss. I carried your pain for so long that I was numb to my own feelings. All I wanted to do was protect you. I never wanted to lose your trust. You were so vulnerable, so fragile. I did everything for you—It was all for you. But my dad had a point..." Ro hesitates. He grabs his bottled water from off the ground. After taking a couple of sips, he sits the bottle back down and stands back up. "He said that if you loved me and it was meant to be, then you would be here for me when I returned. He told me not to change my dream in order to fit yours. I never told you what he told me because I was afraid of losing you. And even more afraid of losing myself in you."

It all makes sense now. This is why he was determined to leave, why he waited to tell me, and why he yelled out that I was selfish back then. It makes perfect sense.

Val's heart feels shattered, torn in two. Her imperfections are taunting her... It's time for her to take responsibility--complete responsibility. She's living a lie, a lie she had created for herself. The lie she told herself for years, over and over again—thinking he was to blame. She knows now that she's the blame—she messed up. Her flaws became his nightmare. She never knew the weight of what she endured when she was younger would affect her this way. She was changing the course of his life without even knowing it. She gave him her weights without ever asking what he wanted.

It was Valerie who begged him to apply at Wayne State for college because she was going there. It was her that was building their lives without involving him in the blueprint...

The pain haunts her like a lion roaring in the night. She grabs her stomach. *I can't believe this!*

It was her that never answered the text messages he sent her that day he shipped out. He wanted her then, but she never came. He did call when he was in the Navy...

Her mind is consumed with despair—her eyes growing wetter by the second. The feeling is recognizable—her heart is heavy, she places her palms over her eyes to hide her face. She shrinks inside herself. It was too late. It was too late for them. She would've weighed him down. She finally understands why he fought so hard to leave. It was the only thing he had ever done for himself. She had crippled him, and he was finally learning to breathe on his own—the military had taught him that. "It's all my fault. I'm so sorry," she muffles into her palms.

He looks at her, "It's not your fault," he replies as he places his hand gently over hers and removes them from her face. He closes the gap between them as he steps closer to her. His chest is right in front of her face.

"It is, she responds," letting out a deep sigh into his shirt as she grabs it with both of her hands.

Romelle lifts her chin with one finger, "I never blamed you—not then and not now." He tilts his head to the side and grabs the back of her head.

Val can feel his warm breath upon her head.He wipes her face with one hand. Then he pulls her forward and kisses her passionately. Valerie falls into his body. Her face leaning into his--she feels every part of his mouth enveloping hers. Paralyzed by his kiss, her body heat rises in the heat of the moment.

She hears the birds chirping around them as they kiss, her ears intertwining with nature. She begins to feel crossed—Fixed between two worlds. A world where there's Romelle, and the other with Rick. The intensity overwhelms her. She pulls back, and her eyes shut tight, her head lowers. Overcome with a flood of emotions. She shakes her head from side to side. "No... I um, I can't." Her mind is racing with thoughts of her husband, the one-night affair with Ro, the guilt of loving another man—she can't let this happen again.

"What's wrong? Why'd you pull back from me?"

Her head hangs low. She had to tell him—tell him the truth, she's been married for two years. The time is now…

August 23, 2019

Rick walks in from taking a jog, like he does every Sunday morning, "What are you doing with that?" he questions, as he motions to the glass in her hand.

Val takes a sip from her wine glass, and the cool chill of strawberry rushes down her throat. "I needed to relax," she replies.

"Where're the children?" Rick questions. As he glances at the time on the clock, the second-hand strokes twenty-five after ten.

"Upstairs watching tv in their room." Valerie takes another sip of her wine. Her brown eyes gaze out the window. She notes the sprinklers that was once soaking the grass has stopped now.

"What's up, babe? You seem stressed." Rick sits down next to his wife.

Perfect. She thinks to herself, sitting on the blue chase by the bay window. Valerie sees a mother bird feeding her baby up in the tree. The nest has been there all summer. She watches as the mother flies away, then comes back again. Was it two or three days ago that bird hatched? She tries to recall when but gets distracted by reality.

Val turns to face her husband. She finishes the rest of the wine. The glass clinks on the glass table as she sits it down. "I need to tell you something," she finally says.

"What?" His eyes are fixated on his wife. He leans forward, with his forearms on his knees and his fingers interlocked. His hair is freshly cut, his face is shaven. His blue and gray Detroit jersey matched his gray and white gym shoes.

Val grabs her goddess braids, pulling them over to the left side of her head—they hang low just past her waist. Her black sundress is floor length. Her legs are crossed as she sits on the couch. Her muscles are tight, and her hands are a bit warm. She wants her husband to know about Romelle. She wants him to support her decision for Nairobi to see her father. Besides, Nairobi has always known about her father before Val married Rick. Val has always kept pictures of Ro in a small album, so her daughter could know who her father was. Val's mother told her from the beginning never to keep Romelle a secret. She wanted Nairobi to know about her father from the jump. Valerie has always talked with her daughter—telling her small things about her father. Of course, Val has always spoken of Ro as Nairobi's father. Valerie would point to his picture while teaching her the word daddy when she was younger. However, when Val married Rick, she told her daughter— Now you have two fathers.

Speaking of fathers, Romelle was puzzled at the thought of having a daughter he had known nothing about. The other day was a shock for Valerie. However, it was much more of a shock to Ro. The idea of finding out he had a daughter this whole time, that would make any man feel angry, betrayed, and hurt to say the least. Valerie wanted to tell him she was married too. However, her phone rang as soon as she was about to tell him about Rick.

"Hello," Val answered. "Yes. Aha. Umm, Ok. Be right there!" Val exclaims as she ends her phone call.

"Look Ro, take me back to my jeep," she snaps in haste.

"Why, who was that? What's wrong?" Romelle questions.

"Listen, I'll have to explain later. Just get me out of here," she shouts as she motions her hands in speech. Her body language was frantic as she hurried along, picking up the picnic items from off the ground.

Romelle said nothing. Just got the items up and made a mad dash to his car. He sped through the town in silence, being oblivious to what was going on with val. Little did he know it was Nairobi's school calling to inform Valerie that she had had an accident on the playground and was complaining about her head.

When Valerie got to her, she had a small knot on her head. Some little boy dared her to jump off the swing while she was swinging. And well, let's just say, Nairobi doesn't like to be challenged by boys.

"About our daughter," she finally says to Rick.

"What about her, " he asks?

"Well, her father is in town... Umm. Back home, I mean."

"Romelle?" he scoffs. His brows raise.

"Yes, of course, who else would I be talking about?" she said with sarcasm. She narrows her eyes at her husband, "I'm really trying to have an honest conversation with you Rick."

"Okay, I'm sorry. Go ahead and finish." Rick slides his gym shoes off and walks them over to the front door.

"Well, like I was saying, Nairobi's father is back from the military."

"How long has he been back?"

"I think about a week or two," she says cautiously.

"How did you find out he was back?" Running his hand across his waves repeatedly, his narrowed face waits on Val's response.

She wants to tell him the truth, right here, right now. But this isn't about her cheating on him; it's about their daughter. She'd have to save that conversation for another day. "I ran into him when I went to the hardware store to pick up the paintbrushes you asked me to grab," she lies. A wave of heat rushes through her body. She tries desperately to keep a calm face. Her palms are beginning to sweat. "Well, Umm, he knows about Nairobi. He—"His eyebrows raise instantly, "So you told him?" he interrupts.

"Yea, I did." She wonders if he's shocked, or he's just play-ing along—she waits for the ball to drop. Rick sometimes masks his emotions, waiting like a thief in the night to let his anger unfurl on her. She's seen his temper flare countless times—punching holes in the walls, throwing small objects across the room, and one time he threw a plate of spaghetti across the room at her. The plate shattered on the dining room wall—the stain stayed on the wall for three days. He always apologizes. And she always forgives him.

"What was his response?" he asks his wife.

"He was shocked, to say the least. He was angry, of course."

"Why would he lose it? It's not your fault he walked out on you," he scolds. "He's the one that decided to go off and join the Navy, not you!" His tone is harsh.

"He did Babe," Valerie said softly.

"He did what?" He folds his arms as he stands there waiting for a response.

His wide stands intimidate Val. "He did try to reach me," she whispers in an almost inaudible tone. "Over and over again."

"How you figure that? I think you would've known if he really did try to reach you."

"He did babe. I know it's hard to believe, but he did. He never even wanted me to get rid of Nairobi. It was me who left him no choice." Valerie drops her head. Bringing up what happened in the past to stir up emotions that she is trying hard to avoid. Her hands feel numb-- she grabs her palms and massages them. She strokes her hands gently to ease her anxiety. She is not a girl who could hide her emotions well, unlike Rick.

Her breath becomes labored, and the last thing she needs right now is to have a meltdown in front of her husband. She wants her marriage to work, but if she involuntarily shows any signs of emotional attachment to Romelle, she will fall to pieces. It will surely send Rick into a brewing tornado—his emotions would launch, twist, and turn into a fury that she did not want to see.

"I don't believe it."

"No, I really didn't leave him any choice. I wrote him a letter and texted it to him the day he left. I told him I was going to terminate the pregnancy, but when he landed, he couldn't respond to me; I blocked him." she states. "And he tried to reach me, calling me over and over again when he was over-seas."

"So, you kept Nairobi away from him? Something doesn't sound right." He scratches his temples. "I thought you said he didn't want the baby at all. That you were left to raise her by yourself."

"I... I was wrong. It's a long story. But I was wrong. He did-n't leave us." Her face is downcast. Val feels her stomach tighten... "He really wants to meet her. And I—"

"So, what are you going to do? Are you letting her meet him? I mean, umm. You have to be sure this is okay for our daughter. This may be too soon and be too much for her. Don't you think?" He grabs a seat on the couch.

She senses her husband's reluctance and apprehension. She needs to reassure him that allowing Ro to see his daughter was the right thing to do. She's already promised Ro he can see his daughter. And with or without her husband's permission, she is not keeping Romelle away from Nairobi this time. "Of course, he can meet her—she is his daughter. I can't just keep her away from him. I have no right, and I have no reason to," she said confidently. Rick's eyes look empty. She can't gauge her husband's emotions or thoughts at the moment.

He's masking his feelings. I have to get him to feel comfortable with the idea of Ro meeting Nairobi. I really don't need my husband shutting down on me right now. She backtracks, "Don't you think I should baby? What if you had a daughter you didn't know about? Wouldn't you want to meet her too?" Her heart feels heavy. Rick must understand her point of view. He must consider their daughter, right?

"Yeah, I guess you're right," he replies. His tone is calm. His shoulders begin to relax. He adjusts his seat and rears back on the couch. "I would want the truth," he finally admits. "I would want to see my child." He crosses his arms as he throws his head back on the couch. "Have you set anything up yet?"

Valerie is relieved to see her husband a bit calmer. Every nerve in her body has been on edge from the moment the conversation begins. "Yeah, I told him next week Saturday, on the thirty-first."

"So, is he coming here?"

"No. I—"

"Where are we meeting him at?" He cuts her off.

We? She never included him or Noah. Romelle wants to meet his daughter. Val wants them to spend the day together without feeling awkward. It will already feel new to both Ro and Nairobi. She doesn't want to complicate things. *How do I say this?*

How can I let him know that we are not meeting here without him getting angry with me?

She planned for a day at the carnival, where they can have fun in an atmosphere that feels safe and inviting to Nairobi. Having Ro meet at her house will make him feel uncomfortable, make Val feel uncomfortable too. Besides, Ro still has no clue Rick even exists. She knows she will have to eventually tell Romelle she's married, but if she brings Ro over now, all her emotions will be on her sleeves. She needs to tell Ro she's happily married, which means she can't keep Romelle in her life the way he wants. She will have to leave him again; for the second time. She will have to let him go, this time with closure.

"I'm taking her to him, she finally says." She pretends to brush some lint from her dress as she anticipates his harsh response.

His brows furrow, his face tight like a pair of new leather shoes. "Oh, me and Noah not invited?" he questions, raising his voice slightly.

"Babe," she replies softly. "This is not about, umm, us right now." Her voice cracks under the pressure of trying to convince her husband to back off. "This is about our daughter meeting her father for the first time. And Ro meeting his daughter for the first time. You really think he's gonna feel comfortable with everyone around?" she exclaims.

"I really don't care about that. I don't feel it should be a problem. You make it seem like it's a secret or something."

"No, that's not it!" She tries to explain herself.

"Well, it sure seems that way to me." His gaze was heavy upon his wife. What is he thinking? "Like for real, what's the problem? Why wouldn't I be able to come? It's like you leaving Noah and me out." His voice grows a bit louder now. His already deep tone rumbles like thunder. He stands up and begins to pace the floor—stopping for a moment, arching his body over the table in front of him. "It's stupid not to invite me. I don't know this man from Adam to Eve."

A thunderstorm brewing fills the air in their home. Val tugs at the idea of telling Rick she will set the meeting up at their home. But that means she will have to first tell Ro she's married. She's not ready for that conversation. She knows her husband has a jealous streak, mostly because he doesn't like her around other men at all. Valerie swings her legs off the couch, and she plants them firmly on the floor. She's stuck between a rock and a hard place. Avoiding the inevitable, she decides to stick with her original plan. Raising her eyebrows slightly, she tries to reckon with him, "Rick, there's nothing wrong, seriously. I feel that they need this time together. I don't have a problem with you meeting him, truly," she lies.

It's Ro I have the problem with. He's the one that doesn't know about you—my husband of two years. I have to first wrap my own mind around how I'm going to even tell Ro I'm married. He's going to be devastated... Her thoughts trail off, broken by her husband's voice.

"I don't have a problem with Noah meeting him either," she continues, "but not on the first day. Nairobi needs this time to spend alone with her father."

"FATHER! Oh wow, so now he's a father!" His eyes are cold and sharp. Calling Romelle a father seems to send Rick over the edge. He walks over to Val who is now also standing. His body invading her personal space, as he fills the space between them, "Wow! You are really this stupid huh? Now he's her father? So what have I been to her? Huh? Answer me!" His once stoic nature is now unmasked.

Valerie is silent, her head shaking from side to side—her eyes sting as they fight back tears. She doesn't want to argue, nor does she want her husband upset with her. At this moment, she just wants peace.

"You must be crazy if you think this a good idea to let our daughter meet a man, she has never met without me! She barely knows him, only by his pictures. So tell me how this makes sense V.?"

Valerie feels his hardened eyes convict her already torment- ed soul. This definitely wasn't the mood she was going for. His defiant tone hurts like hell. Why can't he just let it go? Drop it, for crying out loud? Why doesn't he agree to disagree?

He seems to get colder and colder, no matter what she says, Rick is not taking down. Val retreats to the sofa as her husband continues to throw insults. Her head pounds—feeling like an offensive tackle just gave her a concussion. She massages her temples, feeling the stress of their conversation taking its toll on her nerves. Her stomach feels as if it's in knots. Nothing is going to calm her husband, except him getting his way—and that is not going to happen. Val will just have to sit and deal with his temper in hopes it doesn't get out of control. Much to her surprise.

Rick eventually withdraws to the back patio, and Val eventually succumbs to the only thing that can ease her tension... Her journal.

August 24

Dear Diary,

The house is still. I can't sleep. I've failed at yet another thing. My husband is mad at me, and I don't know how to bring him back. He's sleeping on the couch downstairs. I fixed one of his favorite meals for dinner; pot roast with homemade gravy, sautéed onions with mushrooms on top, homemade mac & cheese, and stewed string beans seasoned with cut-up potatoes and salt pork. I thought the aroma of some good old food would draw him back in—instead, he continued to soak in his anger, drinking too many beers. I even turned to the Lions game. But that didn't bring him back in either, although it would've made him more upset because, of course, the Lions lost yet another game. I tried to entice him to jump in the jacuzzi with me, but he refused.

So here I am, up at 2:35 in the morning, with my husband giving me the cold shoulder. It's thundering outside, with distant rain following behind. Lighting is illuminating the sky. Perfect weather for snuggling, right?

Nope! Not me and my husband. He's too busy trying to prove his point. What point is that exactly?

Well, in other news, tomorrow is the big day. The day my little girl is finally meeting her father. We are going to meet at 12:30 at the carnival not too far from here— only about a twenty-minute drive. Nairobi is so excited. She has been asking daily for the big day. When I told her a couple of days ago she was meeting her father she had so many questions. When is he coming to see her? Did he get hurt in the Navy? Her little mind was overjoyed with emotions. I was so happy she wanted to meet him, and she was excited to see him. And Ro keeps asking about her every day too. He wanted to see her the day I told him about our daughter at Stoney Creek Park. He was anxious, but I told him I needed time, and I wanted to make sure she was ready. I pray everything goes well.

~Val

Chapter 7

The grandfather clock on the mantle chimes twelve o'clock. It is time for Nairobi to meet her father.

"Mommy! Is it time to go yet?" Nairobi yells, running into her mom's bedroom.

Valerie and Rick are sitting on the bed talking when she runs in. Val grabs her daughter. Her frame feels light as she places her on her lap, enveloping her in her arms tightly. Kissing her all over her face, she tickles her daughter until she hollers...

"Uncle, uncle, uncle—mommy stop, I can't breathe," she yells, her breath panting.

"You had enough?" Valerie laughs as she watches her daughter wiggling to get loose.

"Yes," she replies.

Val squeezes her daughter with a tight hug and plants a kiss on her forehead.

"Daddy, why didn't you stop mommy? You didn't save me." Nairobi collapses into her father's arms.

Rick gazes at his daughter. His warm smile would melt any little girl's heart. Rick pulls his daughter up upon his lap. "Are you daddy's little girl?" he questions. His forehead gently meets her forehead.

"Yes, daddy!" she replies with a smile.

"Always and forever?"

"Yes, always and forever daddy," she giggles.

Val relishes at the moment, remembering why she married her husband. It's always a joy to see Rick playing with Nairobi. She loves her husband and daughter relationship—they get along well. Although Nairobi is meeting Ro today, Valerie feels the connection between Nairobi and Rick. She understands his point of view—Rick has a right to feel the way he does—he's been in Nairobi's life for two years now. She knows her husband just doesn't want to lose the relationship he has with his daughter over to Romelle.

Rick starts to move his nose back and forth on his daughter's nose. "Butterfly nose."

"Butterfly nose, daddy," she replies.

They all make their way downstairs. "Noah, you still eating that cereal?" Rick questions his son. He was sitting at the table, spoon in hand, watching cartoons on the TV screen.

"Yeah," Noah replies.

Before leaving out, Valerie remembers her promise. "Three hours, I promise." She walks up to her husband. She lays her head on her husband's chest, feeling his warm embrace—she inhales his cologne. "I love you, babe, more than anything," she whispers softly.

"I love you too, V. more than always," Rick responds.

His heartbeat thumps lightly against Val's face—she captures the affection of emotions that radiates off of his body.

Rick begins to whisper into his wife's ear, "Looking back, I sometimes regret the decision I made before I met you... Marrying you makes me realize the choice I made after Noah's mother died was rash." His tone is solemn. "I made a choice that seemed rational at that time though, by doing what I thought was best for me at the moment..." He hesitates. He traces her soft face with the backside of his right hand.

Valerie reaches up and wraps her arms around Rick's shoulders. On her tiptoes, she reaches his mouth, kisses her husband on the lips softly. She runs her hand on his face with one long-tender stroke, then walks away without a word. She grabs her purse off of the stand. "Come here Noah. Give me a hug baby." With two pecks to his cheek, Val looks at him as she kneels. "Mommy will see you a little later, okay?"

"Okay, mommy," Noah replies. "See you later."

Rick pulls Val close to him for one last kiss before she walks out the door. His arms firmly wrap around her waistline. He closes the gap between them as he leans his body into hers. "You better not be too long V." His warm breath tingles her nose and sends chills down her spine. Her breast is squashed from the firmness of his chest that is pressed up against her body.

"I won't," she replies.

"I'm not playing with you," he said, as he grips her shoulders tightly, bringing her closer. His eyes dance back and forth between her eyes. "Don't get your ass spanked, coming in here all late and stuff, trying to feed me with some lame excuse either, he said with a smirk." He smacks her butt, then holds it in his hands while giving her a steady gaze. His hands still anchored to her bottom, he tilts his head to one side and kisses her ardently.

Valerie indulges in her husband's soft-wet kiss. Standing on her tip-toes, she still feels his firm pecs, pressing up against her full breast. She stares into his eyes as her husband is reaffirming his stance with the look in his eyes.

"Don't be out too late. Tonight is your night to put the kids to bed early. I'll go to the store and pick up the wine."

She glories in the moment as she feels his dominance, his mood, his gesture of masculinity. "I won't babe," she replies. "Three hours, I promise. And if I'm gonna be late. I promise I'll call you." She opens the screen door and begins to walk out...

"Oh, and Val."

Val's legs lock into place as she turns her head--she looks back over her shoulder and keeps one hand on the handle of the knob. "Yea, babe?"

Make sure you stop and get a new coffee pot from the store before you get back because the other one just went out," Rick said. His eyes bolt towards her butt with enticement. He smacks her butt, then kisses her soft neck gently, using his wet tongue to stroke her as he moved down subtly. His body presses up against the back of hers. He towers over her with heat and excitement--he craves her. He craves her body.

Val utters a light moan that comes from the back of her throat. His wet kisses, his body up against hers--she feels his nature rise as he presses it firmly against her butt. The way he dominates her sends shock waves all through her body. The heat of the moment calls out to her. Her pearls throb with intensity-- her clitoris jumps with pleasure.

"I'll see you later baby," he said, as he grips his crotch with one hand and steps back from Val. He leaves her standing in heated passion.

Val's body jolts in shock waves. She wants to stay. She wants to lay her husband down and climb on top of him. She yearns for his desire-- lovemaking with immense pleasure. She loves the way he smacks her butt, the way it jiggles in his hand. He knows exactly what to do to make me want him! The smile across Val's face meets her husband's thoughts. She knows what he wants when she gets home. Any time he gives her that look of want, his eyes gloss over with enticement. He can't seem to stop them from wandering up and down her body. She's all but anticipating the night that awaits her when she gets home.

She's going to be late. I know why he did that to me. Got me all wet and wanting his long-beautiful body over mines. He knows how to start a fire in me.

Val drives towards the carnival about twenty-five minutes away. With all the orange barrels on the road—construction has it down to one lane. People are blowing their horns as they impatiently wait for the person in front of them to move up.

The weather is warm. Val enjoys the cool breeze blowing out the vents in the jeep. Blasting Mary J. Blige's Strength of a Woman album, she sings the tune to all her songs. She'd been listening to her since her 1992, What's the 411, album debut. She recalls how happy she was to go to her first concert with her brother. Her brother was the one who convinced their mother to let her go see Mary J. Blige— her performance at the Fox theatre was riveting.

Nairobi was in the back, strapped into her child booster seat, looking at cartoons on her tablet. Her purple shorts match her purple shirt and purple glitter sandals. Her hair is attractively pulled up in three ponytails, with purple balls and barrettes.

I really want this day to be perfect for my daughter, Val thinks to herself. Her mind envisions how today is going to go. She tries to imagine a day full of laughter, riding on all sorts of rides, and eating cotton candy.

Val has already briefed her daughter on not saying anything about Rick or her brother, telling her to focus on her day with her father. But the truth is—she didn't want Romelle to find out about her other life just yet. That conversation will have to wait.

They finally pull into the carnival parking lot. She pulls right next to Romelle's car—He's standing by the front entrance. Val braces herself...

Okay, here we go! Val climbs out of the truck. The sky is sunny and clear--perfect carnival weather. Val notes the jammed packed parking lot, its people everywhere. She paces in-between cars and trucks, Nairobi's hand clasped in hers.

"Hello Nairobi," Romelle says with a warm smile. He lifts her up off the ground, twirling her around, her arms around his neck and his around her little frame. He embraces her for a moment, then finally pulls back and sets her on the ground. Glancing at his daughter for the first time, he seems to be overtaken by her presence, her beauty, and maybe her resemblance to himself.

Valerie smiles. She quietly enjoys the moment-- the view of her daughter finally meeting her father. She has dreamed of this day, imagining and replaying this day over and over again in her mind. Her eyes sparkling with life, her cheekbones rising, illuminating her thoughts of satisfaction vividly. Val's heart melts with approval.

Neither one is hesitant, it seems. Her face glowing brightly as she stands watching them both connect. Val never meant to keep her daughter a secret for so long. Nor is she planning to keep her marriage to Rick a secret long either. Her thoughts always condemn her for not being stronger, for being so weak, both mentally and physically. She has risked so much already, but today she refuses to let her guilt overtake her. Today she relishes in what she has accomplished—Her truth is set free. Romelle knows about his daughter.

Two birds fly overhead, their wings outstretched widely, as they glide across the sky.

"It's so nice to finally see you Nairobi," Ro said softly. He bends down to meet her eyes. "You are so big. And so beautiful," he says with tears welling in his eyes. "You look just like your mom and me. You even have the same mole on your face as me, right above your left eyebrow," he adds. "And look!" He raises his hand, "You even have my dimple too," pointing to her left cheek. His jawline tilts slightly as his dimple begins to show. His eyes are fixated on his daughter.

"I'm four daddy," Nairobi said eagerly, raising four fingers on her right hand. "I'm going to preschool this year too."

"You are! Well, are you ready for school?" He stands up, clasps her right hand in his as he begins to walk towards the carousel. "I bet you're excited huh."

"Yeah, mommy has told me all about it. I can't wait to meet my teacher and make new friends next week."

"Well, I'm sure your teacher is going to love you. And you'll make plenty of friends. Do you know how to count yet?" Walking up to the ticket booth, Ro pays for three wrist bands.

"I can count to twenty-five. And I can spell my name too!" She looks up at her dad, her smile glows like the stars in the sky on a clear night. As she begins counting, her voice is light and bubbly. Nairobi steps lightly as she skips across the pavement. Her arms flailing, swinging back and forth can make any adult wish they were a kid again.

"That's great! You're so smart!"

A steady breeze flows gently by them. The park is screaming with invitations to ride the rides and buy everything in sight.

"I know," she replies. "Mommy tells me all the time."

They are so cute. Val lingers behind them just a little. She keeps a steady pace, strolling casually towards the rides in the park. Her goddess braids are arranged up in a bun—she feels the heaviness of her freshly done braids, pulling tightly along the edges of her hair. Reaching up to grab her bun, she unwraps the band, letting her braids fall freely.

Children are screaming everywhere. Music blaring through a speaker just ahead—adults are watching their children as they sway back and forth to the beat of the music.

The smell of hot buttery popcorn fills the air. Valerie gazes upon her daughter skipping and bouncing up and down the sidewalk along-side her father. Her ponytails sway to the same rhythm of her steps.

She's so happy. Her polite manner seems surprising to him. I wonder if Ro feels nervous or if he's afraid to be himself. He seems to be having a good time getting to know her. This is all I ever wanted; Ro knowing our daughter, and our daughter having a chance to spend time with her father...

Val's thoughts drift off as she listens to them talk.

"You wanna get on the carousel Nairobi?" Ro asks.

"Yayyy," she replies. Her face radiates in approval. Her eyes bulge out with gleam. "This is my favorite ride." She jumps up and down with excitement.

Looking back at Val, he smiles, "Just like your momma's," he replies. "She loves this ride too." He holds his gaze on Valerie. His charming smile is enticing.

Valerie feels the warmth of his smile, the subtle hint of love reclaiming her as she recalls the last time they went to the carnival. Just months before she found out she was pregnant with Nairobi. She remembers all too vividly, Ro's fearlessness drove her crazy. He went on almost every single roller coaster. "Sure is," she responds.

"Step right up," the ride conductor calls out, holding the gate open for the next group.

Romelle flashes his and Nairobi's wrist bands to the man at the gate. Nairobi rushes in, running towards the middle. "Slow down Nairobi! I don't want you to fall," he shouts.

Nairobi finds her seat upon a zebra. "I got my favorite animal mommy." She stands there waiting for her mom to pick her up.

"You sure do baby, let me pick you up." Valerie reaches for her daughter by her waist, but before she can lift her Romelle cuts in.

"I got her." Ro gently pushes Valerie to the side—lifting his daughter. "I'm going to stand right here," he says, placing his one hand on her back for security. "I don't want you to fall."

The carousel was full of different animals and began to fill up nicely with boys and girls hopping on one animal after another.

"I'm a big girl daddy. I won't fall," Nairobi said.

"I know sweetie. I just want to stand next to you, okay?"

Valerie grabs the pole of the Zebra. She pulls herself up, allowing Romelle to assist her as she balances herself on the animal.

The conductor calls out the rules before he starts the ride. He gives a round of checks to make sure every child was safe, and then the clacking noise starts as the ride begins to move.

Romelle stands there, his left hand on his daughter's lower back and his right hand on Val's.

Valerie looks down at Romelle as her horse ascends upwards, her eyes locked on his. She wonders if he is happy to be with his daughter.

After they rode the carousel, Ro took his daughter all around the park, riding ride after ride. They ran from the Ferris wheel to the tilt-a-wheel, the bumper cars, and now they're running inside the house of mirrors maze. Time appears to have no distance between Ro and his daughter. They are having a ball, laughing, running around, and getting to know each other. Nairobi skips from ride to ride—she even giggles at her dad's corny jokes.

Snapping pictures, Val captures their every move. She even chooses to sit some rides out so the two could have father and daughter time on the rides together. Making today about them two was her intentions—not the three of them. Capturing intimate moments of them—She never wants to forget this day.

"You want some cotton candy baby girl?" Ro asks his daughter.

She bounces up and down, her pigtails flopping around freely. Smiling from ear to ear, she holds her dad's hand as they begin walking up to the cotton candy stand. "I wanna pink one," she says, pointing.

"Can I get two cotton candy sticks and three bottles of water please?" Ro asks. The attendant nods and gives a courteous smile.

As they wait for their sticks, Ro turns to Val, "I thought you and I could share one. You know... Just like we use to." He pauses and waits for a response.

Valerie nods her head in agreement.

"How are you feeling baby?" she questions as she bends down to tie her daughter's shoestrings. "Are you having a lot of fun?" They have to be burnt out by now.

"Yes, mommy! I love it here. I wish we could come back tomorrow and bring N—."

Val places her finger up to her daughter's mouth, cutting her off. "Remember what I told you earlier," she whispers. Her daughter looks back at her dad who's pulling his wallet out his back pocket to pay for the cotton candy and drinks.

Nairobi almost slipped up and said her brother's name. I *don't think he's paying attention.* Valerie hates herself for putting her daughter in this predicament, but she can't bring up her life right now, not today. Romelle will know in-time when they are both alone.

Val's marriage isn't a secret. She loves her husband, but she knows it will crush Romelle, and that part, she's not exactly ready for. Sleeping with Ro was unexpected, and she's been trying to redeem herself ever since that night—That night she slept with him on the pier while her husband and children were at home. Her flesh wanted one thing, yet her mind wanted something different. She can't have her cake and eat it too— Any kind of intimate relationship with Romelle. She lost her chance the day she gave up on him.

"Here you go baby girl." Ro hands his daughter a cotton candy stick. They head over to a picnic table that is just across the way. "You like your cotton candy?"

Val inhales a hint of Ro's cologne as a breeze brush past them. She closes her eyes in a breathless moment of euphoria...

"It's really good daddy!" Nairobi replies.

"Great," he replies, giving her a nod of satisfaction.

Val looks at her watch. Three hours have passed by already. Pulling her phone out of her purse, she notes that Rick has left her a voicemail and two text messages. Her eyes bulge widely in surprise. She wants to leave in haste before her husband responds in a way Val was not ready to deal with. I have to get going, even though I know Nairobi is nowhere near ready. She knows that she needs to wrap things up--keeping her promise to her husband is important. "Hey baby, we have to get ready to go," she exclaims.

"No mommy! I don't wanna go," she cries.

"We have to get going. Mommy has to stop and pick up something from the store."

"But I don't wanna leave. I'm not ready to go." Her eyes are downcast, and her face soaking in discontentment.

Her eyes are glued to her daughter with empathy. She hates to see her little girl pouting. "I know Nairobi, but we have to go." Her tone is soft and empathetic.

"Please mommy, just one more ride. Please, with cherries on top!" she begs. Nairobi gives her mother those unrelenting puppy dog eyes, with her bottom lip poking out.

"Look, how about daddy tries to win you a teddy bear before we go," Ro suggests. His eyes dance between his daughter and Val— watching to see how she feels about him interjecting. "What do you think?" he questions Val.

Val looks at Romelle, then back at Nairobi. "Umm, I don't know baby," she finally responds.

"Please," Nairobi and Ro say in unison.

"Okay. Okay. Okay," she finally gives in.

"Yay!" Nairobi yells out.

"Let's go over to the racehorses," Ro suggests.

They all begin walking over to the horses. Val notes the couple walking hand and hand beside them. Val's eyes drift as she follows them as they pause— They share an intimate kiss. To her right, a young woman strolls with a huge teddy bear in her arms. Her man must've won it at one of the game stations. She notes the wedding band on her hand as she holds it out for her husband to grab. *How romantic.*

Life seems simple. Children stand patiently in long lines, waiting for their turns on the roller coasters. Crowds the lemonade stands, and people are chopping on sugary elephant ears as they walk past. Birds swoop down, feeding on the many crumbs that have dropped to the ground. Couples were riding the Ferris wheel together, kissing in the kissing booth, and holding hands as they stroll through the park. Tired parents and grandparents sat on the benches to take a rest. Fun is in the air, and so is love.

Valerie understands the significance of the day—her daughter making a bond with her father. Valerie takes pictures of Ro and Nairobi riding their last ride. *I'll make a photo album and share the pictures later.*

She grabs her daughter's hand, walking her towards the park exit. She swings her back and forth as she holds one hand and Ro holds the other.

Val feels her phone vibrates in her back pocket. She pulls her phone out and sees three missed calls and five missed text messages. Her stomach tightens as she puts her phone away in her pocket. A barrage of questions from her husband is bound to ensue as soon as she walks through the doors.

Reaching her Durango, Val unlocks her truck with her remote key-fob. She tosses her cross-body purse and sunglasses inside on the passenger seat. "You enjoyed your day baby?" Val asks.

"Mommy, I really had fun! Can I see daddy tomorrow too?" she asks.

"Well, we—"

"Hey baby girl." Ro squats down, coming eye level to Nairobi. "I really had fun with you too. I know this was our first time seeing each other, but I promise this will not be the last."

"Okay," she responds somberly, as she hugs her big teddy bear her father won for her. It's almost as big as her.

"Well, how about you call me tomorrow if that's okay with your mom." He glances up at Val, then back at his daughter. Sweat trickles down his face—he wipes his forehead. "I can't explain how happy I am. Seeing you and spending time with you today made me feel good. I was a little nervous to meet you, but we had a good time right?"

"We sure did daddy," She grabs him around his neck, hugging her father tightly.

Romelle hugs his daughter, his arms around her little waist. He closes his eyes and whispers, "I'll see you next time baby girl."

On the drive home, Valerie reflects on a beautiful day—she finds the imagery of her daughter and Ro overwhelming. It's such a release. I'm so happy they finally met. My daughter knows her biological father now.

Her eyes become wet. She glances in her rearview mirror and sees Nairobi knocked out. She's had a long day—she'll be sleeping until Val has to wake her up at her next stop.

This is all my fault. I really can't believe I've screwed up so bad. How could I'd been so blind? THIS ISN'T FAIR! I loved him. I wanted a life with him. But now it's too late.

Val begins to sniffle. Too late for our daughter to see what her life could've been like with both her mom and dad in the same home. Pulling into the parking lot, she pulls down her visor. Her raccoon eyes look back at her. She grabs a napkin from her counsel and wipes away her tear-stained face. Her solemn mood antagonizes her.

She collects her thoughts before waking Nairobi up and taking her into the store. She feels dizzy, her stomach feels like acid churning. She puts her hand up to her mouth and slowly waits for the feeling to subside.

Val hurries into the store and searches for a coffee pot. She strolls through the aisles. She picks out a coffee pot in aisle four.

Valerie ignores the vibrations of her phone that is once again going off in her purse. She already knows it's Rick, trying to find out where she is.

She heads towards the front of the store, walking down the third aisle, she walks past the pregnancy kits. She pays for her coffee pot and grabs a chocolate bar to add to her bill.

I don't know why I'm feeling sick, but hopefully, my husband doesn't feel like arguing today. I just want to walk in and take a long-hot shower.

Before pulling out the parking lot, Val grabs her phone and sends a text...

Val

OMW!

Just picked up the coffee pot.

Chapter 8

September 1, 2019

Dear Diary,

It's 2:48 AM. I can't sleep. The house is quiet, and I keep tossing and turning. I keep thinking about yesterday. My baby girl had an amazing time at the carnival with her father. All she could do was talk about her day at the park, how much fun she had with her father. When I asked her how did she feel about meeting her dad on our way home, she said it was so exciting, and she couldn't wait to see him again.

Ro texted me last night telling me how grateful he was for yesterday. I saw his eyes fill up with tears, his voice slightly cracking when it was time for us to leave. He made me wanna cry too. Seeing them say goodbye was difficult. Especially when I saw him waving us goodbye from my rearview mirror, it's as if they had not been apart. As if he was there by my side during delivery, instead of leaving for the Navy. They are going to be inseparable. I won't keep him from her. All he wants is his daughter in his life. After I had gotten Nairobi in her booster seat and shut the door, Ro hugged me tightly. Feeling his warm face against my cheek, he whispered in my ear, Thank you for having our daughter. I love you.

It was hard for me. Hard for me to see Ro and our daughter together without thinking of us myself, a complete family. No one can tell me. If they were in my shoes, they wouldn't have the same thoughts as me. No matter how wrong it is. We broke up so abruptly when Ro went to the military. I was so upset that I couldn't talk to him, nor see him off. Now, I know that was such a huge mistake. He didn't deserve it. I thought he turned his back on the baby and me. Instead, I was the one who turned my back on him. I forced a life upon myself that I didn't have to. My trust issues and my insecurities. Why did I have to raise my walls up all the time? Even when I try not to, they're still there.

Why did I have to be so hurt, so embarrassed? It was not my fault. That day years ago was not my fault—I was only fifteen. I couldn't do anything. I couldn't say anything. That grown-ass man knew what he was doing. He was on top of me before I knew it. It's his fault! Not mines! That's why I'm so messed up now. I wish I could rewind the time, erase everything that happened to me before I dated Ro. But I can't. So I'm stuck living in a world that hurt me. That took my innocence away. A world that never asked me what I wanted. Why did it have to happen to me?

Well, let me get some sleep.

~Val

The morning sun beats its rays upon Valerie's sleeping eyes. Her eyes blink as she slowly opens her eyes. She rolls over to wrap her arms around her husband, but instead, she met with a white envelope staring her in the face. She sits up, grabbing the letter off Rick's pillow...

WE NEED TO TALK...

What? What's this supposed to mean? She flips the letter over. Nothing else is written. She throws the royal blue and white duvet covers off to one side and places both feet upon the floor, feeling the gray and white plush rug against her cold feet. She grabs her robe off the bench at the foot of her bed. The robe strings hang down in a bow around her waist. Valerie's footsteps move swiftly across her room, and her eyes move rapidly from one place to another. She glances over to her desk but sees nothing. *Where's my journal?*

Valerie feels the compression of her chest--restriction of air as her lungs struggle to inhale normally. Now I know I left it right here on my desk. What the heck happened to it? Desk drawers open and close back with frantic thuds. Braids fall in front of her face as she kneels to the floor. Moving her hair back with a tight grip of one hand, she moves her free hand back and forth under her bed. The soft carpeted floor brushes her skin with friction as she tries to grab a hard object. She pulls it closer to her as she slowly lifts her body up.

"DAMNIT!" she scuffs. "Where the heck is it?" she cries out loud, holding a notebook in her hand.

The book slams with a light thud upon the carpet. Her butt falls to the ground. She scours her room, scanning from one side to another. She glances over at the bay window. She scans the space under her desk, behind her bed, under the chair, and towards the ledge where she sometimes sits and reads...

"There it is! I don't remember putting it down there. I could've sworn I left it on my desk." she exclaims. She walks over to grab her journal. Did Rick move it? Naw, he would kill me if he knew the stuff I wrote in here. I have to be more careful, she thought.

She puts her journal in her desk drawer, placing a book over it to hide it. The desk drawer slides close without a sound. Valerie pause as she hoovers over her desk with both hands. Thoughts about yesterday fill her mind.

Jumping in the shower, she thinks of Nairobi and her father getting on the racehorses together. Brushing her teeth, she thinks about them bumping each other in the bumper cars. When she sits on the bar stool waiting for her coffee to finish brewing, she thinks of the times where Ro picked Nairobi up and carried her on his back. Even when she made breakfast for the family—cooking eggs and pancakes, she thought of them sharing an elephant ear together and getting white powder dust all over their faces. She smiles and gives a near faint snicker as she reminisces about them laughing and playing together in the park. She knows that her daughter will never be the same. She has two fathers in her life now. Two important men that love her greatly—If only she could say the same thing about her father.

The difficulty in forgiving her dad is the sole reason she doesn't visit her parents nor speak to them much. She loves her mother and father, but the hurt she feels inside keeps her in bondage—resenting the fact that her father let her down and her mother didn't stand up for her. Val thought that a mother would always stand up to her husband when she felt he was not protecting his family. Instead, her mother stepped aside. She said nothing. She did nothing.

Although she would hear faint sounds of crying coming from her mother's bedroom late at night when her parents would think she was asleep, Val would walk up to her parent's bedroom door and wonder what was wrong with her mom. She never spoke a word or questioned her mother. She didn't want to intrude. After the incident, Val felt it was her fault. She felt her mother was disappointed in her—upset with her and blamed her for that night.

Leaving home at fifteen was difficult but necessary...

Keys rattle in the far distance. Val straightens her body up and glances towards her bedroom doorway. Loud thumps illuminate up the steps as her husband enters through the side door. Val turns her head to the side, glancing out the window.

I didn't hear his truck pull up. Maybe he parked on the street. She glances over to the second-hand clock on the wall—Eleven fifteen. She grabs the black hair scrunchie off her desk and flips her head down. She tightly gathers her hair into one big ponytail and pulls the scrunchie on, tying it twice around her ponytail. She straightens back up, tosses her hair back, and walks towards the doorway. She descends the stairs bare-feet in her silver-satin gown that cuts off just above her knees.

"Hey, babe, where did you go so early in the morning?" Valerie's arms stretch around her husband's neck. Her lips meet with his softly.

"I went to my mom's house," Rick replies.

Still holding on to her husband, she walks forward, forcing his body to walk backward until they both plop down onto the sofa. She cradles his hips as she throws both her legs on either side of him. She lays her head on his firm pecs. "I missed you when I woke up babe," she exclaims softly. "I rolled over to wrap my arms around you, and instead, I got your note staring back at me in my face. I was wet for you," she continues, as she starts to give him short-soft pecks across his forehead, his cheeks, and then down his neck. She moves her body up and down with every kiss.

Rick's arms rest upon her soft butt--his grasp is firm as he cradles her bottom with every motion of her sensual rhythm. "Where're the kids," he asks as he turns towards the stairs.

"Watching TV," She turns his head back towards hers and continues her advances. "Don't worry baby, I'll be quiet," she begins. "You left me hanging this morning. I wanted to make love to you, kiss you, and caress you, and feel you inside of me, but instead, I got a cool drink of water to cool me down," She smirks. Her eyes stare at him with benevolence. "Laying in the bed with nothing to do and nowhere to go, I thought about how we would just watch TV and cuddle all day. You know... Like we use to do. You remember that?"

"Yeah, I do," he replies—his voice shutters under her kisses. "I remember a lot of things V." He pants heavily with need as his eyes close to her erotic advances.

She ignores his last statement and continues to kiss him softly on his neck, then caresses his pecs as she continues to kiss his face and then his lips again. She tries to entice him—She yearns to make love to him. "Relax baby." Flashes of heat propel down her lower region. She gently grabs his lower lip in-between her lips and pulls softly. Her lips begin to softly suck on his full lower lip—She knows what this will do to him.

Her advances begin to work. She feels his hands maneuvering up and down her body. He squeezes her butt cheeks together as the sound of moaning comes from the back of his throat. Val feels his nature rise as she continues to move up and down on his lap--her body calls for her husband with intense passion. His jogging pants give way to his firmness--Val feels it touching her perils as he makes his nature rise up and down under her soft silky gown, which rises up her hips now.

Val moves his joggers just enough to let out what is pleasantly waiting for her. She pulls him out with one hand. Heat steams from his nature, which pulsates through Val's hand. His veins immensely throb as she holds the thick package in her hands.

Rick glides his finger under her gown. He moves her stringed panties to one side. She is moist to his touch. He closes his eyes as he lets out a deep-low utterance.

"Umm." Val moans with satisfaction as the pleasure of his touch inside her sends her body right into over-drive.

"You like that baby," Rick questions.

"Yes babe," she replies, her voice in a low whisper.

"You want it baby?"

"Yes, bae," she replies.

Blood rushes to her heart as his nature meets her jewels. "Ahhh baby," she moans.

Val continues to kiss her husband's thick lips. The heat of his thick tongue glides seductively across hers, and his tongue expands in her mouth. She continues to thrust her body in slow motion on top of her husband. Her body jerks as her pearls pulsate in heat and becomes moister with every insertion of his package.

The sounds of lovemaking echoes through the walls of their home as she climaxes.

"Shhhhh," Rick warns his wife as he cups her mouth with the palm of his hand. "The kids..."

Valerie pulls back, lifting her head off his chest. Valerie can sense her husband's discontent. After they made love, he didn't rub her face and talk to her like he usually does. "What's wrong babe," she asked as she glances into his eyes. She can't read him. He's staring out the window--looking straight through her like she was made of plexiglass. "Is there something wrong? You seem distracted."

Rick pulls away from his wife, lifting her off of his lap. "Yeah, It's something I really need to say to you, but I need you to listen to me without listening just to respond."

"Okay..." she replied. Did he find out about Ro and me? Was it him that moved my journal last night? Or was it this morning before he left out? Val tries to gauge him but waits for his response before she gets carried away with her thoughts.

"First, I didn't get to really speak to you yesterday when you got in. I had to leave and pick my mom up from the airport. When I got back, you were sleeping."

"Yeah, I was wondering what happened. I thought she was supposed to get in at one."

"Her flight kept getting delayed. She didn't make it in until six." Ro replies.

"Wow, I know she was mad," Valerie replies, as she shakes her head.

"Yea, she was pretty annoyed." Rick looks over towards the bay window. Quietly, he seems to be waiting to say something else. He looks over towards the stairs. "The kids should be coming down soon."

"After I fed them breakfast, they went upstairs to watch Jurassic World Two. I'd lost my appetite after I cooked. I felt lightheaded for some reason, so I just ate a couple of strawberries... Oh, and I made you a plate of pancakes and eggs and put it up in the microwave. You want me to warm it up?"

"No, not right now. I'll eat later."

"Okay," she replies. The house still lingers with discomfort. She's waiting for the ball to drop any moment. For some reason, Val knows her husband all too well...

"How was Nairobi's day yesterday, at the carnival?"

"Oh, she had a wonderful time." Valerie smiles. She knows where the conversation is going now. He just wants to see how yesterday went.

"How was she with Romelle? I mean, was she nervous?

"No," Val replies.

Oh. So she didn't have a hard time warming up to him?"

She knows he may not want to hear the truth. She pulls her hair back, flinging the long-heavy braids all to one side. "Actually, no, she didn't," she finally admits with caution. She wants to be truthful. Val smooths out Rick's shirt with her palms as if ironing the wrinkles out by hand. She adores the way his shirt fit snug around his firm pecs and his broad shoulders.

His brows furrow as they quickly raise, "Oh." Rick moves the conversation along. "What about Romelle? How was he?"

"He was anxious to see her. Actually, they both got along well, as if they had always known each other as a matter-of-fact." Val leans back on the sofa, realizing she may have said a little too much. She rephrases her words. "Umm, I mean, they both really enjoyed spending time together. I'm glad it didn't feel awkward... For Nairobi, you know."

Rick peers at Val slightly. "Yeah, that's great. Glad our daughter had a great time. It seems like she will be fine visiting him again, huh. I mean, I know she's going to start spending a lot of time with him, right?" Rick stands up and moves to the table to sit by himself. He begins to go through the letters on the table. Opening the first letter and then the second.

"Uhh, Yea, she's going to spend some days with him. I will contact Ro tomorrow to set up some days. He says we need to talk about it, and I think I should be fair. Don't you think so?"

"How many days you think a week?" His curious expression was not hidden.

Val lets out a small sigh. She waits a moment before she answers. She places her elbows on her knees and props her face up with her hands as she leans forward. "I'm not completely sure. But I will let you know what we come up with. I don't know his schedule yet, so I need to take that under consideration," she exclaims.

Rick says nothing. He glances over the second piece of mail before placing it back down. He places his hands on the table and pushes his seat out. Rising up, Rick strolls over to the bay window. He grabs at his collar and unloosens his top two buttons on his polo shirt. His hand rubs back and forth across the back of his neck as he stares out the window. His tall stature compliments his solid physique.

Val walks over to her husband. His stance is wide. His agitation doesn't come as a surprise. The smell of his cologne fills her nostrils. Looking at his stance, she assumes he is contemplating on what to say next. She wants to wrap her arms around him. However, she settles for standing side by side.

"Listen, I know this may be rough on you, but this is important."

He places both hands in his pockets as he turns to face his wife. "To whom? To our daughter, Romelle, or you?" His gaze fixed upon her, his bearded face, is stoic.

Val reaches her hands to touch his, but Rick does not release his hands from his pockets. She retreats and interlocks her hands instead. Valerie knows her husband well. She knows that he feels isolated, helpless, and even agitated, rightfully so. However, she understands this may be difficult and reassures her husband that everything will be fine. "It's important to all of us, hopefully. I will keep you informed on everything babe, I promise. I know this may be difficult and even nerve-wracking, but this is what we should both want—our daughter having a relationship with her father. He's done nothing wrong, sweetheart," she exclaims. She puts her hand on her chest and continues. "He hasn't had a chance or a say in the matter of me having our little girl. It wasn't fair to him. And I just wanna make things right—by allowing our daughter to grow up with her father in her life. Two fathers in her life," she adds. Looking up at her husband, she moves closely in, closing the space between them, as she places one hand on his shoulder. She stares into his eyes. Her eyes dance back and forth between his eyes. "Are you going to be okay with our daughter seeing her father? Are we still a team?"

Rick looks upwards towards the ceiling, then back down at his wife, catching her gaze. He pulls back. "Yeah, we are a team, Val...

He opens his mouth to say something but retreats. Rick turns and walks away, leaving his wife standing there. Heading towards the stairs, he begins to climb them. He stops midway, turning back to look at Val. "I want to meet him this week." Then he continues going up the steps, leaving Val standing there.

Chapter 9

Valerie sits in her jeep. The ignition is still off as she listens to Maxwell play on the radio. She hears her phone vibrating. She reaches in her purse and pulls her phone out. Her eyes are frozen in time, fixated on the messages she sees.

Ro:

Hey! Are you busy?

Meet me in an hour. My place.

26431 Buttercup Ave. Apt. 3250 Royal Oak, MI

She lays her phone down on the phone cradle in her truck. Sitting in front of the drug store, she grabs the bag, pulling out the small white and blue box she just purchased inside. Valerie feels the throb of her heartbeat increase. She begins to rub her forehead back and forth. Four years ago, was it the same feeling? Did I feel this way? She wonders... Is her apprehension warranted; nausea, dizziness, and consistent tiredness?

Her eyes are fixated on the box. The sudden cravings for pickles, is it a sign?

It's September the fifteenth—when was my last cycle? Am I late? She throws the box back into the bag on the passenger seat. Closing her eyes, she throws her head back on the headrest and takes a deep breath in, and then she exhales slowly. It just can't be... Sticking her key in the ignition, she pulls off and heads towards Royal Oak.

It takes Val forty-five minutes to reach Ro's apartment. She sits in her truck for a couple of minutes, waiting for the light-headedness to go away. She grabs the newly bought bottle of orange juice and snaps open the top. Juice trickles down her throat. Valerie closes her eyes as she feels her throat moisten with satisfaction.

She takes in the scenery. Well-manicured lawns and the prestigious look of the neighborhood makes the apartment building stand out. There's a tranquilness that surrounds the building and a valley of trees that streamlines the pathway towards the bridge, which crosses over a pond. Ducks are swimming in groups. There's a young couple, looking to be in their mid or upper twenties jogging along the side of the isolated road. Valerie also notes the couple that was strolling their baby along the bridge. The location is gorgeous.

Val gets out of her truck and walks up to his door, pressing the doorbell. She feels the thin crisp air as she stands, waiting for him to open the door. She zips her purple jacket up to her neck. A man a couple of doors down checks Val out with a flirtatious smirk. I hate it when people stare at me. I know the only thing he is looking at is my butt.

"Hey," Ro says. His hazel eyes catch Val off guard. He meets her with a wide smile showing his dimples in his cheeks.

Moving to the side, he grabs her hand. "I didn't hear you pull up, come on in. I hope I didn't have you waiting long."

"Just a tad bit," she replies, jokingly.

"I'm sorry. I was taking the steaks out of the oven."

"It's cool." She follows Romelle through his door.

Ro slips his hands on Val's jacket and pulls it down her arms. Ro walks over a couple of steps and places it in his closet. "Have a seat anywhere. I'll bring your plate."

"Plate? So when you learn how to cook?" she says, slightly giggling. She couldn't help but notice the savory smell of gravy and the robust aroma of fine food.

"Ha, ha, ha, very funny, I see you got jokes."

Valerie's eyes scan the room from left to right. The mocha and cream room is inviting. Two lamps on the end tables cast a low but warm ambiance. The smell of food grilling fills the air with a mouth-watering aroma. Val pulls the black chair away from the marble table and notes the fine finish as she sits down.

Ro places the plates down on the table. He lights the white candle in the center, then pours red wine into the wine glasses sitting on each side of them. "You have a New York strip steak, a sweet potato, and asparagus smothered in butter. I hope you like it," he says beaming. Valerie smiles with delight. Her face glows from the warmth of her cheeks. Her eyes widen as she takes in the presentation. The aroma was divine. She can't believe he went through all this trouble to cook.

"Lord, thank you for this food…" Ro unclasps his hands and opens his eyes. "Bon appetite."

Val takes a bite of her steak—mouth-watering and succulent. "Ummm, this is delicious. So tender and juicy." She grabs a fork full of her potatoes then finishes it off with the asparagus. "This is seasoned to perfection," she adds.

"Well, thank you, my dear," he replies, nodding his head with reddened cheeks. "You didn't think I could throw down like this, did you? Thought I was a rookie, huh?" A small slurp cascades from his lips as he takes a sip of wine.

"Honestly, I didn't. I didn't think you could cook at all."

Laughing, Ro takes his napkin up to his mouth, holding back his wine that almost escapes his lips. "I can probably cook better than you," he adds, wiping his lips with his napkin.

"Now, let's not get beside ourselves, Chef Ramsey," she says sarcastically. Silence fell over the room--Outside the continuous smacking of her lips. Time goes past, as they both work on clearing their plates.

"You must love it. You haven't said a word," he chuckles.

Taking a sip from her chilled wine, Val washes down the last bit of her food. "This Dinner is really good Ro."

Valerie indulges in another glass of wine as they move to the sofa.

Romelle flops down next to Valerie on the loveseat, their knees touch. "I'm glad you enjoyed dinner, are you stuffed? I notice you didn't ask for seconds."

"Ha, ha, ha. Very funny, Mr. comedian! You know I don't eat two plates. I never have. I leave that part up to you."

She begins to miss the way they use to play and joke around. She begins to feel the empty void of her best friend being away. She didn't know how much she had missed her first love. She recalls all too fondly, the way he used to make her smile through difficult times—the way he soothed her during crying episodes whenever she felt the agonizing abandonment of her parents. Having these thoughts was not good. Missing him was not healthy. She's married. She has a new life now.

"Well, that's not the only thing you've never done, Lol."

"What's that supposed to mean?" Her eyelids raise with curiosity.

He touches her thigh, "Nothing," he responds. "Look, thanks again for letting me meet our daughter. I still can't wrap my mind around having one." He drops his head down slightly, rubbing the palms of his hands together. "I really love her, you know. And I'm sorry I wasn't there when you had her or was raising her—"

"Listen, Ro," she cuts him off. "It's not your fault. I don't blame you. If I'd answered your calls, your texts, or even reached out to you through your family, you and Nairobi would've never been apart." She feels empathetic towards his emotions. His words tug at her heartstrings.

"I can't help it, Val. I've missed so much of our daughter's life, and I promise I won't miss anymore. I really wanna be in her life. I wanna be in yours too." His eyes are steady, feeling warm and inviting. He skims Val's jawline with his fingertips. "I promise to never let you go. Do you trust me?"

His low soft tone compliments his deep voice—resonating down the spine of Val's back. She feels the intensity of his voice. It feels good to hear that he remembers she has difficulty trusting people. The warmth of his touch upon her face intensifies as her heart throbs faster and faster. She remembers how he used to make her feel at ease—knowing how to break her walls down. Her emotions and love for him are unyielding.

Her blood rushes through her body as heat travels down to her sensitive areas. "I do trust you." She bites her lips as he rubs his hands on her inner thigh. How could I just let this man walk out of my life? I was so stupid, so prideful. If I had just picked up one phone call, ran to him before he left for basic training, stopped myself from writing that goodbye letter...

He kneels in front of Val on the floor. His gaze is frozen upon hers as he grabs her hands. "I'm glad you trust me. Ever since that day back in 2015 on the pier, I knew I had to protect you. I knew that I didn't want anything or anyone to hurt you like you'd been hurt that night. I vowed to never let you go and to always be there for you. I know that I left for the military, but that decision wasn't all entirely for me. It was for us." His freshly cut hair compliments his facial features, his neatly cut beard attractively brings out his jawline.

"What do you mean?" Her brows narrow. She begins biting the inside of her cheeks.

"Well, I listed you as my beneficiary on my insurance when I was in the Navy."

Her eyebrows shot up quickly. "What? Why?" she responds with surprise.

"Because Val..." Ro sits on the floor in front of Val. His hazel eyes are intent but mesmerizing. His hands cup hers as he brings them to his lips and kisses the backside of her hands gently.

"I'm in love with you, and I always will be," Romelle continues. "Since we were fourteen, you've been my best friend, my soulmate, and of late, I realize the mother of my child. Call me a fool, but you're the only one for me..."

Romelle lifts one knee off the floor and opens a small black box. "I would love it if you would make me the happiest man alive. Please say you will be my wife."

A bright diamond illuminates before her eyes. Valerie's palms quickly slap up against her cheeks, her brows boost high, and her mouth jerks open without consent. "Oh my god!" I can't believe it—this can't be happening to me right now. Stunned, her eyes remain wide-open with shock. No words escape. Tears slowly stream down her face.

"Awww, I didn't expect you to cry like this baby." He grabs her and wraps her in his arms.

"This is all I ever wanted," she sobs into his chest, crying inconsolably. "I can't believe this! This can't be real right now," she cries out.

Romelle removes her hands from her eyes. He wipes her tears away and cups her chin in one hand. His gaze is drawn to her lips. He tilts his head while cradling hers, he kisses her softly on her lips. "I love you, baby," he whispers, over and over again.

His full soft-pink lips meet Val's. His warm touch, his firm-confident tone arouses her. Her hands ache with the desire to touch and explore every part of his body. She begins to feel sexual throbbing and tingling in her lower region.

Romelle pulls her closer, expressing his burning desire for her. He begins to trace her face, her jawline, and then her sensitive areas.

"I love you too Ro" she finally responds softly. "I always have." She melts into his passionate kiss. Her lips part—She feels the gentle glide of his tongue. Tilting her head slightly to the side, she gives in to the passion as their kiss grows deeper and deeper. Feeling Ro's gentle caress of her full breast, her nipples become immensely stimulated, and her breathing is heavier. His audible moans make her quiver. She arches her back as she moans softly, "Ummm." With Romelle kneeling on the floor, in-between her legs, she wraps her legs around his waist as he kisses her deeper and deeper. He places his hands on her curvaceous hips. The roaring of his moans entices her. Further, her body grows wet—she shudders in pleasure.

Val tilts her head back as he pulls her breast out of her bra. Tracing the outline of her breast, then gliding over her nipples gently—Romelle begins to kiss her neck. Then her soft-rounded breast...

This feels so good. I want him so bad. "Ah," she moans. I feel so safe when I'm with him, free to be vulnerable, so free to be myself, she thought. "Ahh..." Her eyes are closed, and her body lays back on his sofa. She enjoys the pleasures of what was before her.

Wait, what am I doing? I can't do this, not to Rick. Lord, help me—give me the strength to stop. I can't be stupid this time, so weak, so selfish.

She quickly pushes him off of her, grabbing her breast, she places them back into her bra. Tears rush down her cheeks. She claps her palms up against her face to cover her tears.

"What's wrong baby?" His tone is endearing. "Why are you crying?"

She continues to sniffle, wiping away at her tears.

"Did I do something wrong?" he questions.

"No," she replies. She tries to wipe away the tears that fall endlessly. She shakes her head from side to side. Her throat feels constricted. "I just can't." She feels guilt-ridden, her soul aches. Her heart and mind want two different things, but she can't give in to her emotions.

Pulling her hands away from her face, wiping her tears with his thumbs gently, he kisses her cheeks, "Baby stop crying. Tell me what's wrong. Please tell me what's wrong." Ro cries.

She opens her mouth, but nothing comes out. I have to tell him. I have to tell him the truth. I never meant for things to go this far.

"I'm married, Ro. I'm already married!" she finally admits. She begins to bawl into her palms—her lament tears of regret and sorrow echoes upon the apartment walls.

Romelle pulls back, and silence falls over the place. He gets up and paces the floor. His eyes become wet, tears begin to fall down his face. He looks at Val, then turns away, standing with his back to her. He begins to cry out, looking heavenward, "She's my first love—MY FIRST..." Sounds of his fists pounding the wall resonate loudly. "I haven't been with any other woman. How could she do this to me? LORD, WHY? First, she keeps our daughter from me, and now this..." He drops down to his knees, bursting out into tears. "How could I have been such a fool? How come I didn't see this coming? You were all I saw and all I wanted to see!" he shouts.

Valerie walks over to him, meeting him on the floor, "I'm so sorry Ro. I'm sorry. Please forgive me. I'm sorry!" she repeats over and over. She throws her arms around him, trying to console him. She feels terrible —guilty for hurting him over and over again.

He looks up, cupping her face in his palms, his eyes locked on her brown eyes. "You just can't be married, Val. You can't do this to me! You just can't. I'm in love with you. We were supposed to get married," he sobs. "It was supposed to be me— Me and you, husband and wife!" he yells. "I can't let you go— You belong to me!

Chapter 10

Monday-September 16th

Dear Diary,

It's 3:34 am. I can't sleep. My mind is racing a thousand miles per minute. Seeing Ro cry like that yesterday sunk my heart deep into the abyss. I know he's confused. I know he's probably angry as hell with me, as he should be. Telling Ro I'm married was one of the hardest things I had to do apart from telling him about our daughter he thought I had aborted. I didn't do right by him. I've done so much wrong. I just keep fucking over his life. I led him to believe that I wasn't married. I hung on to the thought of us, the what if's, for too long. I'm so selfish. I feel so awful. How can I live with myself? How can I look at myself in the mirror again? When I drop Nairobi off to see him next week, I'm not going to be able to face him.

I love him, but I can't keep doing him wrong. The marriage proposal was sweet but unexpected. We almost made love again. SHIT! I feel like such an idiot. I have a life, a husband, and children. Why do I keep putting myself in these crazy predicaments? Truth is... I never got over you. I don't know what I'm going to do. Should I stay, or should I go?

~Val

Valerie comes upstairs after watching the news and having her morning cup of coffee. Walking into her bedroom, she glances at the time—10:15 A.M. Her children are off to school, and the house is awfully quiet. It's only been two hours since she's seen them off. Rick is a great husband. He never makes her feel that rearing the children up, getting them ready for school, nor dropping them off was strictly a woman's job. They both share in the responsibilities. She knows she is fortunate to have such a man.

Looking at her diary on her desk, Val thinks to write a good-bye letter, but to whom? She doesn't know yet. She doesn't even know if her husband is going to want her after everything she's done to him.

Sleeping with Romelle is unforgivable, the ultimate sin in a marriage. She decides to come back to her diary a little later. She grabs a towel out of her linen closet and glances at herself in the mirror. I really need to lose this stomach— pinching at her stomach fat. She jumps in the shower and tries to wash the memory of Romelle away, making love to him and hurting him. She feels like her life is a roller coaster—traveling high and low, with terrifying twists and turns.

She scrubs her body vigorously—her skin becomes rough from the constant rubbing. She stands motionless in the shower, arms laying across her chest, her eyelids shut. She soaks in the rush of rushing water upon her bare skin. The steam soaks into the glass shower doors. But no matter the temperature of the water, or the scrubbing of her skin, she can't erase the sin from her body, the lust from her mind, nor the pain of loving two people from her heart.

The showerhead gradually slows down as Valerie turns off the steamy water. The sliding glass door slides open, and Val reaches for her towel off the stand. She blots her face first, then wraps the purple towel around her body. She wipes her foggy mirrors in a circular motion with the palm of her right hand as her left-hand rests upon the countertop for balance.

She puts music on to disrupt the quietness in her room. Soothing sounds of the R & B singer Maxwell fills the air. She glances out the window, noting the thick mirage-grey clouds. The tree leaves are blowing back and forth vigorously. I really need to talk to my brother... Mark will be home from his travels in two weeks. Mark is Val's older brother by three years. She can always talk to him about anything—their loyalty towards each other is unbreakable.

Val has been contemplating if she should tell Mark everything; About Romelle, the affair, the unexpected marriage proposal. I have to talk to my brother about the affair. I got to get this off my chest. I know what I've done is unforgivable. Val's thoughts run away with her as she desperately searches for ways to let off some stress. I don't want my brother looking at me like an adulteress little sister. He's never judged me before, but I don't think I can handle his disappointment with me. I always try to make him proud of me, graduating from college, being a great mother to his niece, and not being a failure.

Ugh, telling him is going to suck! Hopefully, I can talk to him as soon as he gets back in town. No, I'll wait a couple of days before I throw all my issues on him.

Valerie gets distracted from her thoughts, noticing the sounds of distant thunder. She walks to the bay window—her blinds are drawn open. She notes how ominous the sky is, light raindrops begin to tap on her window. Flashes of lightning dance across the sky. She opens the window for a moment to feel the wind whipping into her room. The breeze feels refreshing. The air is heavy with moisture.

Val suddenly clasps her hand on her mouth, the instant acid churning in her throat catches her off guard. The queasy in her stomach makes her cautious. She swallows hard as she stands there soaking in the atmosphere. As the wind begins to pick up, Val shuts the window—shielding herself from the storm that was brewing. Rolling thunder glides across the dark purple sky, and heavy rain begins slamming into the roof.

SWV's song; Weak, serenades the room on her Bluetooth speaker. Her phone is connected to her speaker. The song speaks to her soul—battling between what her heart wants and what she knows is morally right is tiresome. She can't believe she's in love with another man—the father of her child, her first love and best friend. But everything inside her says, don't keep falling. Get up, Val. GET UP!

The truth is, she can't help it. No one ever said life was easy, that love would be simple, that everyone grows up and makes all the right choices. Valerie understands this for the first time in her life. Everything is not perfect, and she hasn't made all the right choices. I never planned for any of this to happen. Her eyes grow moist. What type of woman am I? What type of mother would be so reckless?

She places one hand on her forehead. Her head hangs low, in disgust. I have a daughter. What the hell am I teaching her? Tears welling up in her eyes, she can't hold them back any longer. The thoughts of her careless behaviors are unyielding. She falls apart—crumbling in the middle of her bedroom floor. Tears of torment roll down her face rapidly. "Why? Why does this hurt so bad!" she yells out. Her body crumples to the floor, her knees under her bottom. With her face buried into the silver rug, she sobs uncontrollably.

"I need to get over him! I know it's wrong. I can't keep going on like this. It's all my fault! My husband loves our daughter and me. He doesn't deserve this! I can't keep lying and hiding from my sins," she carries on.

She sits up on her bottom, pulling her knees up to her chest, her arms wrap around them, she sobs. Her chest feels tight. Rocking from side-to-side, Valerie sobs dropping her head into her knees. She sulks in disappointment. I'm such a stupid idiot. I hate my life!

The thunderous storm builds and makes a loud crackle sound, startling Val as she looks up. She stares out her balcony window and notes the tree on her front lawn has a broken tree branch, which is now hanging almost to the ground. She continues sitting on the floor and observes the bolts of lightning flashing across the sky, as the downpour of heavy rains, crashes upon the rooftop.

After sitting on the floor for some time, Valerie finally gets up. She puts on a long tee shirt and pajama pants. The storm has slowed down, although she hears claps of thunder in the distance, the weather calls for thunderstorms all the way until tomorrow morning.

Her playlist plays artist after artist. She allows the soft sounds of Celine Dion's, My Heart Will Go On to filter redemption and healing through her heart. She curls up in her bed, her lids heavy and still burning from her meltdown. She feels numb. The pain is no longer intolerable. She knows what she has to do. Allow herself to forgive herself, allow herself to heal. But first, for her to heal, she knows that she must first deal with her past—Deal with her younger self.

Later that afternoon

"How was school baby?" Val questions her daughter as she picks her up from pre-school. The rain had let up from the earlier downpour, but it left the roads slippery as puddles of water line the streets—Val splashes through it as she drives home. The sky is still cloudy and the air thin. It's dangerous on the streets.

As Valerie continues to drive, she notices some wires are hanging down and some trees are toppled over onto the street— blocking the pathway of motorists and hindering pedestrians from getting by safely. Fortunately, DTE Energy crew members are already on the scene. Val's lights had flickered on and off once during the storm, but, she was not one of the thousands of customers who are waiting to have power restored in their homes.

"It was good mommy," she replies. "The storm was so scary! All the students got on the red carpet on the floor, and my teacher read us stories."

"Oh, yeah what kind of stories baby?" She grabs her stomach, feeling the queasiness coming back again.

"Ms. Hepburn read a story about a momma bear and her two cubs. But I don't know the name of it. I forget."

Val drives by more utility trucks as they work to get the power back on at the intersection she is approaching. The traffic lights are not working, so vehicles are treating it as a four-way stop. "What else did you do in school?"

"My friend and I was singing, rain, rain go away, come again another day."

Val giggles at her daughter singing. "Well, I can't wait until your dad picks your brother up so we can all make a homemade pizza tonight." Noah has karate after school that lasts until 5:30 p.m. Valerie passes the drug store where she picked up that blue box two weeks ago...

Valerie immediately remembers she hadn't taken the test. After the shock of Ro's proposal and her telling him she was married, Val really hadn't been thinking of anything else lately.

I'll take the test when I get home before Rick gets in. I haven't been able to keep anything down lately, and I keep feeling nauseous.

She glances in her rear-view mirror at Nairobi. She's already knocked out. Her head is slumped over to one side, and her mouth is open with drool running down her chin. Valerie gives a half-smile. Her love for her daughter was unquestionable.

Val into her driveway, parks just outside her garage door. She throws her keys into her purse and gets out the truck. I'll take the test soon as I get us something to snack on. She opens Nairobi's door, unbuckling her from her booster seat, Nairobi wakes up as Val pulls her out. Grabbing her mom's hand, she walks into the house, still groggy from sleep.

Inside the house, Valerie takes her shoes off at the door. She begins walking over to the kitchen, dropping her purse down on the kitchen counter.

Taking her shoes off behind her mother, Nairobi places her shoes on the top shoe rack. She puts her book bag down in the foyer, she strolls into the living room, grabs her coloring book and crayons from under the coffee table where she keeps it. "Mommy, you wanna color with me?" she asks. She sprawls across the living room floor—tummy side down and turns to the Princess and The Frog coloring page.

Valerie flops down on the chase, lifts her legs up and throws her head back, resting her body for a moment. The room seems to spin before her eyes. "No, not today pumpkin," she finally responds. The churning in her stomach begins again—her body feels weak. She takes a moment, waiting for relentless nausea to subside.

"Noah really loves Karate," Val says out loud. Smiling at the thought of him in his uniform. She loves going to his classes whenever she can. She enjoys watching him compete.

"No, he doesn't," Nairobi replies.

Val lifts her head up from the chase, "What? Yes, he does."

"No, he doesn't mommy."

"What makes you say that? How do you know?" Valerie glances over at her daughter. Eyebrows furrowed, her mouth hanging open.

"Cause mom. He told me."

"He did!" Her eyebrows sprint upwards quickly.

"Yea, I know he only pretends to like it to make daddy happy."

"Really? He said that?"

"Yup," she replies, as she continues to color in her coloring book—coloring all outside the lines.

"I dunno. He said he does it to make dad happy."

"Wow," Valerie responds. "I never knew that. I guess he doesn't wanna hurt dad's feelings. Your daddy loves going to see him, you know. It would break his heart if he found out Noah doesn't even like karate."

Nairobi shrugs her shoulders. "I guess mommy."

Val gets up and walks over to the kitchen. She smells the scented candle she lit when she first went into the kitchen—it fills her nostrils with warm-autumn scents. She opens the frig. "You want juice and some sliced oranges, pumpkin?"

"Yes, and can I get some animal crackers too?"

"Sure."

Nairobi continues to color in her coloring book on the living room floor.

"I need to mop this floor today. It's so sticky." Val feels her feet sticking to the floor. "Hey, did you spill something on this floor sweetie?" Her eyes glued to her floor.

Looking up from her coloring book, "No. But I saw Noah did earlier before we left out for school. Dad said he would get it up."

"Oh, where was I? I don't even remember that happening," Valerie responds.

"You were upstairs in the bathroom."

"Oh," Val replies.

After handing her daughter her juice, some cut up oranges, and animal crackers on a plate, she precedes to the stairwell. Let me take this test. Before ascending the steps, she pauses and looks back over towards her daughter who is still coloring.

"Pumpkin?"

Nairobi doesn't lift her head up from the coloring book, "Yes, mommy."

"I have some things I need to get done. I'll be upstairs if you need me, okay?"

"Ok mommy," she replies.

Upstairs, Val walks toward her dresser drawer. Pulling the blue box from underneath her clothes in the bottom drawer, she stares at the box, her gaze fixed on the big letters that ran across it, Pregnancy Test... She turns and walks towards her desk— stationed at her desk, and she touches her journal—she thinks about writing in it now. On second thought... Naw, I think I'll wait until afterward. I can write about it after I've gotten my results.

She walks away from her journal and heads into her master bathroom. Glancing at herself in the mirror, she places the test on the sink and lifts her shirt up. Feeling her stomach, she gently rubs her hands in a circular motion. Turning sideways, then towards the front again, she sticks her stomach out back and forth—inhaling in and exhaling out, seeing if she notices anything different. I can't be pregnant. Right? I could be coming down with something. The seasons are changing. I always get sick every time the seasons change. Valerie rationalizes the symptoms she has been having of late.

Undressing from her clothes, she slips out of her jeans and sweater and slides on her lavender nightgown. She pulls her door up, turning to lock it as she pulls her panties off. She opens the blue box, taking out the pregnancy kit. Her eyes are glued to the kit; results in three minutes. She can't shut her mind off, *You belong to me*, replays in her mind over and over again. Taking deep breaths, she unwraps the pregnancy applicator. Her hands begin to shake, her heart races, and her head begins to feel warm. She feels the unrelenting sensation of blood rushing towards her brain faster and faster. She takes a deep breath and lets it out slowly.

Valerie begins to sit on the toilet. She takes the test in one hand, "Negative for one line, and positive for two lines...

"I can't do this! I just can't!" she recites out loud. She grips the side of her sink, her arms bracing her as she leans over into the basin. "1…2…3...4...5." She turns on the faucet and runs her hands under the cool water. Still leaning over the basin, she begins splashing the cool water onto her face. She looks up at her reflection in the mirror. "Val... Just take the damn TEST!"

She takes a deep breath—dropping her shoulders down. "Here we go... Again." Sitting down on the toilet, she takes the applicator and leans forward. When she finishes, she glances at the pregnancy applicator and places it down on the sink. "Now, all I have to do is wait." Closing her eyes, she breathes in deeply through her nose... Exhaling through her mouth. "Wait, what? I have to wait here for three whole minutes! Yeah, right, feels more like three weeks."

The anxiety is killing her. The queasy feeling won't subside until she knows. Looking in the mirror, she bites down on her nails, pondering what if it shows up positive. How would I tell my husband? I would lose Rick and Noah. I would have to tell him about my affair with Ro. My husband can't even have any more kids, so I know it'll be Ro's baby.

Rick had gotten a vasectomy after Rick's first wife passed away. He didn't want to ever experience the death of a woman again because she was having his baby, he had told Val before they had gotten married. He never wanted to face that possibility—so Val agreed with no more kids when she married Rick. Val threw away all hope of ever having another child.

To break the stillness in the atmosphere, she walks down to check on her daughter. She pauses and smiles as she reaches the living room. Nairobi has fallen asleep on the floor with her tablet in front of her—cartoons playing on the screen.

Val grabs the device off of the floor, and she shuts it off. She grabs the cover, throw off the couch and places the navy blue throw over her daughter. She gazes at her daughter with glossy eyes—her face reddens, flushing with warmth.

There's nothing she won't do for her daughter. She keeps saying she wants a little sister or brother, but I know it can't be this way. I never thought that she would be my only daughter. I always wanted two or three children. With Rick not being able to have any more children, I know my dreams of having a baby with my husband were crushed the moment I said, I do. Every woman wants to have a least one baby with her husband. Well, that's not going to be me. My fairytale family is blended. "Hopefully, this test comes back negative," she says.

Gray clouds are still hovering over the city. Val looks out her back window and notices patches of dead grass in her lawn. She stares blankly out the window... *Where are the birds, I usually see coming to the bird feeder? It's been almost two weeks. I know I have bird food in there.* Her love, her place of tranquility no longer looks the same. She doesn't see the usual scene of life in her backyard, no life at all— Vacant of all the things that Val considered a breath of fresh air. Now, it was just gloomy and void of beauty and life.

Val looks at her watch, suddenly snapping out her daydream. She looks at the clock; it reads 5:17 p.m. Rick and Noah will be home soon. She heads upstairs to see her test results. When she enters her room, she closes the door behind herself. Bracing herself, she closes her eyes, then opens them up and heads towards the bathroom.

She wipes her sweaty palms on her clothes. Entering in, she takes a moment before she grabs the applicator off of the sink. It feels so far away, but so near at the same time. It's calling her to come and look. Taking a deep breath in, her eyes closed, Valerie stands in front of the test applicator on the sink. She then opens her eyes and looks down...

"Hey V, we're home," Rick yells from the foot of the stairs. "Hurry down."

Oh shit! Val is caught off guard. She passes by her purse and runs out of her room. Racing down the hall, Val comes rushing down the stairs. "What's wrong babe?" Val barely makes it down the stairs without stumbling. "Is everything okay?"

"Whoa, whoa, whoa, Baby! Stop running so fast," Rick says, catching his wife as she misses the last two steps.

"You screamed my name like something was wrong." Her brows were slightly raised. "Did something happen at karate?" She kneels down to Noah and gives him a once over, "Are you hurt, baby?"

"No, mommy," Noah replies. He reaches down in his back-pack and brings out a shiny silver medal. "Look! I won second place in the school spelling-b today." His smile illuminates the room.

"Oh my god, sweetie!" She hugs him tightly, "I'm so very proud of you. That's a really huge accomplishment!" Dammit! She looks up, glancing up at her husband with a wide smile, "He's so smart babe." Val had completely forgotten Noah's spelling-b competition was today. She was supposed to go—she feels terrible inside.

Rick helps his wife up off her knees, pulling her up, "Yes, baby I know. I knew you would be proud of him. He couldn't wait to show you." Rick grabs the medal from his son and places it around his son's neck. "We're very proud of you, son." His smile is radiant. Rick's facial expression needs no words. He is a proud father. "Hey, I have an idea. Let's go out to celebrate."

"Yay!" Noah shouts. He runs up the stairs, "I'll change out my karate uniform and be back in a flash." He darts across to his room excitedly.

"Well, I'll go get changed," Rick exclaims.

Valerie looks at her husband, then towards her daughter. Nairobi is still asleep. Valerie feels compelled to stay behind. She's struggling to find the right words. Her eyes quickly glance downward at her feet. She grabs the back of her neck and starts to massage it. Her voice cracking, "Umm, I... I don't think I can make it babe. I really want to go, but I don't feel so good, and I've had a stressful day." This is the truth.

"Oh babe, I'm sorry you don't feel well," Rick replies. He moves over towards his wife. Standing close, he reaches for her to pull her close to him. "We can stay in. I'll order take-out a pizza or something."

"No!" Val quickly responds. She turns away. Keeping her distance, she fiddles with her braids—stroking her hair up and down. "I'm fine. I just need to get some rest. I don't want you staying home because of me. I'll get Nairobi up and get her ready to go." She begins to wake her daughter up.

Rick rubs his chin. "You sure you don't want us to stay? We can order whatever you have a craving for." His eyes are fixed on Val.

She glances at her husband. "Yes, babe I'm sure. I lost my appetite. I really don't think I'll be able to keep anything down anyway—exhaustion probably." Val's head feels heavy.

His eyes are narrow. Rick starts scratching at his temple. "Ok V. Go lay down. I can get Nairobi up." His tone is uncertain. He turns away to grab Nairobi off the floor.

Valerie makes her way upstairs and kicks her slippers off at the foot of her bed. She glances over at her diary. No, I'll wait until they leave before I write in my journal. She pulls the blanket back and climbs into her bed.

Maybe he doesn't believe me. Was I too obvious? I can't go like this—feeling like I can throw-up at any moment...

OH SHOOT! Val sits up straight. I forgot to get the test and throw it away! Wait, I threw it in my purse. It's safe in there. I'll throw it away outside when I get up—Where Rick can't find it. She lays back down, snuggling under the covers. So much stress and this enormous headache, I need to lay down for a moment. I'll make it up to Noah. I'll make it up to everyone.

Today doesn't feel like a day of celebration. It feels more like a day of gloom. It's just one big headache after another. My life seems to be spiraling down. I love my husband. I know I've made some irresponsible decisions, but I've learned my lesson. I know I want my husband. I just hope it's not too late for us. I hope he can forgive me. I hope he knows that no matter what, I choose him.

Chapter 11

ℰ

Valerie wakes up to a quiet home. The clock on her nightstand blares 10:15. It's been almost three hours since Valerie drifted off to sleep. She climbs out of bed slowly, feeling a little groggy. She notes the full moon outside, peeping between the patches of dark clouds. She hears rolls of thunder still approaching in the distance. Small raindrops dance upon the roof.

Something's off. Val notices something missing. She begins looking on her desk and on the floor. She opens every drawer. Where's my fucking diary at? She opens each drawer again, moving around the contents inside—nothing is there. She goes over to the window where she sometimes sits—nothing is there either. "Where the hell is my stuff? I know damn well I didn't move it. Or did I?" she said.

The raindrops become a little louder as the thunderous storm begins to roll in. Her heart is pounding heavy. Did I move it before I laid down? She rubs her forehead. I don't remember... She paces her bedroom floor before finally descending down the stairs.

Val notices her husband is on the couch. Rick is sitting in the living room—his gaze is fixed, staring into the darkness. He's sitting on the couch with his legs planted wide on the floor beneath him—his forearms firm upon his legs, his body leaning forward.

Valerie walks over towards the lamp, "Babe, why are you sitting in the dark?" She flicks the switch, illuminating the room, allowing herself to see him clearly. His eyes are cold—his face tight. But he remains still. "I didn't hear y'all come in. Why didn't you wake me?" she said. She didn't stand there to wait for his reply. Instead, she continues her search.

She glances over her husband as she paces the floor—still looking for her journal. "I would've put the children to bed," she adds. She begins looking around the dining room, flipping over papers and magazines. She searches the kitchen drawers—opening and shutting each one, but still, nothing is there. She blows her breath out heavily. She pauses, her hands planted on her hips. "Hey babe, have you seen my journal? I thought I left it on my desk in our room, but it's not there.

Rick reaches for the pen off the table in front of him. He taps the pen in the palm of his hand repeatedly. He's speechless. He continues to stare out the window.

Val raising and holding her eyebrows, she waits a moment while waiting for a response from her husband. Nothing... She begins walking back towards the living room—her eyes now focus on her husband intently. "Babe, have you seen my journal?" she asked again. This time being sure her husband hears her. She knows something is wrong.

Did he take it? Is he hiding it from me? Hell, did he go through my purse? If he did, then he knows everything. Please

Lord, tell me my husband didn't go through my personal stuff. Don't tell me my husband has read my journal or found the test...

Val touches his shoulder, "Babe, what's wrong?"

Drawing in a slow, steady breath, Rick glares at Val for a moment, his nostrils flaring. He begins to crack his knuckles. Val notes his veins in his neck bulging outward, he appears to be irritated about something. He turns away without a word.

"Baby, did I do something wrong?" she asks calmly. She was actually scared of his response. She didn't want to find out he went through her personal things.

He looks at his wife sharply and rolls his eyes slightly as he turns back towards the window—still nothing.

Rick's glowering looks frighten Valerie. She has never seen her husband look so angry, so distracted in thoughts that she seems unable to discern or pull him out of. She feels sick to her stomach. The anxiety she feels shoots through the roof. Her palms are sweaty now, and her legs feel weak as if to cave in.

Val sits next to her husband on the couch. Not too close, she doesn't want to intrude on his personal space. She says nothing at first. She looks out the window. Seeing bolts of lightning striking across the sky, she can't see anything more—no visibility, as her view is obstructed by the rainstorm. Her eyebrows squeeze together in a frown—she begins scratching one of her eyebrows. She tries to hide her agitation from her husband's lack of response. His refusal to answer her begins to annoy her. She turns and looks at him. She knows he can feel her gaze upon him. Still, he continues to keep his gaze on the rain pouring down. Deep, rumbling thunder sounds crashes upon the house.

There's a big elephant in the room and Val knows it. She senses his anger rising from off his body. His body is rigid. "Rick?" she finally calls out.

Rick finally turns and looks at his wife. "What?" His tone is sharp, his face sullen.

Valerie's brows quickly raise in surprise. She's never heard his tone sound so absolute. She is taken back. So, *He finally decides to answer me.* "I've been asking you if you saw my journal. I think I lost it. You keep ignoring me. Is something wrong?

Did I do something?" Of course, *I did. That was a stupid question.* She waits for a response. She senses he has her journal, but she can't prove it. She didn't check her purse before she came down the steps. Hopefully, he doesn't have the pregnancy test too.

"Is that the only thing you've lost?" he finally replies. "Have you lost anything else you wanna talk to me about?" His right eyebrow raises up slightly. He glares at his wife with a tight face. He waits on her response.

His passive-aggressive questions disturb her. The air is thick. *Okay, now he's playing games with me. Does he have my test or not? Why won't he just come right out and say it if he does? Does he know about Ro? Which one did he find? The journal or the test? Or is it both?*

She glances over at the table—nothing there. She looks beside him—nothing there either. He couldn't have; he wouldn't just read my journal. But where the hell is it?

"So you fucked him, huh?" he finally blurts out. He glowers at her and then turns his head. Shaking his head, he remains quiet for a moment.

Rick sucks in his bottom lip—A tell-tell sign he is infuriated. She puts her hand on his knee, "I—."

"Get yo' damn hands off me, you fucking slut!" he shouts out as he jumps up.

He does know! Her eyes are wide, and her brows arched high. "Baby, wait, Let me explain."

"Shut up!" he interrupts her. "You don't have shit to say to me V." His face is red. He blasts her with insults. "Get the fuck away from me!"

His insults shock her. Her eyes are burning. Water begins to fill her eyes up. Her throat feels constricted, and her heartbeat races. Her palms are sweaty. She jumps up, her voice cracking under pressure, "But, but, let me explain. Please, let me explain myself, baby. Please don't do this to me!" she exclaims. She reaches out for him.

He shoves her off of him violently. "I told you not to touch me," he says, pointing the finger at her. "You did this shit to yo' self! Did you once think about me—think about us, or our children?" He waits for an answer. After no response, he balls his fists up beside him tightly. His face fiery red. "No! Of course, you didn't. You just thought about yo' self!"

Val sobs into both palms of her hands, her breath panting rapidly. She stands there, her legs feel numb. It feels like the room is spinning. "Please! Just listen to me, baby. I'm so sorry. I didn't mean to hurt you. I love you, babe. I—"

"No Fuck you, Valerie," he says, cutting her off. "Are you sorry for cheating on me or sorry cause you got caught?" He pounds his fist in the palm of his left hand—letting out a deep-hard breath of air. He backs away from Val. He takes the journal from under the couch where he was sitting, tossing it at her, the journal falling to the floor right at her feet, he stands sulking.

She can sense the negative energy churning inside of him. As Rick continues blaring insults at Val, she retreats. Her stomach aches with cramps striking her in what feels like 60-second intervals. Her head feeling heavier and spinning. Her head bangs with flutterings of sharp pains as rick continues to reject her. I can't believe he knows everything. He found out before I had a chance to tell him.

Her plans of telling him everything has flown out the window. He must've read it while I was sleeping. She can't control her tears. She sobs uncontrollably—she breaks down on the floor in front of Rick. She takes in cups of oxygen as she loses her breath. Her violent gasps for air didn't seem to alarm Rick, he just continues to pace the floor—his fists bawled up tightly, he wipes the sweat from his head.

Val looks at her husband and tries to speak, "I-I..." but nothing comes out. She notices Rick grab a bottle of Vodka off the kitchen counter and take it to the neck. Val hadn't noticed the bottle earlier—she was too focused on looking for her journal.

She was too self-absorbed in finding something that her husband had already read.

I'll never forgive myself. He has every right to be upset with me. Her tears are unyielding. Her husband's anger is not quenched with any apology that she offers him. Val paces slowly towards her husband—calculating her every step. She inches closer and closer to him, wiping the snot from her nose with her sleeves, as he continues to take large gulps of Vodka from the bottle. Val places her hand ever so gently upon his shoulder. She hopes he doesn't reject her touch again. "Rick... I... Um--" He turns towards his wife, cutting her off abruptly, "You, um what?"

"I... I'm really sorry. I didn't mean to be unfaithful," she says softly. She notices how red her husband's eyes are. She braces patiently for what she has to say to him. She takes in a deep-slow, steady breathe. "Um, I want our marriage to work. We can go to counseling. I'll do anything you tell me to do." She clears her throat, trying to dislodge the saliva that has built up. "I just want us to work this out."

She notes the coldness in his eyes. His motionless reaction to her words makes her knees wobble. She leans closer to him—smelling the hot liquor coming from his breath. I can do this; I have to tell my husband everything. "Look, I know you're upset with me, and uh, you have every right to be." Her tone is gentle but shaky. With calculating movements, she doesn't want him to push her away again. She has never seen him drink like this before. She doesn't know this man.

Rick stares at Val blankly. He wipes his mouth with the backside of his hand, still holding on to the bottle of liquor. He stands with his chin high and his nostrils flaring. His posture is rough—his legs are planted wide. He remains speechless.

"I don't wanna lose you," she continues. She sees his face remains rigid and his chest rising up and down heavily. "I don't wanna lose Noah. I want our family to work." She drops her head. "I wish I could take that moment back," she says softly. "I wish I never—"

"You wish you never what Valerie?" he snaps. Walking close upon his wife—His chest almost onto hers—closing in the space between them. He looks down demeaningly at her. The invasion of her space is intimidating and freighting. "So how many times did you fuck him? he finally asks. Tell me the truth! I wanna know how many times, did you open your legs up for your baby daddy?!" His tone was harsh and insulting. "Cause we don't even have sex on a regular no more! Maybe it's cause you are fucking him all the time," He snaps.

"It was only once," she responds weakly. Tears are flowing down her face. Her voice is weak and cracking. "I only slept with him once. I promise it was only one time." She cups her face with both of her hands. Covering her eyes with her palms—her face collapse against his chest as he stands over her. He's not changing his stance with any sign of empathy. "I just wanna take it back. I wanna take that day away," she sobs. She wishes he would wrap his arms around her and tell her everything will be ok. But he doesn't.

Rick looks down over his wife, he remains unfazed. "Well, you should've thought about that shit before you opened your legs to him. I don't give a damn about your tears." He pushes her away from him again.

She wipes her eyes, but the tears keep racing down her cheeks anyway. "I know I messed up, babe. It was a mistake," she cries out.

Rick grabs his wife by her chin with one hand—He looks intently into her eyes. "The fuck you are talking about, a mistake? That wasn't any damn mistake. You wanted to fuck him. You wanted to be with him. Listen..." He hesitates. "Do you really want this marriage?"

"Baby, I love you." She looks up at him, her eyes puffy, "I want to be with you. You're my husband. I want my family. I want us."

"Then you call him right now Valerie. Call him right now and tell him to stay the fuck away from you. Tell him you don't wanna see him no more and to lose your number."

"What about our daughter? That's still her father Rick. She's already met him, and Ro won't stay away from her now that he knows she exists." Her tone sounds feeble. She wants nothing more than for this night to end. It's almost midnight and they're still arguing.

"I don't give a damn about that. That's my daughter too!" He pokes her in the chest with his finger with every word... "I'm the one that's been in her life. I'm the one that built this house for you and her. It's me who clothes her and who feeds her every damn day! That's me Val, and not him! So call him now! Or I'm gone!" he yells.

"But I can't tell him that," she blurts out. Her tears showering down her face. "I can't tell him that. Be—Because... I'm pregnant..."

Chapter 12

T he words that had just resonated off of Valerie's lips were crushing like a wrecking ball. She was sure that her husband would leave her now. She doesn't blame him. Even though she wants her marriage to work, she knows it is virtually impossible now that the whole truth is out. Val has just found out moments earlier that she is pregnant. After looking at the test strip, she had no time to really deal with her reality—an unexpected pregnancy.

The storm stopped ragging, and the elephant in the room has disappeared. This moment in time could not be erased. This moment was not an illusion but a nightmare. Her fingers felt numb, and her stomach beckons with vomit. She thrust the feeling of acid churning back down her throat...

Crack! The piercing pain from the blunt force of Rick's hand against her face is unrelenting. Taken off guard, her face burns with the type of pain of a hundred bee stings. Still, on her knees, Val dared not get up. Instead, she sobs uncontrollably.

"You fucking bitch!" Rick shouts. After all I've done for you. After all I've put up with, you have the nerve to tell me you are pregnant!" His eyes are bloodshot red. "You know I had a vasectomy, so we don't need to guess who the father is. I can't believe you," he shouts. "But guess what? I already know that too." He grabs the test out his pocket and throws it at her. "Why do you think I even read your damn diary anyways?"

Did he go through my purse?

"After I finished watching the game and finished my beer, I went to get your keys to move your truck into the garage, and instead of keys, I pulled out a pregnancy test! That's the whole reason I read your diary dummy!"

Val struggles to get up off the floor. Her face is numb—tears and the blood streaming from her nose mixes together and runs down her burning face. She wipes her face with the back of her hand, "Rick, I'm so sorry. I'M SORRY! I didn't think this would—"

"You're a god damn whore," he yells as he slams Valerie to the ground like a linebacker. He stands there as he watches his wife crash down onto the glass coffee table—breaking through the glass, she crashes to the floor.

Glass shatters everywhere—Valerie feels the cuts of glass upon her face. "Rick No!" she starts to yell. "Please don't hit me again, you promised!" Her arms covers her head and face as she crows below her husband. He moves toward her with rage...

"DADDY STOP! DON'T HIT MY MOMMY," Nairobi yells.

Rick turns around quickly, rushing to his daughter, he ushers her back up the stairs. "Sweetie, mommy just had an accident and fell down. She fell on the table, but she's gonna be alright," Rick said.

"But I want my mommy," Nairobi exclaims.

"Go back to bed darling, mommy will be up shortly after we get her cleaned up. She just fell." He kisses her forehead as he ushers her back to bed. "Night, night sweetie. Get some rest ok. Daddy loves you." Rick watches Nairobi climb the steps, until she is no longer visible.

Valerie manages to get to her feet, but she is very weak. Her face is swelling from the hit earlier, and she thinks her left arm is sprained from the fall. She feels her face—speckles of small pieces of glass she pulls from her face. She hesitates as her husband walks up close to her—closing the gap in between them. Her head lowers, her shoulders round slightly.

Rick grabs her by the back of her head— holding her head firmly close to him, her braids are woven in the tight grasp of his fist. Val feels the heat of his hot breath, still reeking of heavy liquor. His gaze is intent—his eyes glower with a menacing look. Her body is shaking uncontrollably—she tries not to flitch.

"Don't call me," he finally says. He lets go of her head, but not before giving her a once over.

Valerie sees the look of disgust all over her husband's face as he looks her up and down. She watches him walk out the front door, not knowing when or if he's going to return. She collapses to her knees and wails in the palms of her hands. "I'm sorry," she screams over and over again as she sobs, her pain ebbing away at her, regret tormenting her very soul.

The next morning Val was so sore she could barely climb out of bed. Her body aches, her nose feels dislocated, and her face burns fiercely. Walking with a limp, she grabs at her hip. Crashing through the glass table last night, she banged her hip pretty hard on the floor—throbbing pain illuminates all through her body. Her back is so stiff it hurts to move from side to side.

She glances at her face in the mirror as she enters the bathroom. She's shocked. She can barely contain herself as her eyes begin to sting and water begins to well up in her eyes. She gazes silently at the many little cuts in her face that the shattered glass penetrated through her skin. There's a bigger gash just above her right eyebrow. The open wound shows the white meat underneath.

She takes a washcloth off the towel rack and runs it under warm water. She then places it gently on the gash above her right eye. She grimaces and shutters her body at the vibrating pain—Careful not to make too much noise since the children were still asleep.

Val makes her way down the stairs to see if her husband was on the couch but can't find him. Rick hasn't returned home and must've stayed out all night. But where? Valerie has not a clue. And she dared not call him. Valerie vehemently feels the discomfort of being alone. The nagging pain of a sensation she has never felt before ebbs away at her mind.

The living room floor looks as if someone had broken into her home and crashed the home Val once knew as a home of peace. The early morning sun shined its rays through the bay window—Val's eyelids are heavy and harshly pierces her eyes. The skyline peeks through the silver clouds and illuminates every morsel of what the previous thunderstorm had left behind.

As Val stares out the window, she notes the branches scrolled across Mr. and Mrs. Santana's yard across the street to her left. The flower pots were toppled over Ms. Sutton's porch just two doors down. The ground looks damp and muddy, the result of a long-hard rainfall.

As Valerie turns around to get a pot of coffee started, she hears the grandfather clock chiming seven o'clock... *Where's my husband.* Valerie thought. Please let him come back home. I can't do this without him. I know I really messed up, but I just can't lose him.

The words, 'I'm pregnant', hung in the air—resonating throughout the house from last night.

I can't believe I'm pregnant with Ro's baby. How could this be? She asked herself. What am I gonna do? This is too much.

Tears fall slowly down her cheeks as she fills the coffee pot with water and places it back on the cradle. She grabs a clean filter and pours one tablespoon of coffee grounds into it.

She pulls her phone from her robe pocket. No missed calls or messages. She slides her phone back into her pocket and grabs a chair at the table. Sitting down, she glances over the table and observes the liquor bottle still sitting there, reeking of the brutal night before. Grabbing the glass bottle, she gets up and tosses it into the trash. She grabs the newspaper off the counter and covers the bottle entirely, careful not to let her children discover it.

The air fills with the soft smell of coffee. Hearing the coffee pot—the brewing is complete—Val reaches painfully into the cabinet, careful not to overstretch her bruised arm. She pulls her favorite mug down and begins to pour her coffee. Lord help me... Val sit at the table drinking her coffee. Her mind concentrates on the dooming thoughts of her marriage.

My husband is never going to forgive me. Heck, I wouldn't either. What man wants a woman who cheated on him? Hell, what man wants to stay with a woman who's carrying another man's child. Shoot, I've hurt two people—Rick and Romelle. How can I face either of them? How can I say anything? I don't know what to do.

Valerie takes a sip of the steamy coffee and sits it back down on the table. She hears the ticking of the clock in the stillness of the room. The muteness of the room gave Val an unrelenting eeriness about her life. The unfamiliar feeling provokes a sabotaging truth about her marriage and about her future with Ro.

I've sabotaged two relationships all at one time. Valerie gripes. Nothing will ever be the same. Not between my husband or me. Not to mention Nairobi. This is all my fault! She cries. How could I let one night destroy my marriage? I'm so stupid. I didn't think about the consequences. I didn't think about how this was gonna destroy my marriage or pull the children apart from both parents. Now what? What am I supposed to do?

Val crumbles into self-pity—her head falling into the pit of her arms. She sobs endlessly from the deepest parts of her soul. Her muffled crying soaks up the sleeves of her robe. She weeps for comport. She weeps for forgiveness.

Moments later, Valerie pulls her phone out of her pocket. This time not to check it—she knows her husband hasn't called or texted her. She knows who she must text...

Valerie:

Can you come over?

Chapter 13

The knock on the door startles Valerie. Putting the mop back in the hall closet, Val takes a quick scan of the room. The once shattered glass on the living room floor has removed. The vanilla-scented wick candles replace the once thick aroma of liquor with a soft-sweet fragrance. Val grabs her bruised hip. The grueling-dull pain bothered her immensely with every stride. She walks towards the door with a limp and notes Rick's house shoes by the sofa and quickly throws them into the coat closet. A half a cup of lemon tea, cold, left to be emptied—she will pour down the drain later.

"Hey, come on in," Val says, opening the front door. She receives a warm hug from her brother, whom she has not seen in over six months. She walks toward the kitchen as her brother comes inside.

"What's up little sis," Mark says, shutting the door behind himself. "I'm so happy you texted me to come over earlier cause I missed my little niece." He scans the room and glances towards the stairs. His oversized shirt hung loosely over his plumped body. His lack of sleep, long hours at work, coupled with the stress of his demanding career, never left him much time to do much of anything. Fast food and microwave dinners were his delight. "Where's Nairobi? he finally asks.

It's dusk out, and when the children awoke, Valerie had already cleaned up the mess that once showed evidence of an abusive night. Her plans of getting the house cleaned and her kids to a friend's house a couple of blocks over before Mark came was a laborious task.

Valerie knows she has to start from somewhere, but once he takes one look at her, the end is where she'd need to begin. She closes the cabinet door as she places the empty black-coffee mug on the marble counter—turning around to face her brother...

"WHAT THE FUCK!" he shouts. "What happened to you Valerie, you better tell me the truth. Mark was now up close to his sister. With bulging eyes, he reaches for his sister's face, and she quickly turns her head to one side.

Mark's body is rigid. He snaps his eyes shut. "I'm g-o-n-n-a KILL HIM! Where is he?" He runs towards the stairs.

"Jr. wait!" Jr was the name that only Val, and their parents called him. "He's not here."

"Then where the hell is he Val?"

"I don't know," Val responds softly.

"Don't lie to me to cover his ass up. Look at your face! Your face is swollen. And your nose, is it broken? Why the hell are you still here, instead of the hospital? This time I don't care what you say I'm gonna get his ass! And fucking kill him!" Mark pounds his fist on the wall behind him.

This wasn't the first time Val had called her brother over. Valerie knows how Rick can be when he drinks. Rick getting angry is one thing. But Rick getting angry coupled with alcohol was another.

"Rick baby, I was just getting my hair done, I promise."

"Then why the hell did your girlfriend just text your phone saying did you make it in?" Rick was holding Val's phone in the air. They had just made love, and Val went to start dinner. She had left her phone on the nightstand in their bedroom.

"Oh." Valerie whispered. Val was left feeling nervous. She didn't want her husband to know she lied—she was still hanging out with her girlfriends from college. He hated they were all single and said single women were nothing but trouble. So after just four months into their marriage, Val reluctantly promised Rick that she would stop seeing them. Besides, she was a newlywed herself, and making her husband happy was all Valerie wanted to do. But she couldn't keep her promise. She was bored, and she began losing her self-worth. She felt trapped.

"I had made a quick stopover at Angie's house just to say hello." Her heart was racing. Telling lies was something she wasn't good at. So she told the truth. "Today's her birthday and even though all the girls were going out for dinner, I told them I couldn't make it. That you and I had plans."

Walking up closer to Val, she could sense her husband had been drinking. Valerie rarely saw her husband drink. Only on certain occasions or when he was overly stressed from work. Closing in the gap between them, "So you lied to me?"

"No baby. I promise I didn't lie. I went to get my hair done, then I—"

CRACK! One slap to Val's slender face, and she was down. "Didn't I ask you to stay away from those sluts? Didn't I ask you to keep away from them?" Rick grabs Val by both arms and pulses her back up to him. "Huh?" His gaze was intense. The liquor on his breath is hot. "Dammit, answer me?"

"Yes baby. I'm sorry. It won't happen—"

Rick violently bangs Val into the wall and grabs her by her throat with his right hand—his other hand pins Valerie's right hand behind her back. "The next time you fucking lie to me, I'm gonna snatch your throat out with my bare hands.

"Baby. You're hurting me." Val whispers. "I can't breathe." Val's head spins, and her breath is labored. She holds on to his hand with her free hand, trying to claw it from around her throat.

"I fucking love you girl," Rick replies, as he covers her mouth with his left hand—muffling her sounds to be let free. "But don't you ever lie to me again. After all I've done for you. I'm changing your phone number tomorrow so you don't have any more contacts with them sluts. And you're calling your job first thing tomorrow to let them know of your resignation."

With his wife still pinned to the wall, Rick kisses her with drunken rage—his fury and love mingles together unapologetically. He controls himself, then gradually releases the tight grip around his wife's throat.

Val coughs violently as she takes in the air that once was taken for granted. Sliding down the wall, Val holds her throat gently while she coughs up what seems like her entire insides.

That next morning, Valerie found one long-stem red rose and a note on the empty pillow that lay beside her. The note read...

I'm so sorry baby. I promise it will never happen again...

And just like that, Valerie knew the idea of having friends was no longer an option. She quit her job and concentrated on being there for her husband, Nairobi, and Noah. No questions asked, she gave the life up she once knew.

"I promise I don't know Mark. He left last night, and I haven't heard or seen him since." Tears are streaming down her face as she stands there helpless in front of her brother.

Mark tugs harshly at his collar, uncovering the MAD DOG, tattoo on his neck—A street name given to him by his boys he hung with in his juvenile days. He stands there stoically looking at his sister. His wide stance and body language say two things...

One, I'm not going anywhere until you tell me everything. And two, I'm still gonna fuck him up.

"Sit down Jr. It's a long story," Val replies, gesturing towards the couch. "I'll get us some coffee."

Chapter 14

Mark was so angry after he heard what happened, he decided to take a walk and he didn't come back until three hours later. He sat on Val's couch, rubbing the top of his bald head. His silence made Valerie nervous.

She taps her fingernails on the coffee table. Valerie told her brother everything—She told her the truth. Nothing made her more embarrassed than to tell her brother that she had an affair, and worst off, she was pregnant.

"Look Valerie." Mark finally breaks his silence. "I-I know your hurt. And I know Rick's hurt too." Clearing his throat, he coughs and signals Val for water. After she returns with bottled water from the fridge, Mark continues. It's something I need to tell you."

Val's eyebrows raise slightly. Her eyes are fixed on her brother's expression. She pulls the long braid that has fallen in from of her eyes and tosses it behind her right shoulder. The room feels a bit toasty, but Val doesn't get up to turn down the heat.

Besides, she likes it a bit on the warm side. "What is it Jr.," she finally replies.

"Well, remember when I was barely calling you two years ago, and you were mad at me?"

"Yeah," Val replies.

"I never told you what happened because I was embarrassed. I never responded to your text messages and could not return your calls because Maria & I was in a dark place." Mark wipes his face with one downward swoop and stares up at his sister. "I cheated on her." He finally blurts out.

Valerie's eyes bulge like a deer in headlights. "What?" Valerie's eyes were stuck-glued to Mark, waiting on his response.

"I don't know why Val. Maybe the same reason any man cheats, I was scared." Mark sighs. Clasping his hands together, he takes a deep breath in, then exhales, blowing his breath out forcefully. "After I had proposed to Maria, I started feeling nervous, I guess. I mean, I loved Maria, but I started having doubts— thinking maybe I was moving too fast. And I—I messed around with someone else."

"Who was it? Someone at the club?"

Mark was known for his days hanging out in the strip club. He was a ladies-man before he settled down and got married. Too many of his families and friends were surprised that he was never the same once he met Maria at the bank. Yeah, of course, everyone was shocked. Shocked that she was Latino, but Valerie didn't care. She always believed that love was colorless and had no boundaries. But Val's family, on the other hand, wanted Mark to marry a black woman. She was the only one that approved Mark's choice. So when it came down to the wedding, there were only ten guests, and it didn't include Mark's mother nor his father.

"No, Val, he replies. I met her at work—she was my coworker. Things started off innocent at first. But then she started flirting with me, and I started flirting with her. Then one thing led to another, and we were talking all the time and meeting up every chance we got. I never meant to hurt my wife, you know."

"Was it just a one-time thing?" Val questions.

"No…"

"No! Jr., tell me you didn't keep this affair going, please."

"I did. For five months, and I feel horrible about it."

"Ahh," Val clasps her hand over her mouth… Trying not to speak, she holds her mouth shut.

"I never have gotten over hurting my wife." Mark continues. "I never thought I could or would hurt her. And after she caught me, I thought she'd never forgive me, especially after we lost our little boy."

"Oh my God, Mark!" Val's mouth flings open. "I'm so sorry. I didn't know."

"No one did. The stress I put her under caused her to miscarry. She was just four and a half months."

"Well, how did y'all get over it? I mean, you still got married."

"It wasn't easy Val. Actually, I don't know if she ever fully got over it. All I know is we worked through it. We went to counseling and we chose never to speak about it again. Well..." He hangs his head low. "Not until now, you're the first person I ever told, besides our therapist."

"Wow..." Val's eyes are empathetic as she listens intently.

"Her sister, Janiah, told her to work it out—that all men cheat. But I didn't want Maria to think that about me. But the irony to that is when Janiah found out their brother Mario girlfriend cheated on him, Janiah told him to leave that slut— Her words, not mines."

Valerie sits back in her chair. Taking in the information her brother just unfurled on her.

"I know I may sound like a hypocrite, and I'm not trying to. But you need to leave Rick. If he keeps putting his hands on you, I'm gonna kill him. I know your hurt—hurt that you hurt him. But he doesn't deserve you lil sis. He needs to get some help. I mean, I know you love him, but is it worth the risk of getting beat on? Or worse, you possibly losing your life?" Mark grabs his sister's hand. "I love you. And I want you to be safe. I'm not condemning you for what you did, and I'm sure you've already done that."

"Thanks Mark. I just need to decide what I'm going to do. It's just hard because I know what I've done is wrong. I know that he won't be the problem. He probably wants out anyway."

"Why you say that Val?"

"You know why?" Val looks at her brother intently. "You know damn well a man is not gonna stay after he finds out his woman cheated on him. My whole image is tarnished."

"I know it's crazy, but why do we do this as men?"

"Do what?" Val replies as she sits up, straightening her posture.

"Why do we make women feel like their terrible-no good women if they cheat? But if a man cheats, it's like we're given a slap on the wrist by society... It's as if all people believe it's a part of man's makeup. Apart from our natural characteristics. When a man cheats—"

"Women forgive you, and men give you a high five," Val finishes.

"Exactly. When I was younger, I was never faithful. Matter-of-fact, I had a wingman. My boys always covered for me and told lies to the women I was seeing—Telling them I was with them all night, I was late cause I was helping them, or the best one of all, my phone really did die. But all the while, I was with a woman. I mean, yeah, my boy came to pick me up, but when we left from my girl's house, he dropped me right off at another girl's house. Too easy."

"But if y'all get cheated on, it's the end of the world." Val shakes her head. "It's really sad how women experience slut-shaming if they cheat, no matter the reason. And men are treated like pimps and players."

Mark tunes one side of his lips up as he shakes his head slowly. "Yeah, sad but true."

"It's stereotypical and sexists," Val scuffs.

"Hopefully, Rick doesn't tell his family. You already know how they're gonna look at you." Mark stands up and checks his phone. "Look, we need to go get some food. I'm hungry."

"I'm not looking forward to hearing from his mom. She's so protective over her son—Grown son, I would like to add. She already thinks her son can do no wrong." Val walks over to grab her keys off of the counter. "Let me run upstairs to grab my coat."Val climbs the steps to gather her belongings. As she descends down the stairs, she notes the jarring feeling of heartbreak. She is immediately thrust into the moment she came down the stairs and found her husband sitting in the dark as she looked for her diary. She recalls the feeling of panic—not to mention the anxiety she felt once she found out she was pregnant. "Chinese?" Val slides her coat on and zips it up halfway before tossing her scarf around her neck.

"Sounds great," Mark replies. Heading towards the door, he turns around to look at his sister. "Look, I know you don't wanna hear this right now. But you need to confront what you've never confronted before."

"Oh yeah. What's that?"

"Dad..."

Valerie stands frozen. Her legs locked, unmovable like a train stuck on a broken track. She feels her body limp, like quicksand. Her eyes locked on her brother, but words are restricted and have no exit way out. Motionless, she's paralyzed into a memory she doesn't want to relive.

After picking up their food, Mark pulls into their parent's driveway—Forty minutes away from Val's home. Val's parents still lived on the west side of Detroit. The neighborhood looks gloomy. There were no children outside, no one jogging the streets. Not even a dog being walked by its owner.

Her parents had moved years ago from their single-family bungalow home to their small ranch style home. It was easier for Valerie's dad to move about. He was now walking with a cane. When he fell at the job, he hit his head pretty hard on the floor. The guys at the plant were the first to see him go down and called for help. Ever since that day, Mark senior has never been the same.

Valerie could feel her sweaty palms begin to sweat. Her heart pounds heavily in her chest. The sound of her thumping heart distracts her—from the acid churning in her stomach that gives way to her throat. Val places one hand over her mouth as she tries to combat the burning sensation—careful not to throw up in her brother's meticulously manicured leather interior.

It's been years since she's been to her parent's home. Besides the occasional phone calls, Valerie shut herself off from both her mom and dad. Closing the doors to their relationship was difficult. She tried over and over again when she was in college. Then, when she graduated. And again, when she married Rick, however, she never seemed to succeed. Valerie could never dismiss the thoughts of what happened to her when she was younger, nor shut the door to her disappointment in her parents. She felt let down, betrayed, isolated, and dismissed as a young girl—telling her parents what happened seem to be the worst decision of her life. Moving out was the only way she could break loose of the hell that she was living day in and day out.

She sits in the passenger seat dazed, thoughts of Romelle encapsulated her—He was her best friend, the only person she could confide in, the person who she trusted with her whole heart. He was always there for her. He promised never to leave her and never once made her feel terrible for what she had to do.

"You ready?" Mark stares at his sister—his hand lays gently over hers.

Valerie is immediately reconnected with the real world. She snaps back into her reality, looks over at her brother, and simply nods her head yes.

"Hey mom." Mark reaches in to hug his mother as he stands in the middle of the doorway.

"Hi baby, so glad you stopped by." She stands to the side to let her son into the house. Her short heavy frame is miniature compared to her son's. She glances at her daughter standing there behind her son. Her warm smile is inviting and endearing. "Hello daughter," she says with a calm and pleasant tone. She stretches her arms out for Val.

Val leans into her mom, halfheartedly with one arm. *Lord help me...*

Dena gestures towards the door with her hand, stepping to one side for her daughter to come in.

"What's up pops." Mark Jr. sits next to his dad who's sipping on some tea. His cover throw lays flat across the lower half of his body.

"Son." He nods at Mark and barely glances over to look at him. His fragile frame is limp, and his peppered hair is almost non-existent. He grabs a Kleenex from the box of tissue sitting beside him on the collapsible dinner tray—he wipes his nose. His recliner sits close to the forty-inch television. His hearing, decaying just as his sight over the years. Age has definitely caught up with him hard. At 71, he barely has the energy to stand up anymore.

"The chemo treatments are a lot on him. But he's managing," Dena says as she grabs a seat in her favorite rocking chair across from her husband.

The living room is small and cozy. Just fitting for the two of them. Her pink and yellow pajamas were faded, and her slippers are worn. But Valerie's mother seems to be content. She was never a worrisome person. Easy to please, and a woman of few words.

"You need me to warm your tea up dear," Dena shouts across to her husband.

Clearing his throat from couching, he responds, "No." His voice is raspy and light.

Valerie takes in the scenery. It's the first time she's stepping her foot in her parent's house. The floor was wooden and creaked with every footstep. The dingy drapes called for some TLC. The bike was clean, nonetheless. Looks as if her mom was doing the best she could by herself. The smell of home-made chili filled her nostrils.

"Hey mom," she calls out. "You made chili huh?"

"Yup. I sure did," she replies as she rocks back and forth in her chair.

Val's once-a-week phone calls to her mom are usually brief. She always asked how her dad was doing but never requests for him to come to the phone. Hearing his voice was not needed. She just wanted to know if he's alive.

Valerie is both anxious and nervous all at the same time. She desperately wants to get up and leave. She fidgets with her braids most of the time. Her freshly re-braided hair is hanging down her rounded shoulders.

She can't relax. She glances at her father sparingly. His demeanor, his physical appearance, she wasn't used to seeing. She feels helpless and pity towards her aging father. She wasn't around to help her mom out with her dad. She wasn't even there when her mom cried for two days straight, overwhelmed by thoughts of losing her husband. She feels guilty and ashamed. Just one more thing to stir in her pot of guilt and misery, sprinkled with a touch of unforgiveness.

After sitting and talking for twenty minutes to his parents, Mark Jr. breaks Val's silence. "So listen mom and dad, we need to talk about something serious. Something that has being bothering Val. He looks at both his mom and dad.

"What is it sweetie," Dena replies, looking over towards her daughter on the beige couch. Her eyes fixed on her daughter.

Valerie waits until her father stops coughing. His loud gasps for air nerved her. She wasn't sure if he was going to catch his breath or suffocate from a lack of oxygen. "He doesn't need an oxygen tank?" she says as she turns back to look at her mom.

"No baby, he doesn't," she responds. "I'm used to it. Scary at first. Thought he was surely gonna die, but after about a month of hearing him hacking like that, you're bound to get used to it. Now go on. What is it you have to tell us sweetie?" Sweetie was the Nickname she gave Valerie when she was five. She was always eating sweets— grabbing a stool and grabbing handfuls of cookies from the cookie jar. Sneaking candy under her pillow so she could nibble on it at night. And begging for more candy after all the candy was gone from her Easter basket.

"Well..." She begins clearing her throat. "Umm. I—um-"

"Val," Mark Jr. says with a stern but confident look. His right eyebrow was raised slightly. His hands clasped together.

Val knew her brother was pushing her to get on with it. Silently letting her know he was there for her. He drove her all this way because he knew she finally needed to release her pain.

"Well, I, um... I came over to speak to both of you," Val begins. Looking across the room at her mom and dad, Val takes a deep breath in and exhales forcefully. "Well, I want to tell you why I don't really visit you. I know that you've asked me to visit more mom, but you also know that I always make excuses why I can't come." She pulls her shoulders back as she sits up straight. She eyes her brother and notes his calm demeanor. Her mom and dad, on the other hand, looks as if Val has a big confession to lay on them—which she does. "When I moved out of your house to stay with Romelle when I was a teenager, a lot changed..."

Val stops and hangs her head low once more. She feels acid churning in her stomach that makes its way upwards to her throat. She swallows hard and wipes the beads of sweat from her head. She closes her eyes and begins to massage the back of her neck with her right hand. The room seems to spin, and the quietness begins to aggravate Valerie without rhyme or reason.

"Go on," her mother argues gently. "It's okay sweetheart, just say what's on your mind."

"You never believed me when I said I was raped. You never even helped me!" She shouts with anger.

"What wait, what are you talking about? We didn't believe you Val?" her mom snapped back.

"Mom, you didn't. Dad said it didn't happen, so you did nothing!" Looking at her dad, "and you, you never even once heard the whole story," she shouts. With tears flowing down her face endlessly, Val finally feels a feeling of release. She feels the urge to push through. "Your friend Darnell was in my bedroom multiple times, but you never thought anything of it. You allowed him to sleep over when he was too drunk to drive home, but you never once knew he would come in my bedroom? You never once knew?" she scolds angrily as tears form in the corners of her eyes. "I know you were drinking a lot," she continues, "but I was your little girl daddy, your only daughter. You didn't protect me. I-I thought you loved me," she sobs…

Val was broken. She was hurt—living in a world where there was never any penalty or restitution for what she had to endure.

She glances up at her brother, his hand now resting on her shoulder. She didn't even realize he had gotten up out of his seat.

"It's okay Val. You got this," he whispers.

Val continues to weep. Her shoulders heave up and down as she tries to compose herself. "I was pregnant mom," she finally says lowly. "I was a virgin, and he took that away from me. You weren't there for me. I didn't know what to do. My friend's mom had to take me to the clinic. It was no way I could have his baby." She wipes her tear-stained face and pushes her braids away that have fallen in her face. "I did what I had to do, you know. Then I decided I had to move out, and that's when I made a hard decision to leave you both out of my life.

All the pent-up anger she felt over the years was finally unfurled unto her parents. No more restless nights of tormented memories. No more resentment. Valerie could now start to live freely. She could finally learn, how to live in peace. But that process, she would find out, would be long and hard.

Chapter 15

Valerie moves towards her husband, "I know I really
messed up Rick. I've tried to be a good wife—I quit
my job for you, cook, clean, and make sure I pack your
lunch for work every morning. I know you love me, but I am
not yours to control. I need counseling, and I think—"

"We can go together baby. I am willing to go too. We can
work things out," Rick replies, cutting his wife off.

It's been three weeks since she went to see her parent's
house. Her conscience is cleared, and her mind is free. She was
gonna walk away free no matter how the night ended. Her
mother's apology meant the world to her that night. They cried
and hugged and hearing her mother's words, *I'm sorry*, released
here from every possible hurt she felt for far too long.

"I never meant to hurt you baby girl. Please forgive me. I just
didn't know what to do," she weeps. "Your father, your u-ug,
your father said to leave it alone. I cried all the time. We
argued, we fought, we were never the same after that day
Valerie," she sobs.

"I know mom," she replies. "I know."

Valerie heard her mother cry at night when her parents thought she was sleeping. The short time she remained at home made her feel like she and her mother lived in some type of hell. Valerie knew how strict her father was. She also knew how verbally abusive he was to her mother too— The daily drunken fits he had were enough to make any person wonder why her mother stayed. But her mother being the humble, she was so quiet and would never go against her husband. She loves him. And he was all she knew. No matter his flaws, she loved him.

"Come here baby," her father whispers. His voice was stern, but weak. "Come here."

Val walks over to her dad and kneels down in front of him."Yes, daddy."

He grabs her hands and places them in his lap. He sits there, looking at his daughter with tears streaming down his face. His hands are shaking, but he continues to clap his daughter's hands. His body is visibly shaking uncontrollably from his already weak nature. "I-umm, I, I'm sorry baby girl," he whispers—He says nothing more. Valerie lays her head lightly on her dad's lap. Needing nothing more, she feels released.

Val's shoulders relax a little as she sighs, her thoughts slowly rolling back to present day. She interlocks her fingers together, glancing down at her wedding ring. Her heart rapidly beats— aches without signs of ceasing. "Look Rick," she responds firmly. "What I was trying to say was, I think you need to see a counselor too, but not to keep me. You are very controlling. You go through my things, and although my diary has secrets in there that I was keeping from you, you still had no right to invade my privacy. You've gone through my things before, but I never said how it made me feel. Like when you always go through my phone, emails, and even my brother's messages. I mean, you never even wanted me to go out with my girlfriends—Not out to dinner, to the movies, or even a birthday celebration, and vacations with my girls were out the question. You know, at first, I thought it was cute. In the beginning, I thought you were so into me. But no, you only wanted to control me. And now..." She stares out the window and sees the neighbor across the street walking her dog. Trying to avoid the elephant in the room, she becomes distracted. The autumn-colored leaves that have fallen to the earth has left the trees on her street almost bare.

"Go on Val. And now what?"

"And now I have no friends Rick," she sighs. "You ran them all away.

"Listen, I'm sorry baby. I'm truly sorry. But I'm not sorry for wanting to be around you, I loved you then, and I love you now. I don't want us to divorce. We can work this out."

"Look, I know you love me. I know I love you too. But honestly, our relationship is too toxic. You have to find healing for you before there can be a you-and-me." Her eyebrows raise slightly, looking for the slightest hint of a fuss from her husband. She doesn't know what his next response will be...

Rick gets up from the couch. His arms fold across his chest. Valerie slowly follows her husband with her eyes as he moves towards the bay window. "Achoo." Rick pulls a napkin out of his pocket.

"Bless you," Val says to her husband.

"Look, I forgive you, why can't you forgive me?" Rick replies as he turns around to face Val. "I'm willing to work things out and move forward. Yeah, I thought about leaving you. I was angry. Shit, I'm still angry with you. But the truth is, I love you. Noah loves you. And I love Nairobi like she was my own. I don't wanna lose my family."

"I need counseling for myself Rick. I have a lot to sort through. I have a lot of hurts inside, and to stay in this marriage right now, it's not going to be in the best interest of any one of us."Val feels her phone vibrate in her back pocket, but she doesn't make a move. Looking at her husband, she begins to speak. "I, umm. I..." She hesitates.

"Rick sits next to his wife, his hands rest upon her shoulder. "What is it?"

"I was raped repeatedly at the age of thirteen.

Rick's eyes are fixed on his wife. He sits next to her motionless. The eerie silence leaves them both paralyzed, without any words spoken between them.

A deep lump begins to grow larger in Valerie's throat. What feels like a knot in her throat begins to constrict her lungs from expanding. She wipes her palms back and forth across her pants leg, calming herself down. She begins to take deep forceful breath's in and out. Valerie glances over at her husband. She notes his stiff face is flushed red.

"I was abused by my father's best friend," she continues, "for two years." Water streams down her face, her heart pounds heavily in her chest. "I finally told my parents when I was 15." She pauses and drops her head, staring down to the floor. The clock begins to chime. It was almost dusk. The sun was slowly disappearing. Looking back at her husband, with tears streaming down her face, she continues. "I had to have an abortion," she cries out.

Rick begins pounding his fist in the palm of his hands. His face is glowing red. The hard pounding of his fists is bound to leave a mark. He grunts loudly with disgust.

"I never got over it. My father didn't believe me," she yells. "I was just a child. I had no reason to lie," she cries.

"Hey babe, don't cry." Rick grabs his wife and pulls her close to him. He places her head upon his chest. Rick embraces her with all his strength. Carefully, he gives her a subtle kiss upon the top of her head. He pulls her braids that have fallen in front of her face behind her back.

With her fists balled up in her lap—She fights the urge to scream. She lifts her head and brushes away her tears. "I hadn't forgiven my parents, especially my father," she whispers. "Well... Not until recently," she adds.

"Huh? What do you mean recently V?"

"I finally went over there two weeks ago. Well, Jr. and I went over there. My brother felt it was time I told them the truth."

Rick was comforting to Val. His voice very empathetic, and it was a huge release to tell her husband the truth about her past.

"What happened when you told them how you felt?" He tenderly wipes her tears that are still falling down her face.

"They both apologized."

"They did?" Rick questions.

"Yes. And although I felt better that night for telling them the truth. I'm still hurting. I'm still dealing with the trauma that time of my life caused." She tosses her behind her shoulders as she begins to stand up. Her legs feel weak, her mind still grasping what's really going on in her life. "Rick, I need counseling for me. I need to work on me, my pain, my issues—forgiving me Rick," she says softly as her eyes intensely stare into her husband's eyes.

"Ok," he responds reluctantly. "If space is what you want, I'll give it to you. I'll let you work on you, and I'll work on me. If that's what you really want," he says to his wife as he carefully walks up to her, closing the gap in between them. He stares down at her, his eyes glued to hers.

Val feels his hands glide across her backside gently. She feels the comforting touch of his palms on the small of her back. He looks intently into her eyes, and she can't help but want to fall into his body. Lord, help me! "Yes, it's what I need," she responds.

"Alright." He kisses his wife on her lips softly before releasing her. He steps back and stands there, looking at her without saying anything. He turns around and grabs his jacket off the couch on his way to the front door. He grabs the doorknob but turns around to Val before he opens the door. "Hey, have you made your mind up if you're keeping the baby?"

Chapter 16

Halloween had come and gone. The autumn leaves had stripped all the trees bare. There was nothing left but barren trees that yielded no warm shelter for birds to hide in their nest. It was harvest time and Valerie's favorite time of the year.

"Nairobi," Val shouts.

"Yes?" Nairobi calls out to her mother. She was playing with her dolls upstairs.

"Come here pumpkin."

Nairobi makes her way downstairs to see what her mother wanted. "Yes, mommy?"

"Can we finally take the Halloween decals off the window and put up the fall decorations, please? I mean, it's only three weeks before Thanksgiving pumpkin," she chuckles.

"Okay mommy, she replied. Can I help you decorate?"

"Of course, you can baby. Takedown those stickers on that side," she gestures towards the right side of the window," and

I'll take down these. She begins to take down the stickers on the left side of the window.

They both take down the Halloween stickers, to prepare for their harvest decorations. The cinnamon apple candles were lite in the candle holders and delighted her nose with scents of apple pie. It was 6:00 in the evening, and Valerie had already cleared the dishes from the dining room table. She made Nairobi's favorite meal, cheeseburgers, and fries. She was enjoying the evening air that was coming through the house. The sliding glass doors are cracked open off the back patio.

"Mommy, I'm done. Can I get the Thanksgiving stickers?"

"Yes, sweetie, grab that brown bag off the table in the dining room." Valerie took the stickers she had in her hand and tossed them in the garbage as her daughter began digging for stickers to put up.

"Mommy," Nairobi cried. "I can't get the sticker to come off this stupid paper."

"Here I come, let me do it for you." Val begins to pull the peeling back off of each sticker. "There, you put them up on the window, and I'll worry about peeling the stickers off."

"Thanks mommy."

Smiling at her daughter, "You're welcome pumpkin."

They continued to work together until they were finished. The window showcased autumn leaves, golden brown stacks of hay, red apples, pictures of boys and girls playing in the leaves, and the words, 'Happy Thanksgiving' plastered across the top.

"Hey, you wanna bake some cupcakes?"

"Yayyy," Nairobi screams.

"I'll take that as a yes."

"Beat you to the kitchen," Valerie exclaimed.

Nairobi takes off like a racehorse in a Kentucky Derby race. "I win, I win," she yells, jumping up and down.

"Oh man, you beat me again." Val grabs the mixing bowl from the top shelf and grabs the strawberry cake mix from the cabinet. "Baby, grab the mixing spoon and the milk out the frig."

"Okay mommy." She grabs the big spoon out of the drawer and then milk from the frig. "What next."

"Hand me the mixing cup over there next to the tea canister."

Nairobi grabs the cup next to the yellow canister and places it next to the mixing bowl.

"Alright, now I'll pour the milk into the cup, and you pour it into the bowl, ok?"

"Okay, I got it mommy."

Val pours the 2/3 cups of milk into the measuring cup and gives it to Nairobi. After her daughter finishes pouring the milk, she then opens the batter mix and hands it to her daughter, "now pour this into the bowl.

"Nairobi pours the mix and grabs the spoon. "I'm ready to stirry it now."

"You stirry the mix and I'll crack the eggs into the bowl."

They continued to prepare the mix and then poured the batter into each cupcake holes in the pan. Valerie places the cupcake pan into the stove and set the timer. "Now, how about you help me put the autumn tablecloth on the table.

"Where is it?"

"It's already on the table. We just need to unfold it and place it on top of the table. And then we can place the fall decorations we brought earlier from the store on the table…"

They both pull the opposite corners of the burnt orange fabric and place the cloth on the table. They decorate the table with fall-themed place settings, an autumn vase, place auburn-colored flowers inside it, then set two fall colored candles on top. "There, perfect."

"Perfect!" Nairobi recites with her arms stretched high towards the ceiling. She chuckles as her mom grabs her up and hugs her tight.

"Do you know how much I love you?"

"How much mommy?"

"I love you beyond eternity," she smiles, then gives her daughter kisses until she says stop. "You wanna watch a movie?"

"Yes, can we watch a cartoon movie!" she shouts.

"Of course, go grab your snuggie and your little bear.

The two of them curl up on the couch, eating cupcakes and watching an evening movie on Netflix. Valerie was feeling better than she had been when she got up this morning. Nausea, feelings of guilt, and not to mention Rick, she misses him and Noah like crazy. It's nothing she wouldn't do to erase everything between her and Romelle.

Val knew her husband needed help, his drinking never showed the most beautiful part of him, but neither did it with her father. She knew all too well about living with an abusive drunk. Valerie didn't want to become like her mother. But in a lot of ways, it was too late. She married a good-hearted man-- but one who drank a little too much. And before you know it, he would be just like her father. Getting away from Rick was the only way she could stand up and face her own demons. The only way she could stop comparing her husband to her father. She knew where Rick would be if he kept his drinking habit. Sure, he didn't drink every day like her father, but she knew by his behaviors of drinking every time he was a little too stressed from work, or when he was upset, that it was soon to follow. She was happy he agreed to see a therapist. But the real question is, when will she gonna call and make her appointment to see one?

November 27, 2019

Dear Diary,

Today is like every other day. Nothing but regrets are constantly going through my mind all day. Thanksgiving is tomorrow, and I really don't feel like doing anything but curling up in my bed and letting the whole day pass me by. That would be great. However, that's what I've been doing for weeks now. I don't know what I'm going to do--I'm separated from my husband, and I honestly feel like hell. To top it off, I don't even know what I'm gonna do with the pregnancy. Abortion laws are changing quickly, however, that wasn't really an option for me. Do I give the baby up for adoption? Do I tell Rome? Whatever I decide to do, I better make it quick. So much going through my mind, all the time, un-relentlessly. I have a headache most days and can barely drag myself out of bed. I think I'm falling into a depression. If it wasn't for my baby girl, I don't think I could take the agony of being alone or dealing with this crap. I'm sure I've failed everybody. Hell! I've failed myself most of all. How did I get here? Just less than a year ago, I was happy, I was at peace, I was a good wife. Now everything has changed.

Rick keeps calling and texting me, but I don't have much to say, so I keep it brief whenever I do answer him. He's determined to get me back-- us back. But honestly, I don't know about that. I can't make any promises. I mean, I love him, but I need time. He's seeing a counselor about his drinking and talking about our marriage, and I'm happy for him. He actually went through with it as he said. Now he keeps asking me if I set my appointment up, and If I'm going to see a counselor? Crap, I can't answer that right now. Between telling someone all my personal business--My unfaithfulness, the pregnancy, about my past, I can't seem to think straight. I feel so drained.

And Romelle, he's so confused about everything. I can barely bring myself to answer any of his texts or calls. He wants to see his daughter. He wants to understand why I didn't tell him from the very beginning that I was married. Heck, I can't answer that question. I can't answer any of his questions. I know I don't want to hurt him anymore. I know I have to let him see Nairobi, but when? I don't know...

I feel like a weight has been lifted off my shoulders in a sense. Telling my mom and dad how I felt all these years was a relief. I had so much built-up animosity against them that I needed to finally tell them how hurt I was. How I felt like they let me down. And how broken I have been all these years because of their refusal to accept the truth. See, for some reason, I feel they thought I blamed them for what happened to me, so they denied the truth. But the truth was, I just needed them to understand how I felt, and I needed them to be there for me. My dad once told me it didn't happen because he told me to tell him if anyone ever abused me. Well, I was a child. Did he think it would be easy for me to tell him if the man kept telling me to keep my mouth shut; to keep it a secret? If he kept telling me he would kill my parents if I told anyone? No, it's not my fault. Finally, telling my parents it wasn't my fault allowed me to release the anger inside me. No one can take away my truth, not anymore. Now hopefully, they can both forgive themselves for what happened to me, because I am finally free.

~Val

Valerie closes her journal and sips her caramel Frappuccino. She sits alone in the coffee house to try and clear her mind— To get herself out of the house. She looks down at her watch, 9:15. It will be time to pick up her daughter shortly. Her school has a half-day due to the holiday tomorrow. She glances down at her stomach and places her right hand gently on her small belly. Her eyebrows knit, Was the doctor right— Fifteen weeks pregnant? She was nearly four months pregnant. What am I gonna do? Time is running out, and I still have no clue...

"Awww, congratulations! how many weeks are you?" asked the coffeehouse attendant."

"Excuse me," Val replies. She sits there dazedly. Shocked, her eyebrows raise, questioning the woman's motives. She immediately removes her hand and stares at the woman standing in front of her.

"I'm sorry, I saw you rubbing your stomach. I didn't mean to assume." She places her hand over her heart, her eyes are wide, and her face apologetic. The hefty brunette stands there with her cheeks flushed red.

Noticing that she must've snapped at the innocent woman, Val tries to redirect her body language. Valerie sits up in her chair with a warm smile and quickly searches for words to say. "I-umm. No. I mean yes..." She shakes her head. "What I mean is, thank you, no worries," she replies. She smiles warmly, reassuring the waitress that she did nothing wrong. "I'm fifteen-weeks."

"You and your husband must be excited," she exclaims. "Well, congrats again, and sorry for startling you," she says smiling, as she walks away to wipe down the adjacent tables.

Val gives a polite nod and stares down at her wedding band still on her left finger. She must've noticed my ring. I would assume it was my husband's baby too if I were her. She turns her ring around her petite finger over and over again. She picks up her cup and sips it slowly. As she sips her coffee, she glances out the window beside her. The city busses are packed with people getting on and off. I wonder where they're going.

The weather is a bit frigid. The news forecaster is calling for light snow flurries later on this evening. It wasn't unusual for it to snow in November. Heck, it was more uncommon for it not to snow by Thanksgiving in Michigan. Michiganders are used to it, and always prepare for winter to hit by the holidays.

Valerie grabs her rose pink scarf around her neck closely and reminisces about when she first met her husband. The same coffee house--a day full of laughs and good conversation. She smiles fondly. Her face glows with delight of thoughts of her husband. His charismatic nature, his pleasant smile... Oh, the tantalizing smell of his cologne. The rush of customers coming through the door blew in the chill from outside. She quickly shivers and snaps back into reality.

She pulls her phone out her small black purse, and googles, **Psychologist near me...** The search yielded multiple results. Hmm, this one seems just about right...

Dr. Stevenson, verified licensed Psychologist, specializing in women. Anxiety, Depression, Trauma. Secure Counseling.

You're not alone. Let our supportive counselors help you during this difficult time.

Valerie screenshots the information and saves it to her gallery. She takes another sip of her coffee. She notes the couple sitting across from her now. They seem like a happy couple. *Yeah, that's the newlywed phase.* She grabs her novel and picks up where she left off. She loves reading. Something she hadn't done in a while, but something she enjoyed doing very much. She still has about forty-five minutes before she needs to pack up and go. However, It wasn't long before she was interrupted, the buzzing of her phone went off in her purse. She reaches in her purse to grab it…

Chapter 17

You never know what you have until it's gone... But what if it was you that never knew who you were because it was you who was lost?

~Val

Thanks giving Day

Valerie has plans to spend time with her parents. She decided that getting out of the house would be good for her. Besides, her brother Mark said if she didn't, he would show up and drag her out himself. Valerie had agreed on allowing Nairobi to spend some time with her father, Romelle. He called over and over again, asking if he could take his daughter over his

family house so they could all spend time with her. Valerie knew that was the right thing to do, so she agreed. She told him to have her back by 8:00 so she could give her a bath and get her in bed by 9:00.

"Hey Nairobi, come get the clothes I ironed for you," she yells upstairs.

It was 11:20 a.m. She only has a few more minutes before Romelle pulls up. It will be her first Thanksgiving without her baby girl. Her first Thanksgiving without her husband.

Val stands in front of the bay window. Barely noticing the light snow that's falling down softly to the earth. She wants everything back the way it was. She longs for her husband when she lays in the bed at night--she tosses and turns feeling the emptiness that sleeps next to her. The stranger that lays beside her is cold, void of comfort, and dark...

Morning comes, Valerie imagines her husband stepping out of the shower in the morning, dripping wet with his royal blue towel around his waist, talking to her about the meetings he had lined up for the week. When she makes a pot of coffee, she misses the way he use to grab her by her waistline from behind, and softly whispers "I love you forever V." The simple things, make Val feel good; like asking what she wanted from the store on his way out of the door, Rick shoveling the snow and scraping the snow off of her truck in the morning, his long embrace, and the way his strong arms felt wrapped around her. She misses the way he used to tilt her head gently to one side to kiss her. She misses him like crazy, flaws and all. She loves him for who he is, not as what she sometimes sees. His heart, his mind, his gentle way of loving her... I know he's a great man, and nothing else matters. Rather I am with him or not, I will always know his heart.

"Mommy, are you ready?" Nairobi asks as she grabs her mother's hand.

"Yes, baby." She didn't see the car pull up in the driveway. "Let me grab my purse."

Val opens the door and steps outside with her daughter by her side. After locking her door behind herself, Val walks up to Romelle's car, where he's standing there waiting beside his driver-side door.

"Hey Val," Romelle says politely.

"Hey Ro," Val replies back softly. He looks presentable for the holidays with his daughter. His chestnut brown dress coat was buttoned halfway up, and his collar stands up, covering his neck. His shoes matched his coat perfectly, and of course, his hairline showed off his freshly new cut.

He tosses his scarf to the side as he reaches down to grab his daughter. "Hey baby girl, how are you?"

"Hi daddy," Nairobi responds. You like my new pink coat daddy?"

"Yes, I do! I love it. And I see you have fuzzy pink gloves and a pink hat to match. Did your mommy pick that out for you?" he smiles.

"Yup, she did."

"Well, your mom has great taste. Let's get you buckled up in the backseat."

Valerie stands there as Romelle buckles Nairobi into the booster seat in the back. She smiles at how well they both get along. It's such a wonderful sight. He loves her a lot. She glances over at the black truck driving pass and almost thought it was her husband coming home. Get a grip Val. You told him you needed time remember? You know he's not coming.

"Okay, well, I guess that's it. 8:00 right?" Ro asked Valerie. Trying to confirm the time.

"Huh, what you say?" Val responds, snapping back from her daydream.

"Have her back by 8:00 tonight right," Romelle repeats himself.

"Oh, um, yeah. 8:00, have her here by 8:00." Val brings her thoughts back into focus.

Stepping closer to Val, "Hey, is everything okay?" Ro said with concern as he leans his head downwards to catch her eyes. His eyes stare at Valerie intently. His concern was warranted. Val is distracted.

"I'm I ok? Yeah, why wouldn't I be?" Val's motionless response didn't sooth Romelle as he continued to stand there and stare at her. "Yes, I'm ok Romelle. I'm fine." She tries to convince him by giving him a fake smile.

I haven't said anything to him about the pregnancy; I've had so much on my mind. I need to tell him. At least, I need to let him know. Even if I decide to get an abortion. She looks blankly into his eyes.

"Okay, if you say so," Romelle replies as he begins to back away. "Look, I don't want to intrude on you and your husband's time, so I guess I better get going."

She knows that this is killing him. She knows that he is hurt. The whole marriage proposal she turned down a couple of months back, finding out she was married. It has to hurt, but there is nothing she can do about that. Nothing she can say to make Romelle feel any better.

"Hey," Val stops him as he grabs his car handle--grabbing him by his arm. "Wait, I-- um... I need to say something to you," she said with hesitation. She feels her heartbeat begin to race as he turns around to face her.

"Yeah, what is it?" He replies. His face is solemn with concern.

"I'm actually..."

She pauses. This is difficult to say. She knows telling him this time about the pregnancy is right, but how will he react? Anxiety is rising up, and she can't stop fidgeting. Her hands begin to tremble, and she begins to second-guess herself. She drops her head down.

"Val, what's wrong?" he says, grabbing her chin and gently bringing it back up to meet his eyes.

Valerie glances into the car window, she catches a slight glimpse of her daughter playing with the doll she brought with her. I have to tell him. It can't be like the last time. He deserves to know the truth. I'll tell him that my husband knows everything too. I want to be honest. He deserves that. She glances back up at Ro. The intensity of his warm hazel eyes invites her in as they had always done when they were best friends. She is captivated by those moments of empathy he showed her when she first confided in him when she was a teen, not knowing where else to turn. He believed her from the very beginning and told her he would protect her. He said he would make sure she is never harmed again. The soft breeze flew past her lightly and grazed upon her face. She relaxes, and knows that she feels safe, "I'm…"**Buzzz, Buzzz.**

Val reaches for her vibrating phone inside her back pocket.

"Hey, what's up Jr." she answers.

"Where are you? You should be here by now. Do I need to come toss you over my shoulder and drag you out that house?" he shouts, on the other end of the phone.

"No, no, I'm on my way now. I was just leaving."

"You better be. I'll call you back in fifteen minutes to know where you're. Bye." He hangs up the phone without hesitation.

"Look Ro, I have to go, that was Mark." She begins to walk off.

"Hey, wait," he says, walking up to her before she could get to her car. He grabs her hands. "What is that you wanted to say to me?"

She hesitates for a moment. Looking at him, she says, "I'm happy you decided to get our daughter. I know she really wanted to see you. So, thank you." She smiles, gives a quick wave and blows a kiss to Nairobi and walks away to her car, with Romelle still standing there.

"You're welcome!" he shouts.

Valerie turns around and smiles, then opens her car door and gets in.

"I thought you had lost your way, big head," Mark says with a smirk as he opens the door for Valerie. He grabs her hand and pulls her to him and gives her a big hug.

"Move stupid," she replies back, shoving him out the way.

"Do you two ever stop?" Diane was waiting in the middle of the floor for Valerie with a big, warm smile. "Get over here baby," her mother says with her arms wide open for a hug. Her red apron was faded and tattered from years of wear.

"Hey daddy," Val grabs her dad lightly and gives him a peck on his forehead.

"Hey baby, Mark senior replies in a low rasping tone. He tries to catch his breath as he begins coughing, but the unrelenting coughing persisted, so he gestures for his water bottle on the stand next to him.

"Here daddy, drink." Val unscrews the bottle top and hands it to her dad.

He clears his throat with a loud-rough cough, and gestures to his daughter to put the bottle down. "Thank you baby," he said, with a more forceful tone.

"Dinner smells good mom," Valerie said, walking towards the kitchen. Her mother was in the kitchen, taking the pan of sweet potatoes out the oven. "Here, let me grab that momma." She grabs the medium-sized pan and sits it beside the golden-brown macaroni and cheese. She stands, salivating over the Thanksgiving meal her mom prepared.

Everything is still cooked from scratch. Golden cornbread, fresh greens with salt pork and turkey legs stirred inside. She cooked sweet potatoes, Mac and cheese, potato salad, and a beautifully glazed turkey with gravy on the side. "Ummm. All my favorites," Val muttered. "You even did the homemade apple pie." She folds her arms across her chest. "Now, who do you expect to eat all of this momma?" Valerie asked smiling.

"Well, of course you know Mark Jr. will have no problem putting any of this away," her mom says chuckling.

It was good to be home, enjoying her parent's company and being with her big brother. Anything to derail the constant insanity that is always captivating her mind. Every day she feels as if she is held hostage by her thoughts. The room is filled with conversation as they eat dinner. Holiday music quietly serenades the room. Dinner forks scrape upon their plates and love finally fills the room.

Valerie looks at her mom and notes her smile upon her frail but tender face. She returns a warm smile and begins to get up to clear the table.

"Alright boys, hand me over your dinner plates," Valerie says, with a hint of authority. "Mark, dang! Did you leave any room for dessert in that belly of yours?" she smirks. Laughter fills the air.

"Of course, I did, big head!" Give me about twenty minutes, and I'll have my pie."

"Shut up stupid," Val snaps back.

"Come on pops, let me wheel you over to the TV so we can watch the football game." Junior begins to roll his dad to the television, and he grabs the remote before settling into the recliner.

"I got it momma," Val says, taking the plates from her. I'll load the dishwasher. You grab the containers so I can put the food away." Val rinses the dishes before loading the washer.

"Thank you dear."

"No problem momma."

After Valerie and her mom work together in the kitchen, Val's mother gestures towards her room. She enters her room with her daughter right behind her. "Shut the door sweetie."

Val shuts the door behind her. "Oh, I remember this, fourth-grade spelling bee contest." She picks the picture up from the shelf in her mother's room.

"Yeah, you won that year. You would've won the year before too if you hadn't been ill. You begged me to let you go to school that day--But you lost to that boy Greg." She stands by her daughter's side.

"Yeah, that was a tough loss. We were the last two standing, going at it for such a long time."

"Thirty-five minutes, to be exact." Walking slowly, she sits down on the foot of her bed.

Valerie glances over at her mom. How can she remember such small details about my youth? Val places the picture back down on the shelf.

"So, what's going on with you sweetie?"

"What do you mean momma?" Val brows knit together. She still feels stuffed from dinner. Her stomach can barely take down the same amount of food— her pregnancy hindered that.

"I can tell somethings bothering you."

Val tilts her head in confusion, "How you figure that mom?" she questions.

"When I asked you where's my grandbaby, you mentioned with her father earlier, but when I said to make sure you tell Rick I said hello, you gave me this interesting look. As if something is going on between you and your husband.

"Well, she's not with my husband. She's with her dad, Romelle." Val stands there with one arm leaning on her mother's dresser. She waits to see what her mother replies with.

"What a blast from the past. He's finally home from the Navy?"

"Oh mom, it's so much you don't know about," Valerie begins.

"I know you two were best friends," she says as she moves up on her bed some more. "And I know you both really loved each other. I know that for sure. I never understood why you two broke it off. And I never asked. But I also know you still love him. So, what happened?"

Valerie tries to fight back the tears welling up in the corner of her eyes. But her eyes begin to burn. She begins to tremble with heated emotions. "Oh mom!" She collapses on the bed next to her mother as tears stream down her slender face. "It's all bad, EVERYTHING! I really messed things up."

"Sweetie." She moves Valerie's braids behind her back and lifts her head up with the palm of her fragile hands so she could see her daughter's eyes. "What did you do?"

The tears roll down her cheeks uncontrollably. "I cheated on my husband with Romelle." Her eyes sting. "I know that losing my husband never seemed possible. I never really imagined us separating. I keep looking out our window, and visions of him pulling up in his truck entertain my thoughts. I miss him so bad momma. I want to see him. I want him to hold me, kiss me on my forehead and tell me everything will be alright." She wipes away a lonely tear cascading down her cheek. "I want him next to me. I yearn to have him near me all the time." She drops down to the floor in front of her mother. "I feel so stupid! I'm living in a nightmare mom, and Freddie Krueger has already killed me. Tell God to please take this pain away!" She sobs without restraints.

Her mother holds her tightly with compassion and care. She comforts her as she rubs her hands up and down her back. "It's going to be alright sweetie. Don't cry."

"How mom? How?" Valarie whimpers in her mother's arms.

"When Junior was three, I got a phone call. It was a young woman asking to speak to me," she begins. "When I asked her who she was, she said Chavona. I didn't recognize her name, but

I was inclined to stay on the phone." She continues to rub her daughter's back, gliding her hand smoothly up and down. "Well, when I got off the phone, I cried. I cried uncontrollably, much like you are right now. But I had no one to call and nowhere to run. So, I questioned him about her.

"What did he say?" Val looks up at her mother inquisitively.

"What do you think he said dear?" She looks intently into her daughter's eyes.

Val places her head sideways on her mother's lap.

"I knew it was true no matter how much he denied it, but I needed proof. So, one day, I tell your dad I'm going to take Mark around the corner for a playdate, and we would be back in a couple of hours. But little did he know, I was going to drop him off for his playdate, and I was coming back sooner than he thought." She pauses for a moment. "Little did he know. My intuition was telling me he would slip up one day. I came home and found the woman underneath my sheets…"

"You caught him with her in your bed mom?" Val voice was loud. Her eyebrows raised high, and her mouth left wide open.

"Shhhhh. Not so loud sweetie. Yes, I caught my husband having an affair," she whispers.

"What did you do?" Valerie sweeps her tears from her face.

"I put him out and told him he would never see Mark or me again." She looks down at Valerie, "I was devastated and embarrassed. Hurt to no end."

"What made you take him back, momma?" Valerie asked.

"You."

"Me?"

"Yes. I found out I was six weeks pregnant with you, and you know what?"

"What?"

"I felt stupid, but I told your father to come back home. I wanted to keep you, and I wanted my family back. I didn't want to raise you both alone. I loved him." She glances out the window, the snow was sticking to the ground. It was dark and a few neighbors had put their Christmas lights and decorations outside their house. "Sure, people talked about me." She grabs her daughter's hand. "But I did what I felt was right for my family. We had only been married for three years, but I loved him. And you can't help who you love sweetie."

"But mom, I'm pregnant. And it's Romelle's baby." Water begins to well up in her eyes again. "I can't believe I'm pregnant, and I don't know what to do," she cries. "Rick wants to work things out. But I don't know. I told him we both need to see a counselor."

"Rick wants you back, that's all that matters sweetie. Sure, his family and of course, his friends, are going to be against it. But it's up to you. What is your heart saying? What is it that you truly want, Valerie? Close your eyes, close your ears, and tune out all the outside noise, and listen to your heart baby."

"But I'm pregnant with Romelle's baby mom! How can God forgive me? How momma?"

This world has no answers for you, only judgment. We all have flaws, and there are no flaws that are better than others. I decided not to give up on your father, on our marriage. I knew that his flaws were not my problems, but God's. I knew the man I loved, in the beginning, loved only me and would do anything for me. So when he cheated, that's his flesh. I could forgive him for that. The stress of this world, his job, and even raising a family wasn't easy for him. He was only 20 when we married. I was 17 and pregnant with Jr. We had to find a place to live cause I knew I couldn't stay at home with momma. She would always say to me, you opened your legs, now deal with the consequence. I had no choice. I had to grow up fast, drop out of my last year of high school to raise my child..."

The world seems to open up with answers, with optimism. Hope of healing and of reconciliation. Reconciliation on forgiving herself. She was hopeful that calling a counselor next week would begin the process of forgiveness.

"Oh mom, I finally get it now. I understand why you stayed with dad and put up with his flaws. Forgive me for judging you. For hating you for staying." She sits up on the floor on her knees and wraps her arms around her mother. She envelopes her with a warm embrace.

Chapter 18

December 18th

Dear Diary,

After speaking with my momma on Thanks giving and going to church on Sunday, I've decided to keep the baby. I really had a breakdown at my mom's, which made me feel a little better. I understand that there is no such thing as a perfect marriage, but it is such a thing as sacrifice. I've learned that you must sacrifice what you thought you knew about being married because it's all fairytales. You must learn that each marriage is different and comes with its own unique set of problems. But, as Dr. Stevens stated, the greater gift of knowledge is learning that it's not about running from your problems but facing them head-on.

Rick has really been doing well. He has stopped drinking, and he has even invited me to one of his AA meetings. When I went, it must admit, I didn't know what to expect. I learned a lot about my husband. I learned things about him I never knew. He is a strong man for having the strength to open up in front of strangers and tell his story. He showed me the biggest gift of all. Introducing me as his wife, and telling his friends there that we were expecting a baby blew my mind to pieces. I mean, what type of man takes his wife back and accepts her baby as his own? Sure, you hear about it in the tabloids all the time. You hear about the countless rappers, singers, athletes, actors, and so forth that have cheated on their wives and sometimes got another woman pregnant. You also hear how the wife stuck by her husband's side, even when the world was talking trash about her decision to stay. But I remember my mother's words... The world will judge you but listen to your heart. I guess I'm the lucky one. My husband listened to his heart, talked to me, and told me he is waiting for me whenever I decide I'm ready to go forth in our marriage. He's staying at his mom's house for now. He calls me every day to check on us. He asks about Nairobi and asks me about how I'm feeling too. He's even left work and brought me soup when I couldn't eat anything else.

Dr. Stevens says to take things as slowly as I need to. I see her every other Tuesday when Nairobi is in pre-school.

Our sessions have been going really good. I've been able to talk to her about when I was sexually abused as a teen. I talked to her about sleeping with Romelle, and I even told her I was pregnant for him. We talk about everything. I even mentioned how I want to go back to school after the baby is born. I want to get my Master's degree in Psychology, helping abused women so they can heal and forgive. I'll go when the baby turns one. I actually found a program where I can take classes online. It's an accredited university and everything. I guess it was a little easier to talk to her than I had initially thought. Although, a little scary, I'm excited about my journey, going back to school, and helping women overcome tragedy. I'm still learning how to forgive myself and learning how to fly freely. Just as the birds in the sky.

I haven't made my mind up just yet about my marriage, but I have made strides to make sure he gets to spend time with Nairobi. She and Noah need to be around each other, regardless of what's going on in my marriage.

I'm finally meeting up with Romelle to tell him about the baby. With him being in the reserves, our timing is not always good. Every time I want to go to his place to tell him is his weekend to go to his military duty. I was trying to tell him when our daughter was at Rick's. She spent the night over at Rick's mother's place, and Romelle is finally home to talk privately. I hope this day goes well.

~Val

Later on that day

With Christmas less than a week away, Valerie was excited about the holidays. She had invited Rick and Noah over two weeks ago to help trim the tree. The attractively arranged presents sit under the tree in front of the bay window, and stockings hang handsomely from the mantle.

The children replaced the harvest stickers in the window with Christmas stickers. The dining room table cover and centerpiece is now decorated red and green. The multi-colored lights hung from the top of the porch, and lights sparkle brightly from the tree on their front lawn. The street was lined with an array of colors, and decorations showcase brightly from house to house.

Old man winter was in full effect--six inches of snow on the ground and snow angels sprawled out in the lawns where every young child lived. Snowman's were big and small, fitted with scarves and button eyes. But most of all, life was illuminated on Harvard street. Happiness and glee were splattered upon every home, and the Christmas spirit feeling was everywhere.

Val grabs her keys from off the kitchen counter and heads for the door. It's still daylight, and she has about a forty-five-minute drive to Romelle's house. She wraps her scarf around her neck and pulls her gloves onto each hand. She opens the front door and locks it behind herself.

"Hello." Val answers the call blaring across her Bluetooth dashboard.

"Hey, how far out are you?" Romelle asked.

"Hey, I'm about ten minutes away now."

"Okay, I was just checking. I know It's a little rough out there. I wish you had let me come to your house so you wouldn't have to come out this way."

Valerie smiles, knowing that he always was so concerned about her driving in the snow. "Look Ro, I got this, I'm not a kid, you know. I'll be there in ten, ok?"

"I know you're not a kid Val, I just worry about you driving in this snow," he says softly.

"Yeah, I know. I'll be there soon," she reassures him, then she taps the screen to disconnect the call.

Val glides onto his street and pulls up in front of his apartment. She hops out the truck and steps up to his door. She rings his bell, and he quickly opens the door.

"Hey, come on in. You finally made it. You had me worried."

"I told you I got it," Val snickers.

Ro takes Val's coat from her, walks over to the closet, and hangs it up. "Here, sit down on the couch," he gestures towards the sofa as he goes to sit down. "You look thicker," he says with his, eyes fixed on Valerie. "You putting on a little weight?"

"Oh, umm, just a little bit," she replies cautiously. Tugging at her shirt, she sits down beside him.

"Well, it looks good on you. I mean, it's cute." He shakes his head and rubs the tops of his waves with one hand. "What I meant was, you look nice. You know, I don't mean to imply anything—I'm not trying to disrespect your marriage."

"It's ok. Really." Val looks at Ro with reassurance.

Romelle breaths out a sigh of relief as he glides the palms of his hands back and forth. "Have you eaten? Are you hungry?"

"No, I ate already." Val pulls her sweater down, conscience not to show her small bulge in her stomach that was now showing. She notes the scent of vanilla in the air. "What's that smell, Vanilla?"

"Yeah, my plug-ins are plugged into the walls."

Valerie begins to get nervous. I don't know how to say this. Just say it, and stop wasting time. Valerie scoots back on the couch a little more, trying to get comfortable. She tosses her braids behind her and glances over to Romelle who was watching the football game on the TV screen.

"Mannnn! Why you didn't call that Ref! That's an interference," he shouts at the screen. Tossing his hands up in the air.

"Ro," Val says lightly.

"Yeah, what's up?" Ro glances over to Val but back towards the screen. He jumps up quickly off the couch, "Interception, YES! NOW THAT'S WHAT I'M TALKING ABOUT MAN!" His voice seems to echo through the walls. "TOUCH DOWN!"

Valerie remembers fondly the love of sports that Romelle always had when they were teens. He played football and basketball in high school and won MVP during his senior year. Valerie loves his joy for sports—As a cheerleader, she enjoyed having a front-row view of her boyfriend running the ball down the field and running the ball down the court. He could've went off to college. Valerie always knew that his commitment to her and their relationship was why he didn't leave her to play sports for the universities trying to recruit him. He sacrificed his dreams to stay in Detroit with Valerie. She knew that she would sacrifice her life for him if it came down to it because he sacrificed his.

"Hey, are you done screaming at the TV yet?" Val tugs on Romelle's shirt. Her eyes looking up at him, she waits for a response.

"Oh, yeah, sorry about that Val. You know how I get a little carried away anytime I see Detroit playing," he replies. His half-smile highlights his dimples. He sits back down next to her. "What did you need to talk about?"

The room was warm from the electric fireplace glowing adjacent to where they were sitting. "Can you turn your ceiling fan on please?" Val questions. She rubs her sweaty palms across her jeans. Sweat forms under her armpits and begins to stream slowly down her arms. Val clears her throat, releasing the tight constriction.

"Since when do you get hot? You always complain about how cold you are, so I turned the fireplace on for you."

Val shrugs her shoulders, and she begins to feel self-conscience about her stomach.

"Come on girl, just say it." Tell him.

"Well, remember on Thanksgiving when you picked up Nairobi?" she begins.

"Yes," Ro replies, looking intently at Valerie.

"Well, when you asked me if everything was ok, I said yes. But..."

"What Val? What's going on?" Romelle says, his voice concerned.

The air was thick, and Valerie's throat is dry--she grabs the bottle of water Romelle had sat on the table earlier. "Ro, I'm pregnant."

Ro's eyes narrow, his brows knit together. "You are?" he says with a low. He looks at Val for a few moments, then turns his head to face the TV. His jawline clinches, his veins in his neck protrude visibly. He claps his palms together and breathes out forcibly. With apparent irritation, he tries to calm himself.

His left leg shakes up and down rapidly. Looking at the floor, "I'm happy for you. Congratulations," he finally responds.

Val sees he is visibly distraught. "It's yours Ro," she replies, looking at him for a reaction.

Ro's leg stops shaking, no longer vibrating the carpeted floor. Turning his head slowly towards Valerie, his right eyebrow arched high. "Wait, what did you just say?" His body is motionless, his mouth still wide open, he waits for a response.

"The baby is yours," Val finally repeats.

"Don't do this to me right now Val. I already have to deal with the fact that I can't have you, and now you're just playing with my emotions." He stands up and paces the floor.

Val remains on the couch and watches him pace back and forth, watch him throw his hands upon the top of his head.

"It is Ro, the baby's yours?"

He stops pacing, "How can you be sure? You slept with me, yes. But you were also sleeping with your husband."

Val stands up and walks over to Romelle. "First, I felt so guilty for cheating on my husband with you, that I couldn't bring myself to sleep with him. I just made up excuses every time he asked me."

Romelle folds his arms across his chest and glares at Val.

"And two," she continues. "My husband can't have any more children. He got a vasectomy after his first wife passed away during childbirth. He never wanted to go through that kind of pain again. So, he got the procedure done way before we even met." She gestures towards her stomach, pulling up her shirt— Her small baby bump visible for him to see.

His mouth drops open, and his arms collapse beside him. With his arms outstretched and widen eyes, he reaches out to grab Val and feel her stomach. "Val, are you serious right now? This is my baby?" he questions.

She grabs his hands and places them on her stomach, "Yes, this is our baby." she responds.

Ro is speechless, his mouth still open, his hands on her belly. "Oh my god, Val. I can't believe this. How far along?"

"Nineteen weeks."

He steps back, "Huh? Why are you just telling me this? How long have you known?" he questions.

He's gonna be so hurt. I've already done so much. She grabs her shirt and pulls it back down. "I found out in September."

"Val, Damn, not again!" he shouts. "We can't be going through this again. Wait, so are you even keeping the ba--"

"Romelle, listen to me." She grabs his hands, "Calm down."

"How do you expect me to calm down right now? How do you think I should feel Val? Because right now, you're the only one with all the cards in your hands. You're the only one that can decide what you want to do with the pregnancy. You're the one that's married. So, heck, it doesn't matter what I want or how I feel. You don't give a crap about my fee--"

"Ro stop. I'm keeping the baby!" she finally shouts. She closes the gap between them. I'm so sorry Ro. I'm sorry all this happened, and sorry things are so messed up. This is not how I wanted things to be. Please believe me." She steps back… She turns away and sits on the couch.

"Wait, what about your husband? Does he know?" Romelle asks as he follows her to the couch and sits next to her.

"Look, a lot has happened. Without telling you everything, I'll tell you the shorter version. He found my pregnancy test. And my journal," she adds. And well, he knows everything about us.

"What happened? Tell me he didn't put his hands on you?" Romelle's chest moves up and down rapidly.

Valerie stares at Ro in silence. Valerie recalls how much he has tried to protect and shield her from being hurt. "Well, long story short, he has moved out. I've been on my own since October—Just me and Nairobi."

Chapter 19

December 20, 2019

After Valerie dropped her daughter off at school, she climbed into bed to take a nap. After only twenty-five minutes, she is awakened to a nauseous feeling, sourness churning in her stomach and moving slowly upwards into her throat. She places her hand over her mouth and waits patiently for the nausea to subside…

Valerie rolls over and lets her legs dangle from the side of her bed. Her feet outstretched, she slides her feet into her lavender slippers. Yawning, she stretches her hands upwards towards the ceiling. She stands up, grabs her robe off the end of her bed, and walks quietly over to her bay window. Snow flurries fall lightly to the earth. She sits down on the bench that sits in front of her window and watches the snowflakes dance from the sky. Her older neighbor, Ms. Luvington, is out with her Bichon on her daily morning walk. *Her dog is so adorable. I think I will get one for Nairobi, since she keeps saying she wants a pet.*

It's Friday morning, so many cars are gone from their driveways—People are off to work, and children are attending their last day of school before Christmas break starts. She shivers slightly as she feels the cool breeze fighting its way through the window. Val tugs at her robe tight, covering her bare chest. She watches a truck slowly glide down the snow-covered street. The black truck reminds her of her husband's truck—for a moment, caught in a daze, as she imagines him pulling up into her driveway...

The sound of his keys unlocking the door, the scent of his cologne lingering in the air as she greets him downstairs are overwhelming to think about. The soft caress of his firm arms and the firmness of his chiseled chest is all but an illusion but fills her mind with hope.

Valerie gets up and heads toward her bathroom. The room is silent; the stillness of the house entraps her with her own thoughts. *I really miss my husband. I miss our talks, and my family. I miss my life...*

Valerie stands at the base of her tub, twists the knobs on, and plugs up the tub with the stopper. The tub starts to fill with warm water. The vanilla-scented bubble bath sits on the edge of the tub. Valerie opens the top and pours the liquid into the tub. The sound of the water rushing into the basin is soothing to her ears--Sounding like an ocean of waves. The scent of warm vanilla fills the air. She begins to take her robe off, hanging it on the hook of her bathroom door. She slides her slippers off, but as she grabs for the spaghetti straps of her slip, she stops midway. Staring at herself in the mirror, she takes a long deep breath in and blows it out slowly. She places both hands on her round stomach--the fullness of her belly is now noticeable. She's no longer able to hide her pregnancy.

"I don't know what you are, and I don't want to know," she begins as she looks down at her stomach. "What I do know is that I want you to be healthy. Things may not be the way I planned, but I'm still happy to be your mother. I thought I would never have another child again, but here you are. I can't say I'm happy about how things turned out, but I can say I can't wait to see you, hold you, and smell your soft skin." Val slowly steps into her tub, careful not to slip and fall. She sits down gently, shuts her eyes, and lays her head back. "Ahhhh, this feels good." She rubs her stomach tenderly with bubbles from her bath and hums a lullaby song to her baby. She learns to accept the idea more and more each day that she is really having another baby.

Snow is still coming down outside. It has been snowing since eleven o'clock the previous night. Driving Nairobi was definitely a challenge. Cars were sliding everywhere, and tow trucks were out on the road, helping cars get unstuck. Valerie had slid a couple of times herself. She never did like driving in the snow, yet winters in Michigan was always something that she looked forward to. She loved the snow, the season, and the holidays it brought with it. Christmas was right around the corner, next week Wednesday.

Valerie is looking forward to watching her daughter open up her gifts. Romelle is going over to bring his gifts at seven in the morning, and he had told Valerie how much he looked forward to being there with his daughter. Valerie had to decide to let Romelle come over for Christmas to see his daughter open her gifts.

As Valerie walks down the stairs, she shifts her laptop from one hand to the other. She enjoyed a nice-warm bubble bath and soaked her skin until the creamy body wash made her smooth skin silky. Once down, she glances toward the door, thoughts still fill her head--imagining her husband walking through the door. Every step towards the kitchen is slightly daunting as she tries to flush the memory of that night out of her mind—The screaming, his fists, her body crashing through the living room table.

Val pulls down the coffee filters and takes a scoop of coffee out of the canister, and brews a fresh cup of decaffeinated coffee.

Val grabs the TV remote off the table. The sound of chimes from the grandfather clock interrupts the silence—The clock strikes ten o'clock. She turns on the television—The ten o'clock news is on. She turns, grabs a mug from the cabinet, and then pours the coffee. She stops midway and places the pot back down.

"Just in—A twenty-seven-year-old woman was killed this morning shortly after she dropped her two small children off at school," the news reporter announced, as she stood in front of an elementary school. Valerie's jaw drops, "Wow! That's my baby's school!" Her pregnant frame stands frozen at the moment. "Authorities tell us that she was in the school this morning dropping off Christmas cookies she had baked for her son's class," the reporter continues. "We are told she also briefly sat in her daughter's class after dropping off homemade cupcakes for her six-year-old daughter's holiday party. The Principal told us off-camera that Ms. Sundusky was a mom who always volunteered at the school and was very friendly." A picture of the woman flashes across the screen. "Local authorities said that that slippery road conditions have more than likely played a part in the terrible car accident. There is no more information given to us at this time, but we will update you as soon as more information becomes available."

Valerie's hand quickly rest upon her chest. With widen eyes, her thoughts hang in the air from shock. "This is so sad. Just terrible!" Valerie stands in front of the TV screen frozen. "She was so young. Who's gonna raise her children? I can't imagine leaving my children that young."

She hits the power button and the television goes black. She walks away, shaking her head in disbelief... **Buzzz. Buzzz.** Valerie picks up her phone...

After chatting with her mother on the phone and checking on her father, she thinks of ways to stay busy. She vacuums the floor, wipes down the kitchen appliances, and then sprays and cleans the bay window and the patio sliding glass doors. Her empty coffee mug sits in the kitchen sink, and her small plate of leftover breadcrumbs sits on the countertop.

Valerie sits with her legs propped up on her chase by the bay window. The blinds pulled back, the brightness of the morning and the falling snow illuminates the whole room. Her laptop sits on her lap. She googled the words, Masters degrees in Psychology. I want to help abused women, and I know that I could be a great counselor for women—Women need empathy, understanding, and an active listener that can listen without judgement. I never knew that helping people would be my passion. Going through what I've gone through, I think this is a career choice I should've made a long time ago.

As she continues to type and search, Val grabs her phone next to her and plays some soft music to distract her from the dreadful silence in the room. As she hums the words to a 90's R & B song, she glances at the universities that offer online degrees in Psychology. "Here's a university that doesn't have a high tuition rate," she said.

The smell of scented candles fills the room with a light aroma. The house is clean, filled with love, and the joyful season of gratitude warms the room with Christmas decorations throughout her home...

Later That Morning

Valerie drives cautiously through the streets to pick-up her daughter from school. School lets out at noon, concluding the school year until after the Christmas holiday. The normal fifteen-minute drive is taking Val much longer. Lord, I should've kept her home today like I started. But noooo, my daughter had to wine and play the guilt trip on me that she wouldn't be able to see her friends for two weeks. I wish her teacher had never told her that she would see her students back in two weeks. Val's thoughts ran away with her as she drove through the snowy streets of Macomb Township.

Valerie tugs at her seat belt, adjusting it around her swollen belly. She glances in the rearview mirror what seems like a thousand times. Her hands clutch the steering wheel tightly, and her palms are sweaty. Her breath is labored. "I can do this. Nothing is going to happen to me..." BEEEEEEP! Her eyes stare up at the rearview window—A green truck sits behind her. The man in the truck motions her to drive. "I-I'm sorry sir," she mouths to the man behind her.

Val releases the breaks and slowly accelerate past the red stop sign. She keeps a steady pace of fifteen miles per hour. This is no longer a trip to get my daughter but an escapade to escape from the other drivers on the road. Her hands twist around the steering wheel tighter. Her deep, purposeful breath fogs up her windows. Let me turn this defrost up higher. She motions towards the nob, increasing the air, and the windows gradually begin to clear...

"OH MY GOD!" Her foot quickly hits the breaks, her truck spins, BEEEEEEP! She grips her steering wheel, her life flashing before her eyes. Her tires screech and slide across the street and abruptly stops at the side of a curb of a busy intersection. Two cars collide. The sounds of metal bending and glass shattering rings in Valerie's ears. As she stares from the safety of her truck, she takes a deep breath in and blows it out slowly. "Thank you," she said, looking up towards the sky. Valerie saw one car spinning out of control as she was passing through the intersection. She was grateful she was able to move out of the way in time.

Val slowly turns her steering wheel, her foot on the accelerator, and travels towards Nairobi's school. "I'm coming baby," she said as she glides slowly through the snow. Five minutes away. I can do it. Valerie is scared. Scared for her life. She grips her steering wheel even tighter. The leather forms a bond to the palms of her hands. Two minutes away. She stops at a red light. She takes deep purposeful breaths as she tries to calm herself from the anxiety she feels. Her sweaty palms glide across her pants leg as she tries to cool them down.

BEEP! BEEP! "Are you stupid or something? The light is green," an angry man screams from out his car window. Val hadn't even noticed the light turned green, nor had she noticed the cars pulling out from around her to go by.

Valerie slowly pulls off, noting the school in the short distance ahead. She pulls into the school parking lot and shuts the engine off. She lets out a deep sigh as she leans back into her seat and allows her head to collapse on the headrest. "Thank goodness today is her last day."

Chapter 20

Christmas Eve

It's the night where children are sent to bed early, and children beg to stay up just a little longer, trying to get a glimpse of the jolly big guy. "Mommy, can I please stay up?" Nairobi cries.

"No baby. Santa won't come unless you're asleep," Valerie replies. "Now, I've read you a nighttime story, sang a song to you, and tucked you in really nice. Besides, it's already nine o'clock. You were supposed to be asleep already. "Val sends her daughter off to bed with her gentle motherly-kisses upon her daughter's forehead. "Now go to bed pumpkin."

Valerie waits until she knows that her daughter is good and sleep and begins to wrap presents...

The red and white Santa plate sits on the glass end table by the sofa—nothing but breadcrumbs left. The small glass of milk sits half empty. The fireplace glows in the dimly lit room, the sounds of fire crackling against the logs. The coziness and quietness inspires Val to read on the carpeted floor in front of the fireplace.

Val has picked up reading again. She's an avid reader—reading two or three books a month. She loves women's fiction, suspense novels, and dystopian novels. For the last couple of days, she has enjoyed reading in the morning and at night when her daughter is asleep. She sits there, indulged in her story, turning page after page. Her suspense story has her imagining what will happen next.

One hour has passed by quickly. She walks towards the steps. When Valerie reaches her bedroom, she hesitates. The short walk to Nairobi's room is brief. The door creaks up slowly. Valerie smiles as she peeks into her room and finds her daughter still asleep. The stars light up her ceiling, and her pink bear lays tucked tight between Nairobi's arms. Val slowly shuts the door back.

She walks into her room and walks into her closet. The purple sweater looks promising. Val grabs it off the hook and pulls it over her head. Fluffing her satin pillows, Valerie turns down her bedding. She climbs into bed, the coolness of the sheets, brushes against her bare legs. The burnt orange flames illuminate, Val places the fireplace remote back down on her nightstand. She takes her pen and opens her journal.

Dear Diary,

I've decided what's best for me, without feeling guilty. No more guilt. No more pain. This is my life, no one else.

Everyone has flaws. I don't judge others for theirs, and I'm not going to let anyone judge me for mines. I've prayed about it. I've thought long and hard about who I'm going to give my heart to. My whole heart. I know that Ro wants me to be with him, being I am pregnant with our second child. It makes sense for me to be with Ro. But Rick also wants me back. He's been through counseling as I've asked him to do, and surprisingly, he has stuck with it. I was shocked that he even forgave me, wants to still be with me, actually wants to save our marriage. It also makes sense to stay with my husband, work on our problems and stick by our vows. To death do you part.

My mother said that forgiveness is not about what others think, but what your heart says. I must follow my heart. I must be true to myself. I'm at peace now. It took me a long time to get here. And I know I still have ways to go in rediscovering myself-- understanding my true purpose. For every woman that already knows her purpose, I applaud them. Hopefully, one day I will too.

~Val

Valerie closes her journal and places it by her side. Her eyes gaze down on her belly. She lifts her sweater up, the circular motion of her hands moves in rhythm, gliding across her stomach from one side to the other.

"La, la, la. La, la, la. I love you my sweet baby. I am here, so very near, you can hear my-soft-whispers," she sings. Soothing herself and her baby, Val eventually drifts off to sleep.

Christmas Day

"Hey, It's Ro," he responds from the opposite side of the door.

Locks click, "Hey Ro, come on in," Val said as she opens her front door. Her face glows as she smiles at the barrage of gifts

Romelle has in his arms. His arms carry a huge box and a Santa bag into her house with ease.

"Merry Christmas Val."

"Merry Christmas Ro," she replies kindly.

"I have to take her jeep out the box, but it won't take me long to set it up."

"Ok, that's fine." Valerie had decided to allow Ro over early because he wanted to be there to see Nairobi come running down the stairs. "Hand me your coat, I'll hang it in the closet," Val said.

"I'm so excited and nervous all at the same time," Ro begins as he takes a seat on the sofa. "I mean, I know I met her already, but this is different."

"You'll be fine, Ro."

"You sure? Do you think she'll like my gifts I got her?"

"Yes, I'm sure," she exclaims as she plants her hands on his hands. "She is going to love them."

The lights of the Christmas tree is blinking red, white, and green. The aroma of homemade cooking is in the air. Jingle bells and other favorite Christmas tunes play softly in the background.

Romelle looks around as he takes in the scenery with childlike wonder. "You sure know how to decorate and make your home look warm for the season. I mean, it even smells like

Christmas, whatever that means," he chuckles. It smells so good, like my mother's homemade cooking."

"Well, thank you! I like to think that I've learned my way around the kitchen over the years," she smiles.

Romelle gazes at Val, his eyes dance upon hers, as if he's admiring her beauty. "Well, look at you!" Romelle places his hands on her belly. "You getting bigger now, and you even have a pregnancy glow."

Valerie's cheeks redden. "Thank you. I'm twenty weeks now, and I just love my, I mean our little baby already," she says as she rubs her belly.

"Wow! You really getting up there. I can't wait to see him. Or her," he said softly. "Can I?" Ro asks as he gestures his hands towards Val's belly.

Valerie places his hand on the side of her stomach, and then she places hers on top of his. "You feel that?" she questions.

Romelle is still, his eyes intent on her stomach. "Yes! Yes, I feel the baby," he shouts. His dimples show as he smiles. His eyes sparkle with amazement. "Man, this feels so weird, but like, in a good way, you know?" he exclaims.

"Yes, I know. Even though I have experienced this before, it still feels so new." She smiles up into Ro's hazel eyes. Silence falls between them...

"You are so beautiful," Ro said softly, breaking the silence between them. "I mean everything about you." He gazes into her eyes as she continues to smile at him. "I can't believe you're having my baby again."

"Me either," she says as she drops her head back down to her belly as the baby continues to kick her. The feeling of every move, every flutter, every kick makes them both smile and live in the moment.

"Um, I better get the box open so I can set up Nairobi's gift," Ro says reluctantly. Neither one of them takes their eyes off each other. He sits on the floor and sets up the gifts...

Twenty minutes go past before Romelle returns to the sofa with Val. She hands him a hot cup of cocoa...

After talking for sometime on the sofa, the clock chimes on the eight o'clock hour.

"Where are you going?" Ro asks as he grabs Val's hand.

"To wake our daughter up."

"Can I wake her? I mean, I am here, and this will be my first time," he said with a huge smile. "And I know that's what you've wanted me to do all these years."

The smirk on his face made Val want to hit him. "Shut up! You get on my nerves," Val snaps back. She can't help but fall for his big hazel eyes, and his dimples. "Go, Before I change my mind!" She waves him off towards the stairs. It's the second bedroom to your left.

He lifts her sweater, exposing her stomach, and kisses her stomach with six small pecks as he recites the words, thank you, with every kiss.

Valerie steps to the side so Ro can get up. She pulls her sweater back down.

Moments later, Nairobi comes running down the steps. "Mommy, Mommy!" she yells. "Did Santa come?"

"Look for yourself," she responds—her hand points towards the empty cookie plate and half-empty glass of milk.

"Yayyy, he did come mommy!" She rushes to the Christmas tree and barrels her way to the biggest gift she sees. "A Barbie jeep!" Her hand rips the big red bow off of the jeep. She jumps inside, "Wow!"

"You like your gift baby girl?" her father asks with a grin.

"Yes, daddy. I love it." Nairobi hops out the jeep and rips through her presents on the floor—A Barbie house, Barbie dolls, a baby doll, a bag of new books, a jump rope, and more.

Valerie and Romelle smile with joy as their daughter shifted from gift to gift. The delight in their eyes was apparent as two parents were satisfied by their child's pleasure. They laughed, they smiled, and most of all, they enjoyed one another's company.

The sounds of laughter fill the air. The smell of southern cooking grew stronger in their nostrils—the smells of honey-baked ham, homemade mac & cheese, yams, and greens soaking in salt pork was all too tantalizing. Two fresh, homemade apple pies sit nicely on the countertop. Valerie's home was no longer the same without her husband Rick. But Val made it a home that her daughter can still enjoy.

After Nairobi opens her gifts, she asks to go outside and play in the snow. "Please, I promise to wear my snowsuit," she pleads, tugging on her mother's shirt.

"Little girl, you just opened your presents. Don't you wanna go upstairs and play?"

"Yes, after I play outside mommy." Nairobi jumps up and down. Her ponytails swing back and forth.

Valerie sits back. She begins to rub her stomach. Her eyes glance back and forth between Ro and his daughter. "Sure, I don't care pumpkin," she finally said.

"Yayyy, thanks mommy!" Sounds of thunder erupt as she runs up the steps to grab her clothes.

"And don't forget to wear your thermos," Val shouts.

"Hey, you look exhausted. How about I go outside and play with her, and you take a little nap," Romelle suggests.

"I am tired. But I have to finish preparing dinner and set the table." She continues to rub her round belly up and down.

"Don't worry about it. I'll help. I can cook, you know?"

"Oh so you got jokes, huh?"

"Funny. Very funny Val," Romelle chuckles. "I'm serious."

"Okay. I'll take you up, upon your offer," she says yarning. "I feel so tired, just give me an hour."

"Is there anything I can do?" Ro questions, with his hands planted on her belly.

"No. Go head outside. I'll be alright."

Val rubs her stomach, lifting her shirt so she can have skin to skin contact. I don't know why I feel so weak. I can barely do anything without feeling so exhausted. I mean, sure, I felt weak with my first pregnancy, but why the heck am I so extremely tired?

Nairobi and her father both run outside. Ro grabs and tosses his daughter in the air. "Wait daddy."

Romelle tosses his daughter into the six inches of snow. They both leave boot imprints in the middle of the yard. The street is lined with cars as families visit for the holidays. There is snowman after snowman, standing up in yards, up and down the streets.

"Come on daddy, let's make snow angels."

"Alright," Romelle replies.

They make snow angels. They make a big snowman with button eyes and a carrot nose. They even chase each other down the street, as they throw small snowballs at each other. When Valerie tells her daughter it's time to come back in, Ro stays outside. He grabs the shovel and begins to clear Val's driveway and the sidewalk in front of her house...

Later that evening, they all sit down to eat. "Girl, this dinner was so good!" Romelle exclaims as he loads the dishwasher.

"Well, I'm glad you enjoyed it," Val responds.

"It was on point. The meat was tender and juicy, and glazed to perfection. The greens were seasoned well, the yams and

Mac & Cheeses were literally to die for. I can't believe you know how to cook so damn good."

Laughing, Valerie grabs the trash off the table and dumps it into the trash bag. "I might've left home early when I was a teen, but one thing I didn't leave behind was momma's recipes."

"You are right about that! I need to call your mom and thank her."

The day had went smoothly. Nairobi was happy. All that was missing was Valerie's nightcap to end the night with. She and Rick use to enjoy it when the children were fast asleep after playing with their toys. Rick would pour them some wine, and they would sit by the cozy fireplace... DING, DONG.

Romelle looks over at Val. His eyebrows raised. "Who's that?"

Val shrugs her shoulders. She slowly walks over to the door, each step cautious. Now, who in the world can this be? "Who is it?" she said. The peep hole in the door obstructed by the big Christmas Reef. The door slides open slowly. "Yes?"

"Can I come in?"

Val stands there, her hand on her stomach. Her eyes are intent as she tries to figure out what's going on. "Sure," she said, as she opens the door wider.

Water rushes through the dishwasher as Ro turns the knob. He stands patiently in the kitchen.

Val shuts the door and walks over to introduce them. "Rick this is Romelle, and Romelle, this is my husband Rick." Her body is motionless. *I wish I could just disappear right now.*

"Hey, what's up man," Romelle said, still standing in the kitchen.

"What's up?" Rick replies. They both stand there for a moment. The big elephant in the room is apparent.

The stillness in the room makes Val uneasy. "Merry Christmas Rick, Where's Noah?" she asks. Her tone is very polite.

Rick looks at his wife, "We need to talk," he scoffs, with a wide stance and his arms folded across his chest.

Chapter 21

Dear diary,

Today was a good day. I actually loved spending time with Nairobi and Ro. The way Nairobi smiled as she opened each present from us, and the way Ro gleamed with so much love just melted my heart. It was truly an endearing sight. I know that he is thankful for her, and I know he is also thankful for being a father. It shows every time he asks me how we are doing. Not a day goes by that he is not calling me. Checking on me, our daughter, and the baby. He is actually so full of excitement. He keeps saying how he is ready for the baby to come. He, of course, doesn't want me to have the baby earlier. But he is eager to get this part over so he can hold his baby. He says he doesn't care what the sex is, as long as the baby is healthy. But when he said that earlier today, I just looked at him without saying a word. I know all men want little boys to raise. I know that he has a girl already, so I know he secretively wants a boy now.

Speaking of earlier today, why the heck did Rick just show up without calling? What makes it so suspicious, he came late, and he didn't have Noah. Now granted, this is his house, and he can come if he pleases. But he usually calls, and he always comes with Noah so I can see him. Now the day I tell him that Romelle would be over to spend time with Nairobi because I didn't want to split our time on Christmas, he decides to show up. I think it was just to see Ro. Like what the heck he wanna see him for? We weren't doing anything, and matter of fact, Ro was loading the dishes when Rick came over. Rick asked to speak with me, talking about, we need to talk. He could've called me.

Anyway, Ro told our daughter and me goodnight and then left to give Rick and me some privacy.

Rick asked me why Ro was still here. I told him that Ro was helping me clean the kitchen, as he could see. I told him to sweep the kitchen floor, wiped down the counters and stove, and then loaded the dishwasher. It seemed like he only came over to see what I was doing, asking me a million questions like; was Ro here when Nairobi woke up, what time did he come over, what did we talk about, what did we do, what were his plans concerning the baby? As if he doesn't already know. I told him that Ro knows I'm keeping the baby and that he wants to be in his child's life. Then he asked if Ro and I were getting back together. I just felt bombarded by too many questions at that point. Today was not the right time to talk about us nor about any future plans that I have. So, he basically told me he will give me more time to think, but I needed to let him know soon. Well... That's like him trying to control me. I already know what I want to do, but today was not the time to address it.

Anyway, I'm exhausted. The main thing is my daughter was happy. She had a great time today with her dad and loved her gifts.

~Val

Val rubs her stomach as she says a prayer over her baby before she drifts off to sleep.

January had come and gone fast. Michigan was experiencing snowstorms after snowstorms. The weather reports had predicted this though, saying this will be one of the ugliest winters that Michigan has seen in a long time. Schools have been closed off and on due to the bad weather. Valerie has been very cautious about taking her daughter to school. She doesn't want to get into an accident—-The anxiety, and pictures of the mother of two, who lost her life during a car accident, still haunts her every time she has to drive.

Romelle has been working as a recruiter since he's been home, and because he is in the reserves now, he leaves out for Washington once a month to report in.

Valerie has been focused on staying mentally healthy for her baby. She doesn't want to focus on anything right now except for her daughter and the unborn baby. She talks to her mom more frequently, and her brother Mark is out of town working for the next three months...**BUZZZ. BUZZZ**.

Val puts her journal down to answer her phone. "Hey Jr."

"What's up little sis?"

"Nothing much, just relaxing," Val said. "What about you?"

"Work as usual. You know how it is. Got me working like a slave."

Val chuckles. "Well, think of it this way. You work four days a week and got three days off to do whatever it is you want."

"Yeah, like what?"

The clock chimes ten, and the house sounds like an orchestra of church bells.

"There goes that stupid clock!" Mark said.

"Shut up, stupid," Val snapped back. You act like you don't love my grandfather's clock."

"Shit, I don't. I hate it actually. Make me feel like I'm being called to church!"

"Hate! That's such a strong word." Val replied. The orchestra of noise ends, and Val continues their conversation. "Look, it's a lot to do in London. You can visit Jack the Ripper Museum, Buckingham Palace, The Tower of London, Big Ben, you know, EVERYTHING!" she shouts.

"Listen, who the heck I'm gonna do that with? My wife not here," he exclaims. "So, doing all that is cool if you got someone to do it with."

"Yea, I get it," she said as she stares out the window.

Val sits with her legs crossed on the sofa, talking with her brother for about fifteen minutes before he has to get off the phone. Ro will be over to get her at 11:00. He told Val he had to take his mom to the bank and the store first. She has time to concentrate on her daily journal log before he arrives, so she opens her journal.

Dear Diary,

Today is February 18th. I'm now 27 weeks pregnant. I can feel my baby moving, although I don't know if I'm having a girl or boy yet. I've decided I want to be surprised.

Ro has been going to my doctor's appointments with me, and he gets so excited when he hears the baby's heartbeat. The baby moves around A LOT!

I can barely breathe, my stomach is so big. My doctor says I am big for 27 weeks. I actually look like I'm already eight months, but I'm going on seven months next week. My stomach is huge, honestly. I have to sleep sitting up now cause I feel like I'm suffocating whenever I try to lay on my back or my sides. I can't zip my coat. I can't even see my feet, not to mention tying my shoes.

I'm not complaining though. I actually love it. It makes me happy to know that I am carrying a baby inside of me. The feelings of joy, warmth, and unconditional love is what I feel. I'm going to be so happy when I finally see and hold my baby. And don't let me get started on how my daughter feels. Nairobi touches my stomach every day. She even tells me she is gonna help me feed the baby. Lol! I haven't told her I'm breastfeeding the baby just like I did her. Ro knows I am because every day he's asking me questions. How do I feel? How is his baby? What type of diapers to buy? What type of breast pump I want? He is too funny. Adorable actually. I told him we can go shopping for the baby today, so he's actually on his way now to pick me up.

~Val

Valerie closes her diary up just in time. She sees Romelle pull up into the driveway. She stands up to grab her things. Her black purse sits on the end table. She grabs it and pulls her lip gloss out. The lip gloss glides across her dry lips. Valerie smooths it in, her lips moving back and forth upon each other, as Val moistens each inch of her lips. Ding. Ding... "Coming, just a sec." She wobbles over to the door. The door slowly opens. Val's face lights up with a warm smile.

Romelle stands there with his Black button-down coat, his red and black scarf, and his Black skull cap pulled down to his eyebrows. His eyes are gleaming with a loving smile. "Come on in," she said.

"Hey, good morning beautiful." His arms reach down to hug Val, his arms around her waistline.

"Hey Ro." Val stands on her tiptoes to reach him around his neck. She feels his firm pecs against her breast.

"How's my baby?" he questions as he pulls up, wrapping his arms around her stomach.

"Good, just active today as usual."

He pulls her sweater up, allowing her stomach to show. He rubs across her stomach in a circular motion, "That's my boy! I know you in there kicking your mom and all, but be gentle to her, for me," he said, as he continues to massage her stomach gently.

"Boy! What makes you think we're having a boy?"

"I just know." He pulls her sweater back down as he reaches in to give her a kiss on her forehead.

Val feels his soft lips upon her head, gentle and endearing. Her cheeks flush red as she tries to grab her coat.

"Here, let me get that for you," Romelle said as he takes her coat and pulls it around her. "Oh, I can't zip your coat up," he said as he tries to pull her coat together.

"I know, it won't zip anymore because my stomach is too big," she replies as she rubs her stomach.

"It's okay," Ro smiles kindly. He pulls her hair back and wraps her scarf around her neck and places her black skull cap over her head. She is wearing her hair in its natural state now, the long natural curly texture of her hair is soft. Taking a break from the braids, she usually wraps it up in bantu knots after putting coconut oil in it to keep it naturally curly.

As he helps Val into the jeep, she grabs her stomach, careful not to let her stomach hit the dashboard in front of her.

"Thank you," she said, as she sits down. She watches Romelle walk to the driver's side door and hop in her truck. This was the second time she let him drive her jeep. The first time being two weeks ago at her doctor's appointment.

The drive to the local shopping center is short. They think of baby names as they drive along. The streets are packed with commuters, and the snow is plowed to the side of the curb. People are bustling their way through the streets, as old man winter blows its fury of winds along the streets.

"It's cold out here. I can't wait until it's summertime again," Val said as she stares out the window.

"Yeah, tell me about it," Ro replies.

"What do you think of the name, Amya?" Val asks Ro.

"Cute. What about Ronald?" Ro replies.

"That's nice. How about Viola," Val said smiling. She looks at him with her eyebrows raised. Hoping for a yes. She likes the idea of having a girl with the letter 'V' like her.

"What about we do this," Ro starts. "If it's a girl, we name her Viola. And if it's a boy, we name him Romelle Jr." He glances over at Val as he looks back and forth between her and the streets.

Val sits there in the seat, adjusting the seatbelt from around her tight stomach. She looks over at him, her eyes are hopeful. "Yea, sure. That's fine with me. I actually like that idea." Her smile of satisfaction lights the atmosphere between them.

Ro grabs her hand and kisses it. "Thank you."

In the store, Romelle grabs everything in sight. "We need a car seat." He shows two different ones to Val. His arms hold a light teal car seat and a yellow one. "Both are unisex," he said.

Val points her hand, touching the teal car seat, "This one."

Ro throws it into the basket. They continue to walk in the baby aisle. "What about this crib? you like it?"

"Actually, I like the one next to it. It's white with teddy bears on it."

Romelle looks at her—frozen solid. "You sure?" he asks as he stares at her with one eyebrow arched high.

She smiles at him, nodding her head up and down.

He breaths out a heavy sigh. "Ok, but so that you know, I hate the teddy bears." He grabs the big box and slides it into the cart. "Let me do it. I got it." Ro grabs the basket from Valerie and continues to push it for her.

"Oh look, let's get this baby tub. It has a mat inside so that the baby won't slide down in it." She points towards the tub on the counter. "These were not out when Nairobi was born."

Ro picks it up and puts it into the cart. As he continues to walk, Val leads him down the clothes isle. They look at onesies, and Ro throws twenty in the cart—all different neutral colors and patterns. They pick out baby socks, hand mittens, caps, and ten packs of undershirts. They picked up baby lotion, baby bottles, a breast pump, nipple pads, pacifiers, baby towels and face rags. Ro throws five packs of diapers in the cart and five baby wipe boxes. He left nothing out. Everything that Val told him a baby needed, he grabbed.

Valerie reaches for one of the bags. "You sure you didn't buy up the whole store," she said as Romelle loads the car seat into the jeep.

"Sit in the Jeep babe, I got it," Romelle said as he walks Val over to the side. He holds the passenger door open and helps her in. "Start the jeep and turn on the heat so you can get warm."

After loading everything in the jeep, Ro takes the buggy to the buggy section and walks back over to the jeep. He climbs into the jeep and turns to grab Valerie's hand. His hazel eyes stare at hers—his look is intentional. "As long as you got me, you don't have to worry about anything," he begins. "I don't need that stress on you like the last time. And I don't need anyone buying my baby anything. This is my baby and my responsibility."

Chapter 22

March 8, 2020

Snow falls lightly upon the earth, and the bare tree branches sway lightly as the wind blows through the air. "My stomach is huge, honestly. I have to sleep sitting up now, cause I feel like I'm suffocating whenever I try to lie on my back or my sides. I can barely fit any of my clothes. I can't even see my feet, not to mention tying my shoes. It's like I have five basketballs in my stomach," she laughs. "I was not this big with Nairobi," Val explains to Ro over the phone.

Romelle is in Georgia. This time for four weeks. He had told Valerie as soon as he found out he would have to go in for an assigned mission in the field. He would be out by the time she had her next appointment with the doctor. "You can't be that much bigger, I just saw you not that long ago."

"That was three weeks ago. Trust me, I'm much bigger now. I look like a whale," she added.

They both burst into laughter at Valerie's stories of how huge she feels now that she's getting closer to her due date.

"I wish I could face-time you. But right now, you know how it is. I'm barely getting a signal out here. Every time I try, it says reconnecting."

"It's fine," Val replies.

"Well, you're thirty weeks now," Ro said. His voice is full of joy. "How have you been feeling? How's the heartburn?"

"It's getting worse. I literally take Pepcid tablets all day, every day. And my stomach feels so tight and itchy."

"Why is that?" Ro asked.

"My doctor said it's because my skin is stretching. So, it's normal to feel tightness, and she gave me a script I had to fill for the itchiness." The clock chimes seven o'clock.

"I just love that sound. Every time I hear your clock, it reminds me of church bells," Romelle said.

"It does?" Val replies as she straightens her back on the couch.

"Of course it does. Remember when mom used to take us to church when we were teenagers?"

"Yeah, I do," Val replies. She twirls her hair with her finger.

"We used to love to hear the clock chiming on the hour every time they had a service..." He trails off.

"Who would've..."

"What?" Romelle asked. "Who would've what?"

"Nothing." Valerie just stared at her daughter on the couch as she watched her cartoons.

"Who would've thought we would have had children together?" Romelle said softly.

"Yeah," Val replied in a whisper.

"My mom," Romelle starts. "My mom knew we would. She used to always say we were perfect together."

Val's brows fringed together. "Seriously?"

"Yeah!" Ro replies.

"And what did you say when she said that?" Val questioned. She had stopped twirling her hair. He had her full attention. So, she waits for him to answer. The silence on the phone made her feel anxious. "Ro, what did you say?"

"I agreed with her."

Valerie had no idea he felt that way about her when they were teenagers. She knew he was her best friend, but so many girls liked him back then, and he was popular on the basketball and football team. She was shocked when he asked her out on a real date when they were seniors. She always felt like she wasn't good enough for him that he could do better.

"Hey, where's my little girl at?"

Val knew why Ro wanted to change the subject. Ever since she told him she was married, he tries his best to respect her boundaries. She knows he's still hurt, angry even. He tries to keep their conversation about their daughter. Anytime it looks like they are about to reminisce about the past, he shuts down and changes the topic. "She's right here, watching cartoons on the floor," she finally said.

"Let me speak to her please."

"Nairobi?"

Nairobi turns around, "Yes, mommy?'

"Here, come get the phone. Your daddy wants to speak to you."

Nairobi paces the floor as she talks to her dad. "Where you at daddy?" she asked.

`"I'm in Georgia right now baby."

"When you coming to see me?"

"Soon, hopefully. I'm supposed to leave out of here sometime next week. What you do---"

"Daddy, what you say?"

… Nothing but static.

"Daddy, I can't hear you. What you say?"

"Let me see the phone pumpkin." Val reaches for the phone, barely able to move. "Hello... Hello..."

The silence on the other end continues. Val labors to catch her breath.

"What's wrong mommy? What happened to daddy?" she asked.

"The phone. It got disconnected," Val replies. It's actually time for you to get ready for bed pumpkin."

"Oh mommy, can I please stay up to finish watching tv?"

"No, pumpkin. I'm exhausted. You have to get ready for bed. You already had your bath at six o'clock, so it's time to get in the bed." She watches her daughter pout as she climbs the stairs. "I love you sweetie," Val said to her daughter.

"I love you too mommy," she replies, as she continues to pout as she climbs the last few steps.

"I'll be up shortly to read you a story and kiss you goodnight," she shouts. But there was only silence that met Val in return.

Val glances down at her swollen belly. Her stomach sits upright as she begins to rub her stomach. Barely able to breathe, her lungs feel restricted. *Why am I so huge?* Her stomach sits up on her lap, like a beach ball. She can't see anything below her, not even her own daughter when she's laying on the floor beneath her coloring...

Val's eyes begin to sting as she fights back the tears welling up in her eyes. Her pregnancy hormones were beginning to unravel without a cause.

Valerie gets up, fighting the barrage of different emotions in her mind. She decides to take a bath and call it a night. She feels exhausted from the heaviness of her stomach, she begins to slowly climb the steps, holding onto the rail. Each step seems to pull her away further from the top. Her knees throb with every step.

It's getting harder and harder to climb these steps, she thought. The weight of the baby is heavy on her slender frame, her pelvic floor aches. Her stomach is much larger than her body now. As she continues to use the rail to pull her weight up the stairs, she holds underneath her belly with her right arm. Her breath accelerates faster like a woman running a marathon. "Come on, you got this," She said, reassuring herself. She tries to encourage herself up the rest of the stairs. As she reaches the last step, she stands there, desperate to catch her breath. Her head is sweating, and her body is overheating.

She makes her way to her bathroom. Her 36 double HH bra hangs from the door hook. She takes her shirt off and hangs it up. She bends over sideways to reach the water nozzle, as she turns it on for her bath. She sits on the tub to reach the stopper, and then she pours the bubble bath into her warm water. The scent of vanilla fills the air. She climbs into the tub; her head relaxes as she soaks her aching body. "Awww, this feels good," she said as she closes her eyes. Her back muscles relax in the warmth of the tub. Her ankles feel tight and full of pressure. She can't wait to climb into bed to prop them up on her sturdy pillows.

Val opens her eyes and glances down at her left hand, staring at the ring around her finger. The paleness looks weird to her, something she hasn't gotten used to yet. The lightness of that finger is going to take some getting used to. Her stomach sits high above the water. She takes the bubbles and rubs her hand around all sides of her belly. "What if I have you with no one by my side?" she begins to talk to her baby. She continues to rub her stomach. "I don't want to be alone. I'm so scared and worried. What if your dad is out of town because it's his weekend to be on duty or in the field?" Tears roll down her cheeks. She sniffs, trying to stop her nose from running. "My brother is out of town. My mom can't help me because she can't leave my dad by himself." She begins to cry— her stomach moving with every movement. "I can't do this alone. I need your father here with me. It just can't be like the last time," she cries.

Val sobs endlessly while in the tub. Her emotions are all over the place--and for good reason. Nothing that she is used to is the same. Thoughts of not having Romelle around is killing her softly. She cries more often than not, most days, keeping her frustration and stress bottled up inside. She hasn't called her Psychologist in over a week. But she knows she needs to do something about that and fast.

After her bath, Val throws on a long white and purple t-shirt. She climbs into bed holding her journal and finds a comfortable position. All her back pillows sit upright on her bed, positioned to support her weight as she sleeps.

March 8, 2020

Dear Diary,

Today I saw on the news that there is a deadly virus that's affecting people all around the world--Corona Virus. And the death toll has been rising since January of this year. I didn't watch the news much, but I heard something about it in February. But now, it's getting even more serious. The governor of Michigan is talking about shutting down schools so we can start practicing social distancing by staying at home, as China did in late January. I hope that things get better soon. I hope we don't have to experience being put on lockdown like China.

~Val

"I have to get to the doctor," Valerie insisted. "My appointment is in three days." The early morning sun shines brightly into Val's home. Nairobi is still asleep and due to wake up shortly.

"We know Mrs. Augustine," the woman said on the other end of the phone. "Because of the Governor's Stay Home, Stay Safe order, we are calling to push all non-emergency appointments back."

"So, my regular scheduled appointment is considered non-essential?" Val asked.

"Yes, Mrs. Augustine, which has been prohibited by our Governor's office." If you are experiencing any problems that are considered life-threatening, we ask that you go to your nearest hospital or call 9-1-1."

"This is crazy," Val cries. She places her hand on her head. The disbelief of how terrible things have gotten has left Val in a state of worry.

"I know this is a lot to take in. Everyone is trying their best to practice social distancing. Our doctor is asking that you be patient with our office for now." The lady on the other end clears her throat." Excuse me, I'm so sorry," she said. "Dr. Gray is available to speak with you by phone, however, on your scheduled appointment date. She will be calling to speak with you and to see how you are doing."

"Ok. Well, thank you," Val replies.

Valerie places her phone down on her table. She sits at the dining table, rubbing her stomach. It's been over a week since Valerie last spoke with Romelle. Neither her calls nor text messages have gone through. She hopes that he is released to come home this week. She has been a nervous wreck since Nairobi's school was shut down three days ago. Her brother is stuck in London, and although, his company was willing to let him go home early, there is a travel ban, halting most flights from other countries. It's not even safe right now. The US. is not allowing people to leave from over there and come back home so easily. Thank goodness for Rick, who has come to bring her what she needs. He has been a life savior shopping for her and Nairobi. With Val's constant pain in her back, it's almost impossible for Val to shop for herself.

Whenever Rick cannot help her, she either uses her local grocery store delivery system or drives to do a pick-up order, hoping it doesn't cancel on her—which often times it does cancel, with the influx of online shopping during COVID.

It's warmer out now. Snow has not been seen for a while, and spring is just around the corner. Birds have started coming out, and Val has seen people going out for walks more. With more and more businesses shut down and people told to stay home, people spend more time in the house with their families playing board games, cards and watching movies. There has also been a surge of many people creating dance videos with this fairly new app and posting their new videos on social media. People are doing anything they possibly can to stay mentally healthy while they are practicing social distancing. But Valerie has not been feeling her best, both mentally and physically. Her mental wellness is unstable as she begins to fear the worst.

Chapter 23

April 9, 2020

6 weeks to go

Valerie opens her frig, "We are in the middle of a pandemic," she said, as she stood in the kitchen. Valerie takes some food out to warm up for dinner. She had left the door open for Romelle once she saw his truck pull up in her driveway. "I was scared the government wasn't gonna let you come home. You were supposed to come back three weeks ago," Val cries. "I kept sending you text messages and calling your phone."

"I know. I'm sorry," Ro exclaims as he shuts the door behind himself. "It was hard getting back home, and to top it off, none of us had any signal to call out. "You know I would've called you. I missed talking to you and my daughter so much."

Val takes a frozen pizza out of the box and sets the stove temperature to 400 degrees.

As Val continues, Romelle stands in the foyer and opens the closet door. He grabs a hanger for his coat. "Val," he said," as he walks towards the kitchen. "Turn around, don't be mad at me." He turns her around and pulls her closer to him. "Look at you!" His hands are placed on her round belly. I know I've been gone for like a month, but you must've grown like three sizes since I last saw you," he said.

"Boy stop. No, I have not!" Val replies, trying to pull away.

"Are we having twins?" he chuckles. His smile is wide--His teeth illuminates his perfect set of white teeth.

"Oh, you got jokes?" She stands there with her hands on her hips, propping herself up, so her back has support from her heavy stomach. "Hee, hee, hee. No!"

"No wait. Let me look at you. That's really my baby in there," he said smiling. "I can't believe it." His dimples deepen as his smile widens. His gaze remains on her stomach. "I didn't get to go through this with you when you were pregnant with Nairobi. How many weeks are you now? Thirty-four right?"

"Yeah, true," Val replies. And yeah, I'm thirty-four weeks.

"Was Nairobi this big?" he questions. "Were you still slender everywhere else? Well, you know... Your stomach is so hard and round." Ro stands fixated in amazement as he holds her stomach in his hands.

"Well, actually no. I wasn't this big with her," she replies. "I was slender still, but she was not nearly as big. I actually find it hard to breathe sometimes. And I'm having sharp pains more frequently now."

"Pain, what pain? Are you ok?"

"Yes, I'm fine," she replies. Probably just early Braxton Hicks Contractions. I'm on bed rest now, so I don't go into labor early."

"Bedrest? Is the baby ok?"

"Yes, my doctor said it's normal. It's because of the baby…"

The baby is so big. She takes a breath, and her lungs feel crushed under the weight of standing up with the baby. She holds on to the counter with one hand on her back as Romelle continues to hold her stomach up from the bottom. Her stomach sits in his hands, but Valerie can't see anything. But the support of his hands makes her feel like so much pressure has been lifted off her pelvis.

"Is she sure? I mean, do you need to see someone else?" he said with his eyes intent on Val.

"Yes, Dr. Gray says everything is normal Ro, calm down. She said to take it easy. Because of the pandemic, things are a little hectic right now, you know? I'm so scared of getting sick in the clinic or hospital. I just prefer to talk with my doctor over the phone." She takes a deep breath in to catch her breath. Her legs feel weak from the prolonged standing, and her ankles hurt from the increased water she has retained. "I haven't been able to see my doctor since January. I missed my February appointment because I was too sick to go."

"That's when you had that fever and was throwing up all day, right?"

"Yeah. Then my March appointment was canceled due to this pandemic. So, I haven't even had my ultrasound appointment. But that's my fault because I didn't know if I was keeping the baby. I have been to the doctor twice. Once in November and once in December with you."

Ro pulls his hands off of her stomach and tries to wrap his arms around her waist. "I can't hug you like I used to anymore, but will still try every time I see you," he said, as he reaches his arms around her.

Val wraps her arms around Ro's neck as much as possible. As she adjusts her stomach, she tries to fit her arms comfortably around him, but it's no use; she can't do it. She stands on her tiptoes as Romelle reaches down, embracing her warmly.

"Dammit Val," he whispers softly in her ears. I love you so much. I mean you, our baby, and Nairobi. I don't know what I would do without ya'll. I want everything to be ok. I don't want anything to happen to you or our baby." He grips her tighter, Val's stomach is the only thing standing in between them, despite standing even closer. "I know you're still married, but no matter what you choose to do, you will always be my baby, forever." He pauses. The room is warm. He rocks Val from side to side. "I don't want to lose you," he finally continues. "I-I would just die without you. Please make it through this pregnancy."

Val feels a tear from the corner of his eye fall slowly down onto her cheek. She feels his heart beating rapidly—his concern, his nervousness, and most of all, she feels his love. "Nothing is gonna happen to me or the baby Ro," she gently whispers in his ear.

"My back is hurting, I have to sit down," she said as she pulls away from Ro.

"Here, I got you." Romelle grabs her arms and places the other on her backside as he ushers her over to the sofa. "Here, sit here."

Val reaches down to grab the armrest and slowly sits down, letting her back lead the way. She tries to catch her breath.

"You okay?" Ro asks. His eyes looking down at her.

She tries to catch her breath. "Ye-Yeah, I'm good. Just tired. I can barely stand long, or I feel like my back is going to cave in." Her long pink nightgown showed how her stomach protrudes out from her body.

Ro stands there with is eyes widen. "I-I-um, I can't believe this. I mean, I feel like I just saw you. I knew you said you got bigger, but I didn't imagine this big." He stands there with his mouth open as he looks at how her stomach sits up while she sits on the couch. "You can't be comfortable. This must be difficult for you."

"I know. I knew you were gonna be shocked." Val's eyes fall downward. She begins to rub her stomach, her hands moving in a circular motion. She doesn't know if Romelle is disgusted by her. She knows that not all guys find pregnancy a beautiful thing that two people create. They don't take it as a human being that God has stored in a woman's womb. Instead, some men can't stand how the mother of their baby looks—The same woman that they impregnated. The woman that they decided to make love to and the same woman carrying the life they helped to create.

Romelle drops down to his knees in front of Val, "Look, I think you're beautiful. Even more beautiful now that I see you pregnant with my child," he begins as he rubs her stomach too. "I missed out on all of this last time, and I'm just happy I get to go through this with you. I like your——." He stops and gazes into her eyes. "Look at me Valerie," he says as he wipes a fallen tear away from her cheek. "I love your stomach just the way it is."

Val's eyes sting as she tries to fight back the tears. Her eyes well up with water, ready to flow like a steady stream. She sniffs to control herself.

"Valerie, I love you. I loved you then when we created Nairobi, and I loved you the day we created this baby, that day on the pier. Val..." Tears roll down his face, his dancing eyes gaze heavenly upon Val's. "Val, I still love you now. You were my baby then and you will always be."

Valerie's eyes flow—her tears falling endlessly. She covers her eyes with both hands as she allows herself to just let go and cry. Her emotions unfurl as she lets out her tender thoughts of worry. Her doubts of feeling fat. Of feeling un-pretty and her thoughts of being unloved.

The smell of pizza fills the air. The aroma smells of Italian sausages, green peppers, and mushrooms. The stove starts to beep.

"The pizza is done. Help me up so I can get it." Valerie said, as she stretches her arm upwards for Ro to grab.

"No, I got it. Let me do it. Just sit there and relax," Romelle demands.

Valerie stands up and hobbles over towards the stairs. She grabs her back and holds on to her stomach to release some of the pressure.

"What are you doing," Ro shouts as he runs over to Valerie. "What you need from upstairs? I'll get it for you." He stands in front of Val on her steps.

"I was going to wake Nairobi so she can eat dinner."

"Well, let me go get her," he said. "And besides, you're supposed to be on bed rest."

She can barely get a sentence out without having to take a break mid-sentence. So she just flings her hands at him, ushering him to go ahead, and she begins to walk back to the sofa to sit.

Moments later, Romelle comes down with his daughter. Her tired eyes are red. She has her pink satin bonnet on and her pink pajamas.

"Hey pumpkin," Valerie said as her daughter comes over to her.

"Hi mommy," She places her head on her mother's stomach as she hugs her.

"Come eat Nairobi." Romelle has the table set up with saucer plates and glasses filled with lemonade he pulled out the fridge. "Come on baby," he says as he grabs her hand and gives her a push from her back. "You good?" He walks her over to the table.

"Yes, I'm good," Val replies. She wobbles over to the table with one hand on her back while Ro holds her by her other arm.

They sit at the table eating dinner. With Val on bed rest, she had more pop in the oven and fast food delivery orders than usual. The house was filled with plastic plates, and cups which kept her from washing dishes. Nairobi had a stock of lunchables, chicken nuggets, and of course, her favorite—PB& J sandwiches.

"So, you heard that the Governor closed all the schools in Michigan for the remainder of the school year right?" Val ask, as she finishes the last bit of her pizza.

"Yeah, I did hear that. This is so terrible. But necessary to keep our daughter and other students safe.

"I know the teachers are overwhelmed with all the online work they have to produce as well as work from home, and not to mention helping their own children, if they have any."

Romelle takes a gulp of his lemonade. "Yeah, cause don't Nairobi's teacher have a six-month-old, a two-year-old, and a nine-year old?" he asks as he puts his glass down on the table.

"Yeah, and she has a thirteen-year-old step-son that she is also helping with his schoolwork."

Ro shakes his head. "Man, that's gotta be a lot on her. She practically has a newborn and two-year-old to tend to and chase, and no babysitter to help her. Then she has a child in fourth grade and a child in eighth grade too. You know what her husband does for a living? Maybe he's working from home and can help out some."

"Nope," Val said, shaking her head. "He's a Sheriff. Which means he's an essential worker."

"That's sad. I feel sorry for her. This is a lot to take in."

"Yeah. It truly is," Val replies."

Romelle grabs Nairobi's plate, "You done sweetie?"

"Yes daddy. Can I go watch cartoons?"

"Sure, go ahead, if it's ok with mom." He looks at Val.

"That's fine with me pumpkin. But first, you have to give me a kiss," Val said smiling.

Nairobi runs over to kiss her mom, and plants one on her cheek. She leans in to hug her mom, and as she pulls away, she rubs her mom's stomach. "Mommy?"

"Yes," Val replies.

"How many babies are in your stomach?" She continues to rub her mom's stomach.

Val's eyes widen, and her brows raise. She looks at her daughter, "One baby. Just one," she replies as she turns and looks at Romelle.

"Okay. It's just, you know. Your stomach is so big." Nairobi runs and grabs the remote.

Standing there frozen like a statue, Ro's mouth is wide open, but nothing comes out.

"Yeah, tell me about it," Val said. She rubs her stomach. "Look!" she said grabbing Ro's hand. "You feel that?"

Romelle's hand is placed on the side of her stomach. He stands there with his hand on her bare belly. "Oh my god. I feel it. He's kicking you." He feels the imprints of the kicks and see's Val's stomach move as her skin is stretched out like the baby is trying to break free. "Whoa! Look at that!" Ro is amazed at how Val's stomach moves and stretches. Her belly becomes a ball of commotion—-Life moving from within in radical waves of synchronous movements.

"I need to talk to you about something Val. Let's go over to the couch so you can prop your feet up." Val grabs Valerie and helps her up.

The clock chimes at the stroke of seven. Partly cloudy skies shows the sun peeking through. The elderly couple across the street sit in their rockers as they soak up what's left of the day. There are little birds playing in Val's yard. Weeds are displayed across her lawn. She has not been able to restart her lawn service since the non-essential order went into effect.

"What do you need to talk to me about?" Val asked.

"Well... Us. I don't know what's going on with you and your husband, and I don't want to pry, but I need to know how we are going to do this?" He sits on the edge of the sofa with his hands clasped together, his legs wide.

Val sits attentive, with her legs up on the chase. Her hands are clasped together and sit restfully on her stomach. "Yeah, I know. This isn't fair to you, and I'm sorry I haven't been honest with you about my marriage." She rests her head against the chase and lets out a long sigh. She glances up at the ceiling. "I don't really have any answers about my marriage right now. I'm honestly trying to focus on the baby right now, you know?" She turns to look at Ro. "It's weird saying anything now because I'm still pregnant."

"I get it," Ro replies. "Well, I want to help with my baby as much as possible. It would be better if we were in the same house. I know this may be a strange question, but I want to know if ya'll can spend the night with me at my apartment? Just for a few weeks or so. That way I can be there to help you and also help with the baby and our daughter."

Valerie turns to look at her belly. Her black sundress once was a dress to wear outside. She wraps her hands around her stomach and rocks her body slightly from side to side. She soothes her baby, with gentle-calming motions of love. I want to tell him what I've decided. But not until I've spoken with Rick. He is my husband, she thought. And he deserves to know first...

Chapter 24

He places his hand on her stomach that sits so round and plump in front of his face. "Hey son, this is your father," Romelle begins. He grabs and holds Val's stomach. His lips touches her bare skin with soft, sweet pecks. "I love you son, and I can't wait for you to get here. You have a whole world waiting on you out here, and I'm gonna show you everything. I'll teach you how to play basketball and how to tie your shoes," Ro continues. "I'll teach you how to drive a car and how to tie your tie. I'll help you when it comes to dating girls and teach you what not to say. I'll teach you how to treat them right, and I'll teach you all about using protection. I'll teach you how to shave your beard and how to line yourself up too. I'll be there when you walk across the graduation stage and when you get your first job.

Val stands there in front of Ro as he continues to kneel in front of her talking to the baby. This is endearing. He really is the sweetest person I've ever met in my life. Missing out on my pregnancy with Nairobi must feel like torture to him. I can't imagine what he's going through. But I will definitely make sure he's there for our delivery. Her thoughts run away with her as he continues to talk to and kiss her belly.

She braces herself with both hands on her back. She stares out the window while Ro continues to caress her belly. Forty-seven degrees is not that warm, but it's better than old man winter striking. It's eleven in the morning, and Val can't seem to find a bird flying anywhere. She notes storm clouds gathering on the horizon. That's odd, I thought the forecast called for sunny skies today. I guess I was wrong.

"I feel So weak," she said, with labored breaths. She can barely get a sentence out without having to take a break. Why is everything so blurry? Valerie steps to the side, holding the bottom of her stomach--careful, so that Ro could get up without bumping into her stomach.

My head pounds and my knees are killing me, she thought. At thirty-four weeks, all she can think about is having the baby and having her body back to normal.

"Hey, what's wrong babe?" Ro asked, his hazel eyes fixed on hers with concern. "Are you alright?"

"Yeah. I just need to sit down," she replies, reaching for the sofa. She has been sleeping on the sofa ever since the doctor put her on bed rest. It was too much stress on her body to keep climbing the stairs.

"Let me get you bottled water. You seem hot." Romelle helps Val down on the sofa and goes to the kitchen. "You want some fruit? I can bring you a bowl of grapes too if you want."

"Sure," Valerie replies. "Just make sure you wash them off first, please." Val rests her head back. Her body feels exhausted, and she hasn't made it through the afternoon. "I can't take nothing for this headache, but if my head keeps pounding like this, I'm gonna take something for it. I don't care," she said, massaging her temples.

"Here you go." Romelle hands her bottled water. "Try to relax and get some rest. That might help your head feel better."

"Thanks," she replies as she twists off the cap. She drinks the water down in large gulps.

"You were really thirsty, huh?"

"Very," she replies, as she hands him back the bottle. She grabs the bowl of grapes from him and places it on top of her belly. "Can you close the drapes too?"

Ro closes the drapes. The room becomes much darker. "Is this better," he asks Val.

"Yes. Much better. I know it's not extremely sunny out. But the little bit of light we do have is killing my eyes."

"Well, I'm about to go set up the baby bed and hang the clothes up in the room. The baby hangers are still in the closet on the shelf, right?" Ro asked.

"Yes. And oh, can you please set up the baby bags and other items on that empty shelf too?"

"Yeah, I got you." Ro kisses Val on her forehead and heads towards the steps. "Hey Val." He turns and looks at her.

"Yea."

"You know I love you right?"

"I know," she replies. She watches him head up the stairs. I love you too, she thought…

Dear Diary,

Ro came over at 10 this morning. He's upstairs working on the baby room. He is so excited about the baby. I would've never imagined this. I love when he talks to the baby every day. He kisses my belly, and it warms me. It's such a good feeling. I can't get over how good of a father he is already, and our baby is not here yet. I know Nairobi is, but to see him with a baby that's not even born yet, well, it's indescribable.

I'm 34 weeks and looking like I'm ready to pop. I'll be 35 weeks in a few days. I've been on bed rest for a while, and I have slept on my couch ever since. I'm grateful that Romelle and Rick have helped me out so much. I didn't need this much help with my first pregnancy. I was not this big, and I was not on restrictions. I still went to school and I worked while I was pregnant.

Nairobi is over at Rick's house. She had been asking to see Noah and Rick for a couple of days. I miss my baby already. I can't wait to see her tomorrow. Rick is more than happy to get her any day for me. When he called and found out how sick I was feeling yesterday, he finished up with one of his online courses he teaches at the University, and he drove right over here. He's lucky is able to work from home because although colleges are closed, he can still take his campus classes online. But it's still a lot of work for him because he already has two online courses he teaches.

COVID-19 numbers are increasing daily, and so are the death tolls. People can't even visit their loved ones in the hospital if they get sick. I hear that husbands can't visit their spouses in the hospital when the wife gives birth. I truly hope that changes in the next couple of weeks. Romelle will curse somebody out if they don't let him see his child being born. Cutting the umbilical cord is all he talks about. We are not married, so I pray it's not an issue for him to be there with me.

If I could tell another woman in my predicament anything, it would be this... I never thought that one night of being unfaithful to my husband would lead me down this road. Not only a broken marriage but a baby that I created from that one night. This is a difficult and quite embarrassing situation, to say the least. Here I am, pregnant with someone else's baby. We created one life almost five years ago. And here we are in 2020, having another baby and I'm not married nor in a relationship with him. Don't make the same mistake as me. Don't let one night cost you a broken home. Don't let your love for one person go on forever. Close that door. Make peace with it and move on.

Yeah, I know many men get caught cheating over and over again, and their woman forgives them. We see it with rappers, singers, sports athletes, actors, and with our politicians too. But how many men are willing to forgive a woman? Women are called sluts, hoes, and floozy and tramps. But what do I see men call other men that cheat on their wives? They get called players, playboys, and pimps. They are looked at very differently than women. Yeah, you may think I'm lucky. But I'm not. They both have forgiven me. But the question is, have I forgiven myself?

~Val

The sky is darkening, and the storm clouds begin to roll in. Val is asleep on the sofa. The church bells of the clock strike two. Val awakes out of her sleep. As she slowly begins to open her eyes, her lids blink as she adjusts to the sight in front of her. Romelle is laid across her floor beneath her. His body lays in a peaceful state. He looks so peaceful. I don't wanna wake him, but I do have to use the bathroom.

The armrest becomes Val's leaning post as she rocks and scoots herself towards the edge of the sofa. She leans over on the armrest and pulls herself up. She steps lightly pass Romelle—Her cautious steps towards the bathroom is calculated.

As she passed by the kitchen, she looks out her sliding glass doors and notes how the wind bustles about with force. The vigorous blow of the wind sways the tree branches from side to side—the thrusting wind whistles upon her windows as it begs to be let in.

Val turns left and opens the bathroom door. The tiled floor is cold upon her bare feet. Her body begins to cool. As she washes her hands, Val glances into the mirror. She splashes water upon her warm face. The coolness travels down her body with delight. Val dries her hands and pulls the door open.

The house is silent, and the rooms feel empty. There are no children rustling upstairs. No thumping of feet running down the stairs. No one yelling her name.

She opens the freezer door. As the cool breeze blows out of the freezer, Val stands frozen, her head enjoys the cool breeze. She closes her eyelids and enjoys the moment of serenity. This feels so good, she thought. She pulls the ice cream from the freezer and then walks over and pulls open the silverware drawer...

"Ouch!" She drops the ice cream carton on the floor and grabs the bottom of her stomach with both hands. "Oucccch," she screams. The unnerving pain throbs as she stands patiently waiting on the pain to subside. She takes deep, mindful breaths in and blows them out her mouth slowly. She wipes her warm forehead as the pain eases up. That was terrible. "We're ok baby. Momma's here," she said sweetly as she rubs her round belly.

The cold ice cream tingles Val's tongue. "Ummm," she said, as she takes a spoonful in her mouth. Clips of news feed about the Coronavirus comes across her phone as she scrolls through pics on her social media timeline...

Stay home, Stay safe challenge. Don't give up, keep going after your dreams. My thoughts on COVID-19. Don't forget to practice self-care during this pandemic.

So many people are staying productive. She loves the positive vibes that come across her timeline. Social media posts have given many people a way to stay connected. A way to communicate and to send positive messages of hope.

The phone line rings on the other end. Valerie waits for her brother to pick up his phone.

"Hello."

"Hey Jr! How are you," Val said.

"I'm good lil sis. What about you?"

"I'm ok. I miss you brother. I wish you were here." Val takes another spoonful of ice cream.

"I miss you too girl. How are you feeling? You still experiencing nausea or pain?"

Val has kept her brother up-to-date on how she has been doing almost every day since she's been on bed rest. "Well, I still get a lil nauseated from time to time. And I'm still chewing heartburn relief tablets like it's candy." She was afraid to tell him about the pains in her stomach because she knows it will cause him to worry. There is no cause for alarm, she told herself. She just wanted him home.

"Alright, let me know if anything changes."

"Okay," she replies. "What's that noise in the background?"

"That's just the TV. I got this old murder, death, kill movie on," he said laughing.

"Yeah. Never was my cup of tea."

"I know. You always hated my movies. Pissed you off when dad told you to let me watch my movies, and if you didn't want to watch it to go to your room." He chuckles echo through the phone.

"That wasn't funny then, and it's not now. You should've let me watch my—."

"Val... Sis?" Mark waits for a response.

Val breaths heavily through the phone.

"Sis, are you ok?" Mark said. His voice sounds anxious with concern.

"I'm here bro."

"What happened?"

"Nothing. I just bit my tongue eating this ice cream," she lies.

Chapter 25

Valerie takes a bath towel out of the linen closet and walks into the restroom. Most of her items are downstairs now. She pours the bubble bath into the water. The steam fogs up the mirrors. She grabs a scrunchie and pulls her natural hair back into a ponytail. She pulls her dress off and places it on the back of the door. Her leg raises slowly as she enters the water. Her body submerges into the hot water with grace. Val takes her rag and drains the water over her stomach. She rubs her stomach with each splash. The bubbles encircle her body. Soft music is playing in the background. Just light enough not to disturb Romelle. She lays her head back as she feels her body relax. The tension in her head begins to subside. She hears the chimes of the clock. I hope that clock doesn't wake him up.

Your dad thinks you're a boy. But I don't know what I think. I'm always so confused. My thoughts are always scrambled. But the one thing I do know is that I love you. I feel so stupid, she thought. She loads more bubbles onto her round belly. What was I thinking that night? Why did he look so damn good? Why did he smell so damn good? Lord why? Thoughts fill her mind rapidly.

I know why? Because I never got over him. I never expected him to come walking back into my life. I'm so scared...

She sniffs as tears roll down her cheeks. The guilt of having a baby outside her marriage taunts her. Conflicting thoughts of loving her baby, yet knowing how the baby was conceived, is the guilt that she lives with every day.

"Ochh!" Val grabs her stomach. Billows of air are forced out her mouth. "Ouchhhhh!" The tightness intensifies more the second time. She cries; her emotions, her pain, her guilt is all too much for Val to disgust right now. "This is too much Lord," she cries out. "I can't take this, I can't take it," she cries...

A soft knock at the door is muffled by the soft music and Valerie's cries. The door swings open slightly. Still, Val continues sobbing.

"Baby, what's wrong?" Ro says as he enters the bathroom.

Val's shoulders are hunched over, her hands cover her entire face. She continues to sob even more.

Romelle bends down on the tiled floor next to the tub. He hesitates to touch Val. Her vulnerable state, her naked body seems to make him take extra precautions. Romelle gently reaches over and grabs her hands. "Baby, I overheard you crying. I don't mean to pry. But please tell me what's wrong." He kneels on the ground, pleading with Valerie until she opens her eyes.

"I... I-I feel so stupid," she finally says.

"Why? About what?"

The music continues to play in the background—Mary J. Blige's, Love No Limit, serenades through the speakers. The bubbles have all disappeared, and scented candles fill the air with a warm vanilla scent.

"About everything, Ro. About you. About me. About our baby!" she cries. "I was married. I had a family, and I broke us all up. It's all my fault!" she yells.

"It's not your fault," Ro says, as he places his hand on her face and wipes her eyes. "It was my fault. I should've known. I never asked you any questions." Ro continues. "I knew it was too good to be true. No way you had waited for me. I should've never made love to you that night. But I wanted you. I missed you. I missed us."

"No," she replies. It's not your fault. I was stupid. I was stupid because I knew from the moment I saw you that I still loved you. That I still wanted you. And now look—one night. Just one, and we have a baby on the way. That was so selfish of me," she continues as the tears stream down her face endlessly. She glances up at him. "Ro, I wanted you. I wanted you then, and I knew it was wrong. I was torn, and I was conflicted. I shouldn't have let it get this far. Now, I messed up your life. Rick's life. Noah's and Nairobi's life too. Everybody's life," she exclaims. "I can't help it."

"Don't say that Val," he says. He lifts her chin with his hand. "Val, you didn't mess up my life. You're the best part of it. You gave me Nairobi. And you're giving me my son, well I think it's a son," he adds. "There is no other woman for me. Ever. I love you and there's nothing you can do to change that." Ro's eyes fill with water as he continues to talk. "You're the only one for me," he said as he gazes into her eyes.

"I love you Ro," she finally says.

Romelle grabs her head and plants it on his chest. His arm wraps around her. Tears from his eyes fall upon Valerie's face warmly. "I love you too," he whispers.

After a moment of calmness has come over Val, she reaches her head up and gestures towards her towel. "Can you let my water out please?"

Ro reaches for the stopper and then grabs her towel off the rack. His tall frame looms over her and pulls her up out of the tub, careful not to let her fall. He takes her towel and begins to dry her off.

It's the first time that Valerie has been naked in front of him since that night. As she stands there with water dripping from her body, from her nipples, and down every curve of her body, she feels a sense of protection. She likes that he is drying her off. She stands in the middle of the floor with her stomach hanging out in the air as Romelle makes his way around her body.

"Thank you Ro," she smiles.

"No need to thank me." His hazel eyes glazes over her beauty. "I love your body, and I love your beauty." He tries to wrap the towel around her body but to no avail. Val lets the towel fall to the floor.

He smiles as he continues to stare at Val. The soft music playing glides their bodies together. He takes his tee-shirt off and flings it to the ground. He rocks her from side to side, as Anita Baker's song, Angel, plays in the background. He looks down at Valerie, gazing at her lips. "Can I?" he asks.

She says nothing. She slowly leans up on her feet, as Ro begins to meet her halfway—His arms stretch around her body. She feels the soft sensation of his lips travel all through her veins.

His tender touch as he clasps her chin. His gentle caress calms her spine. As she continues to rock in motion, she feels his tongue meet hers. They lock in a connection that only the two of them will ever know.

He was her best friend. The only person she told about her rape and impeding abortion from that rape. He always treated her like the love of his life. She shared things with him that she had never told a soul. He was her soulmate. He was her first love. He was her destiny. The only thing that stopped them from being one was Valerie's past, which crippled her ability to speak her truth. Going after her first love when he left for the military, instead of running away from him, is an ebbing pain that won't go away. Expressing to him her love and hiding the truth about their daughter was a mistake. Noting worse than having a love that was meant for you but letting it go without a fight.

Her naked body rocks in synchronous motion as Ro guides her to the rhythm of the song. She turns around slowly in the direction of Ro's hand. She leans her back up against his chest as he wraps his arm around her chest, and he wraps the other hand under her stomach to help give her support. She enjoys being in the moment. Just living in the moment of peace and serenity. Thunder rolls in the distance as the storm rolls in...

"Ouchhhh!" Val cripples downward towards the floor as she holds her stomach.

"VAl! What's wrong!" Romelle walks over in front of her.

"Ouuu. Ouuu. Ouuu," she says over and over again.

"Look, we need to get you to the doctor," he insists.

"No, I'm fine. I'll be ok. Just help me to the couch." She feels her knees buckle. The pain is much worse than earlier. She doesn't understand what's going on. But she thinks the pain will cease when she sits down to relax.

Ro grabs her dress off the hook and walks her out of the bathroom. His arm holds her up. "Here, let me put this on you."

Val reaches her hands up to slip her dress on...

"Nooo! Romelle!" she screams. She is hunched over, both palms to the floor.

"What's wrong! Val, tell me." He glances down to the floor. "Val, what's that?" he asked. His eyes are wide as Val looks up at him.

"My water, It just broke!" A warm gush of water flows down her legs and onto the floor.

4:35 pm

Romelle drives fifteen minutes to the hospital. When Valerie called her doctor, she told her to go straight in. Ro grabs her bags by the front door and helps her gently into the car. She is in anguish most of the way there. "Romelleeeee," she screams.

"We almost there Babe," He reassures her as he grabs her left hand. "We'll be there shortly. Hang in there. He drives what seems like forever, but he gets her there in one piece. The storm was in full force. There were trees knocked down and branches sprawled across busy streets. Traffic lights were turned into four-way stop signs.

Val holds on to her truck handle as Romelle speeds his way through traffic. Even though traffic is light, Val feels like there are too many cars on the road. "Oh my god! Ro, hurry!" She pants her breath in short bursts of air. She breaths in deeply and blows out the air in slow spurts. Her seat is pushed back and reclined at a seventy-degree angle, which allows her room between her stomach and the dashboard.

"I feel the baby's head Ro," she said with a weak tone. She can't stop the flow of tears that streams down her face. "I can't take it. The pain!" she shouts. "The pain! Stop the pain, Ro, Please" Val squeezes his hand tight.

"Hold on," Ro said as he wipes her face. "This really about to happen? I'm bout to have a baby!" Ro said in a low whisper. His tone is feeble—Nerves give way to the reality that Val is having his child. He glances over at Valerie constantly as he tries to drive and observe her every move. Water trickles down the side of his face. He wipes his forehead with the backside of his hand and grabs Val's hand once more. "Are you hot? It's hot in here," he said before Val could answer. He cracks his window. Gusty winds creep their way into the jeep. "Drive, you idiot!" he explodes with anger as he sounds his horn. "Sorry, babe. I didn't mean to yell. Keep breathing in and out slowly," He says as he rubs her belly in a circular motion.

"His head," she yells. "I feel it! I gotta push!" Mother nature forces the baby downward. The natural urge to push causes Val to bear down while she is still in the truck.

The parking lot is full when Ro reaches the hospital. He dashes out the truck and calls for a wheelchair. He grabs Val and lifts her out of the truck.

Val sits in the wheelchair holding her stomach as the elevator doors close. The hospital staff had taken their temperatures and had given them both face masks as soon as they entered the hospital. The pandemic changed the trajectory of life as the world knew it in just a small amount of time. A small ding sounds, fifth floor, the number on the elevator glows. As the elevator comes to a halt, Romelle follows beside Val as the nurse rushes her over to a labor and delivery room.

The nurse helps lift Valerie on the bed. "We got the call from your Dr. Gray, who informed us you were on your way in. So how many weeks are you Mrs. Augustine?" the nurse asked as she grabs a gown from the cabinet.

"I'm... I'm, thirty-four and a half weeks," she said with labored breaths.

"Here, let's get this gown on you," the nurse said.

Romelle lifts Val up from the bed. He slides her dress over her body. Then he snaps the gown on around her. "Go ahead and lay down," he instructs Val. He lifts her up from one side and slides her panties off.

"Mrs. Augustine, I need to ask you a few questions," the nurse Daniels begins. Give me your full name and date of birth please.

"Valerie Augustine."

"How old are you?"

"Twenty-four," she replies. Her twenty-fifth birthday was less than two months away.

"How many pregnancies have you had?"

"Three." Val glances at the long hand on the clock. Five twenty-six. She watches as the second-hand goes around and around. The room birthing suite is equipped with a baby monitor, a baby bed, a rocking chair, and all sorts of hospital equipment. The room smells of sanitizer—freshly cleaned and freshly mopped. She hears faint cries of newborn babies being delivered. She knows that sound very well. I was here at this same hospital when Nairobi was born, she thought. She closes her eyes as she feels another contraction coming.

"And how many births, Mrs. Augustine?" the nurse asked.

"One,"she replies slowly, as she breaths through another contraction.

Another nurse walks into the room and goes to the sink to wash her hands. "Hi, I'm Nurse Hathaway, the head nurse here, and I'm going to see how far along you are." With a face mask and blue gloves on, she begins to check Valerie's cervix. "You sure she's just thirty-four and a half weeks?"

"Yes, that's what her chart says," nurse Daniels replies. Her box braids are pulled back into a bun.

"Wow, you must have a big baby in there!" the nurse said, with a warm smile.

Ro stands there next to Val, holding her hand. His arm flexes as Val squeezes his hand tighter and tighter.

"Sir, are you the father?" The head nurse asks as she looks at Romelle.

"Yes, I am," Ro replies.

"Ok, I need you to step outside."

"Why?" Valerie asks panicking.

"We have to protect you and the baby. We are asking everyone to understand that with this pandemic, we can't afford to jeopardize the mother or the baby," she replies.

"Nooo," Val starts to scream. She grabs Romelle's arm tight. "Please don't put him out, please!" she yells.

"Look, I'm in the military. I didn't get to see our firstborn delivered," Ro begins. "I need to be here for her this time. I need to see my baby delivered. I need this!" he exclaims with emotions. "I need to cut the cord."

"Thank you for your service," the nurse said with an honorable salute. I also served for twelve years.

"Ouchhhhh!" Valerie screams. She yanks on Ro's hand with a solid grip.

"Ok, don't push. The baby's head is right there," Nurse Hathaway exclaims. "She's fully dilated," nurse Hathaway exclaims to the other nurse.

The nurses scurry as they prepare to deliver the baby. A rush of nurses fills the room, and the Doctor runs in, calling for stats.

Dr. Gray scrubs vigorous friction under the warm water. The suds cover her arms and hands. She grabs her mask and blue gloves out of the box on the wall. She is gowned and walks right over to Val. "You ready to have this baby?"

Val nods as she blows out a breath slowly. She can barely see her doctor over her round belly from her angle.

"Sir, I need you to help her hold her legs back please, as she pushes."

Romelle grabs the back of Val's leg. He grips her hand with the other. He gazes into Val's oval eyes. "You about to have my baby," he says with a smile.

"Bare down and push on your next contraction," Dr. Gray said.

The nurses stand at their stations. Everyone ready to perform their duties when the baby arrives. They didn't have to wait long. Valerie pushed three times, and on the third push, the baby was out.

"A healthy baby boy," Dr. Gray said, as she lifts the screaming baby up.

The warmness of his body upon her bare skin feels soothing—Tears stream down her face like a running faucet. "My baby," Valerie said softly.

"Look at my son!" Romelle said with a wide smile. "He got my mole just above his left eyebrow. Wow! I have a junior." He rubs the baby back as he feels the touch of a newborn for the first time. "You did good baby." He leans down and kisses Val on her lips, as tears streams down his face. Looking into her eyes, "I love you so much!" Thank you. Thank you for giving me my son," he said with tears upon his face. He leans in, closes his hazel eyes, and kisses her with the sweetest kiss.

Valerie's heart melts as she feels his love unfurls like the depth of an ocean. She feels his warm touch on her face as their lips continue to lock with a soft caress. "I love you beyond eternity," she whispers to Romelle.

"You want to cut the cord dad?" Dr. Gray stands there with scissors in hand.

"Yes!" Romelle smiles as he grabs the scissors and cut in between the clamps. The look on his face is priceless.

Val's ability to give birth naturally is stunning. With no meds and with no outside help from the use of a vacuum, forceps, or the use of an amniotic hook, she was amazing. Giving birth made her feel happy.

Romelle Junior's body lay warm on her breast. The skin-to-skin contact soothes and comports him. With tears still rolling down her warm cheeks, she smiles at her son and kisses him over and over again. "I love you always Junior," she said in a low voice. "Ouchhhh!" Valerie screams.

"VALERIE!" Romelle screams out.

Epilogue

New York City

She sits at a coffee house sipping coffee. She slides the man sitting across from her a picture. No ring on his left hand. His clean, slender face looks to be about twenty-five. His low tapered fade accentuated his deep burnt umber eyes. His dimples are attractive.

"Mother was a great woman. A great mother," she opens up. "She used to make the best strawberry pancakes for me when I was a little girl. And she never once missed reading me a bedtime story and tucking me in at night." She wipes away a lonely tear that has fallen from the corner of her eye. The sun is brightly beaming down onto her slender face as the cool breeze blows slightly past her bronzed skin.

"I remember she used to let me pick my clothes out, and she would iron them. I would help her change the house decorations from one season to the next. When I wanted cupcakes, she would pour cupcake batter into the mixing bowl, and I would pour the milk, and I stirred it until my hands went numb." She gave a faint smile. Her dimple on her left cheek shows deeply upon her face. She scratches her left eyebrow, just below her mole. "We were a team."

"Whatever happened to your father?"

"After mother's passing, I remember my dad & Step-dad sitting in our living room talking. Talking for a long time," she continues. "Rick hands my father a letter, which at that time had no meaning to me. Well, not until I got much older. I was still so young, but seeing my dad break down." She takes a deep breath.

"Seeing my dad breakdown the way he did after reading that note inside the white envelop still makes me cry to this day. That's a day I will always remember."

She turns her head towards the street, watching the hustle and bustle of commuters going by. A city bus stops to pick up the passengers waiting at the bus stop across the street from her. The street is lined with people moving along—cyclers zoomed past her in a hurry. Everyone is bustling without a care in the world. The world just keeps moving along. Time never stands still.

She smells the coffee freshly brewing inside the coffee house. I should go in and grab another cup. A tear rolls down her face. She takes a deep breath in and blows it out slowly. Turning back to the journalist who was recording her every word on his tape recorder, she sighs. "My father cried heavily at the funeral," she continues. "Not too long after, the twins and I went to stay with him.

"Oh, where was that?" The Journalist asks.

"We stayed in an apartment, but not far too long. Daddy bought a house—A house big enough for all four of us."

"Do you still see or hear from Rick?" Mr. Ottis asks.

"Yes, it's wonderful having two fathers. I could see him and Noah anytime I missed them. Noah still keeps in touch too. He still lives in Michigan —An E. R. Doctor at a trauma hospital in Metro Detroit."

"That's wonderful. What about your brothers?"

"My brothers are both living in California, finishing their final year of college and Playing basketball. They both have dreams of going pro."

"Nice! Where do you think they'll go?"

"Well... Romelle Jr. wants to play for the Lakers. You know... Be like his favorite player, Kobe Bryant."

"And Ronelle wants to play for his favorite team—The Detroit Pistons."

The journalist nods his head in satisfaction. "And you?"

She smiles—bright as the sunny powder-blue sky they were sitting underneath. Her dark curly hair rests softly upon her thin shoulders. She glances at her smartwatch on her dainty wrist. "Well... I'm a Psychologist here in New York," she finally answers, as she looks up at Mr. Ottis. "I counsel women and young girls who have endured childhood trauma."

"Seems like you all turned out just fine, Nairobi." He gazes at her fondly.

Her cheeks redden. "Yes, just fine indeed."

The Journalist glances down at the table. "Is that the letter you brought me," he says, gesturing towards the white envelope lying beside Nairobi's hand.

Val reaches down into a bag sitting on the ground next to her. She pulls a purple journal out of her bag. "Yes," she replies, as she glides the letter and the journal over to him.

"He opens the white envelope and pulls out a letter."

March 29, 2019

Dear Nairobi,

I am writing this letter to you. Rick and your father Romelle, just in case something happens to me. With this pandemic, I'm scared to death of getting sick. People are dying by the thousands. I have severe headaches. I'm always nauseous, and the sharp pains in my stomach are overwhelming me with anxiety. On top of that, I have preeclampsia, but I'm too early to deliver—The baby is at a greater risk of death and need more time to develop.

I cry every night, knowing that there is a possibility that my baby won't survive or that I can potentially get infected by Coronavirus.

Romelle was in-love with you from the first moment he saw you. And when he discovered we were pregnant, he was thrilled. He wanted to do everything with me; go to every doctor's appointment, buy a crib and a baby car seat too. He brought so many clothes, diapers, and wipes that there is no need to have a baby shower. He is elated to have a baby. You can see the sun every time he smiles. He said there's no way he would miss the birth this time. The thought of being there to cut the cords is all he can think of.

If I don't make it, I want you to know I have truly enjoyed watching you grow. I truly enjoyed being your mother pumpkin. I love you Nairobi. I love you more than words can say— beyond eternity. This world was nothing until I had you.

If I don't survive this, tell my baby I love him, and I wish I could've had more time. But I will always be there in spirit, smiling at everything my children do. Children are a blessing, and if I had to, I wouldn't change anything. Sometimes mothers may not understand why certain things happen. But having a baby is the best gift that God can give you.

Please tell your father that I will always love him-- beyond eternity. And anytime he sees a bird to think of me, and know that it was God's plan to set me free— Now I can truly spread my wings and fly free.

P.S. When you get older, tell my story—Take my journal and write it in a book—Flaws and all. Leave nothing out. I want to share My Life Without You, so that you will always know how much I really do love you Nairobi. I trust that you will put it in the right hands.

With Eternal Love,

~Val

{Always and forever your mother}

Author's Note to Reader

Redemption & Forgiveness

My Life Without You is not about hating or loving a character. In this story, we find a woman who is torn between two men. Both men play a major role in her life that you cannot erase. Valerie was created to speak on topics that are not always easy to speak on or acknowledge.

Before judging the main character, what do I see when I write her story? I see a woman that has humanistic flaws.

In a world where we are judged by many things including; the color of our skin, our sexual orientation, and by the choices we make in life, people's flaws are the first thing we see and immediately judge. I love to see people overcome their challenges, flaws, and most importantly their past.

I could have written the story from a different perspective (the husband cheating), which has been told a thousand times. However, this story is not about accepting infidelity from men because we assume that this is what men do. It is not about creating a story of bashing men for being unfaithful, but instead about one woman's journey of forgiveness, both with herself and with others.

Women are judged harshly for being unfaithful, but in our society today, it is not uncommon for women to forgive their husbands for cheating, even when it leads to him having a baby outside his marriage.

Both men and women have their flaws, and all people need help overcoming trials, tribulations, hurt, and temptation.

There will always be a victim, victimizer, or the person that has stood by and judged others for their flaws?

We live in a society that oftentimes, we hear about infidelity and immediately judge. I did not want to write a story of a husband's infidelity—We've read it too many times in books or in the tabloids or splattered across television screens. This novel is not to bash a man or a woman, but to understand one's choices to forgive.

Rick has forgiven his Valerie, instead of closing to condemn her forever for her flaws? Life is about forgiveness.

Remember the song by India Ire: Wings of forgiveness? This song was perfect for this story and spoke to the themes of redemption & forgiveness. I felt there was no other choice to be made when choosing a song that embodies the messages of this story. So thank you Ms. India Ire for blessing us with such a strong-powerful & beautiful song.

Rick has forgiven Val... And Val has forgiven herself.

We must take the time to heal...Forgive yourself & forgive someone else.

The message to forgive is deep and powerful. Only some are able to truly master the gift of forgiveness Forgiving others but also forgiving one's self. Forgive and be healed.

~Adrienne Edwards

Reading Group Questions

Remember, every person is entitled to their own opinion and have drawn their own perspective. Please respect each other's opinions and have fun conversing.

1.   The title of this novel is called *My Life Without You*. Why do you think the author chose this title?

2.   Valerie Augustine is the main character. What similarities/differences do you see in the story if the roles were reversed?

3.   What were your first thoughts about Val, Rick, and Romelle? Do you have those same feelings at the end of the story?

4.   The pier was mentioned as a place Val visited twice. What symbolic message(s) do you see?

5.   Rick seemed like the perfect husband at the beginning of the story. When did you see signs that he also had humanistic flaws?

6.   Val experienced childhood trauma in her life. How does this significantly impact and play a role in her decision making in her adult life?

7. What similarities/differences do you see between Val and her mother?

8. Val initially judged her mother for staying in her marriage. After Val's mother explained why she stayed, do you believe this had a positive impact on Val's outlook on her mother and marriage? Why or why not?

9. Explain how any character may have been valid or invalid on judging another charters flaws.

10. What were your thoughts after Val's brother disclosed his infidelity in his marriage? Do you believe the conversation helped Valerie? Why or why not?

11. Val decided not to stay in her marriage. Why do you think she decided to leave?

12. When Val finally made her mind up for who she chose, who do you think she picked; Rick, Romelle, or herself?

13. The author listed redemption and forgiveness as themes in the story. What other themes do you see?

14. What gender biases did you see in this story? Do you see them in our society today?

15. If the roles were reversed, do you think the wife would forgive her husband and stay?

Acknowledgements

There were many moments in 2020 that had derailed my writing. The world was hit by a pandemic. We lost a basketball icon, Kobe Bryant whom I watched when he first entered the world of NBA. The world came together again for yet another uprising march for equal rights for Blacks, while many people and companies stood in solidarity for, Black Lives Matter Movements to end police injustice. All this happened in one year, and in the same year, I started my Doctoral program. Through those dark moments, I had someone cheering for me and supporting my dreams as a writer.

My husband, Antonio, stood by my side, read my manuscript, helped me with our boys, and was an ever-present support for me both mentally and emotionally. Thank you for being more than enough. Thank you for being my sounding board and the love of my life.

To my ideal readers; Antonio, Ileena, and Stephanie. I appreciate your countless hours of combing through my manuscript and giving me feedback on my characters. I know that I took you on a roller coaster ride of emotions, but without your honesty and reliability, I would not be where I am today. Thank you for all of your support.

To Junior. Thank you for your patience. Thank you for allowing me to be a part of your world. I am proud to be your mom.

To my readers, thank you for your support and thank you for allowing me to enter your minds with a world full of possibilities. See you in the next novel.

About the Author

Adrienne L. Edwards

Adrienne Edwards self-published her first short story collection, "Broken Into Pieces," in 2014.

Edwards has her Bachelor of Arts in English Literature, her Master's of Arts degree in English and Creative Writing with a concentration in Fiction.

She stays in the Metropolitan area of Detroit with her loving husband and children. She loves teaching and mentoring young women. She is also an entrepreneur that enjoys helping writers become published authors.

Stay in-touch with the author:

Website: www.adrienneedwardsauthor.com

Email: contact@adrienneedwardsauthor.com

Social Media handles:

Facebook: Adrienne Edwards

Instagram: adrienne_edwards_author

Upcoming Story
Mirror Image

The air is heavy with emotions ready to unfurl at a moment's notice. "Black Lives Matter! Black Lives Matter! Black Lives Matter! That's all you hear these days. I'm quit sick of it, if you ask me. I'm tired of these black people thinking that their lives is the only one that matters." The lady sitting on the first row chuckles with the man sitting next to her. Her curly blonde hair reached the small of her back. Her thin frame sat upright in her chair as she continued to talk without conviction or discretion. It was as if she owned the whole court room——She spoke with an air of confidence.

Who is she? The court room is crowded with people everywhere. As I turned around, I saw many of my friends, neighbors, and even my co-workers standing in the back. They arrived an hour ago, but of course, the family and friends of the white officer who locked my son up, fills the whole right side of the room. Twenty minutes before I can see my sixteen-year-old son walk out those doors. Hopefully, he's not in cuffs. I don't know if I can take seeing him in cuffs again…

Devin, a six-foot one, two hundred and thirty-seven pound, offensive tackle for Malcom X high school and is well known in the city of Detroit. Girls always throw themselves at him.

Simply put, he's a ladies man, that has a reputation for his tough-boy exterior.

Devin never backs down from any fights either—He didn't always start them, but he always finished them. His mother, Emani, doesn't understand why anyone would want to try her son. She doesn't understand that that was just the nature of the beast, living in a hood, riddled with gangs.

"Devin is no saint, but he didn't rob that electronic store. Another black kid, wearing a hoodie, hanging with his friends, in the wrong place at the wrong time," Emani whispers to her mother.

Carol sat quietly, patiently waiting to see her grandson Devin walk out the doors to the left of her. She glances up every ten seconds, waiting to see the guards usher her only grandchild out, hopefully for the last time. It's been a long time since she had him home with her. Twelve and a half months to be exact. She had gone to every last one of his trials with her daughter Emani. Her golden age, and frail body, left her feeling exhausted most of the time. But she never let that stop her from showing up for her Baby D.—That's what Carol called him when he was a baby. Although, he towers her five foot-one statue, he's still her Baby D…

"Momma, what time is it?" Emani asked her mother. She of course had to leave her phone in the car since cellphones were not allowed in the courtroom.

Carol looks down and pushes her sweater sleeve up over her watch, "It's 8:56," Carol responds.

"Okay, they should be getting started in a few minutes." Emani's pencil blue skirt comes just above her knees. Devin's face is displayed on a button that sits on the left side of Emani's white blazer. "My stomach is growling," she whispers to her boyfriend Ryan.

Ryan sat very calm, but his stocky body is intimidating and usually made people around him uneasy. "I told you to grab something before you got here," he said with haste.

"I know babe," Emani responds under her breath. Her voice barely above a whisper.

"Well, after you drop your mom off at home, how bout we get something from Coney Island. You feel like a corn beef sandwich and chili cheese fries?"

"Sure." Emani glides her hand up the side of her hair— Laying some loose strands that keeps falling into her face. Her long, natural, loose coils are pulled up into a tight ponytail.

The chatter and commotion in the court room always make Emani nervous. She turns around to look behind her for the umpteenth time. Not sure who she's looking for, but the uneasy feeling of sitting in the courtroom always rattled her nerves— Waiting for her son to come out. Waiting to hear the prosecution and defense team argue back and forth. And she longed to see those horrible handcuffs off of her son and released back to her—It's overwhelming. She covers her eyes and runs them down her slender face as she lets out a slow exhaustive breath. Her eyes are closed; her face is warm with anxiety.

Ryan grabs Emani's hand and clutches it gently. As Emani glances over to Ryan, his eyes stay planted in front of him. No words needed to be said. What was understood, need not be explained…

Emani sighs heavily, as she rests her head gently on Ryan's broad shoulder. She always feels safe in his arms. They'd been together ever since they met six years ago at a concert at Heart Plaza. She had just completed her CNA training and was celebrating with some friends of hers…

The warm summer air and cool breeze feels good flowing through Emani's hair. As she moved to the R & B music, her hips swayed effortlessly to the rhythm of the beat.

"Hey, that guy over there is checking you out girl," Emani's friend, Deonna yells through the intensity of the music blaring over the speakers.

Before Emani has a chance to even respond, Ryan walks right up to her. "Hey! What's your name?"

The scent of Creed Aventus cologne elevates her senses with pleasure. "Emani." Her rose colored cheeks glow from the mixture of nervousness and delight. His white tee-shirt fit snug around his chiseled chest. His muscular biceps protruded just below his sleeves. She couldn't conceal her eyes dancing all over his body as she continues to dance. "What's yours?" she finally responds.

"Ryan. He takes a sip out the red, plastic cup he's holding in his hand. "I like the way you move," he says as his body leans in towards hers.

His bright smile and youthful face distracts her. "I'm sorry, I didn't hear you," she yells over the loud music.

He closes the distance between them. His tall frame towers over her by at least a foot and a half. "I said, I like your dance moves." His voice is deep and husky.

Emani smiles as she looks up at him. "Oh, thanks!" She blushes and waits for him to make the next move, which didn't take too long. She continues to talk to Ryan and danced until her feet hurt. They ended the night exchanging numbers and have been inseparable ever since...

Emani jerks her head up off of Ryan's shoulder as she sits up straight. Her eyes glance over to the door where the guards are unlocking the door that will usher her son out. Her heart pounds rapidly. Her eyebrows knit together with anticipation as she awaits her son. Sweat dribbles down her armpits uncontrollably. The doors are opening, and she catches a glimpse at one male guard approaching the guard inside the courtroom. He whispers something to the tall. Caucasian guard and proceeds to go back to the door. He unlocks the door and disappears.

What is taking them so long to bring my son out? Where is my son? I can't take this much longer. I just want this nightmare to be over. My son has gone through one court date after another. He has been sitting in that jail, behind bars for too long. This court system is horrible! First, he sits in there for eight months before his trial even begins. This so-called justice system really doesn't have any justice for my son. My Black son. They just look at him like he's another black kid on the streets with no money, no common sense, and no parents in his life that cares for him. A hoodlum. But they're wrong. They couldn't be anymore wrong. What ever happened to innocent until proven guilty? Yeah, right! How about, if you're black, you are guilty until proven innocent. No one could've told me in a million years that I would be going through this with my son. I hear countless stories about black males being racially profiled, wrongly accused of crimes they didn't commit, beat and sometimes even murdered from the hands of cops that was too trigger happy. But damn! Here I sit. Another black mother, trying to convince the world that my son did not do what he's accused of. He may be guilty of something alright. Guilty of being black. But not guilty of non-of-these charges they are accusing my son of. I just want a fair trial. A fair, unbiased look into the evidence or the lack there of. A chance for my son to be given fair treatment in this trial. Is that too much to ask for? I want my son to come home. Home with me and momma.

The door locks begin to rattle. It's a moment before the husky guard on the opposite side opens it and steps through. Emani's eyes are glued to the open doorway that hide inmates, otherwise behind closed doors. The courtroom settles down as conversations begin to halt simultaneously. Emani's mother grabs her daughter's hand as they both lay their eyes on Devin. Emani's face becomes flushed as she takes in her son. Her eyes sting as they become wet with tears. She tries to hold them back—She inhales very deeply to calm herself down. She feels the tight grip of both her boyfriend, Ryan, and her mother Carol squeezing her hands…

My son. There he is. I'm over here. Can't he see us? Why isn't he looking back over here yet? Did he see me looking at him when he first came out and scanned the room? It's like he saw right through me. He looks like he's losing a little weight.

Or… Is he gaining more weight? I can hardly tell anymore. He looks so different now. His once trimmed face, now has hair on it. He looks rough. Who's braiding his hair in there? I didn't see him with his hair braided the last time. I guess he wanted a new change. I know this is hard for him. She shakes her head. I don't know if this is harder for me or him. It seems like every time we talk on the phone, he's the one telling me, everything is going to be alright ma, and stop worrying so much. How can I not worry? How can I not stress? He's my son. My only son. Oh, wait, I think I saw him glance over here. Did he see me this time? My mom won't stop tearing up and I can't console her because I don't have the strength. I barely have enough strength for myself. I'm tired of wiping my own eyes. Every time I wipe them, they become wet again. It's just a vicious cycle of never-ending tears the whole time he's been in there.

"I just hope this is coming to a close soon. I can't wait for the jury to find that boy guilty of all charges, lock him behind bars for a long time or just throw away the key permanently," the white lady in the front row said firmly.

The woman bore a striking resemblance to someone, but Emani just can't put her fingers on who. Even the man she sits next to—Her husband presumably…

Her voice sounds so familiar. Where did I see her before? Do I know her? It's like deja vu. I feel like I've been here before all of a sudden. Been here with her—That woman. She needs to shut up. How can she be so rude? How can she just assume she knows what my son did or did not do? How can she be so judgmental? I bet she lives in some suburban neighborhood, with her suburban neighbors, with her perfect little family. I bet she never saw pain or struggles. She's just some uppity white woman with absolutely no clue in what we go through. She just hears a story of a black kid and believes whatever the media says. If she had to walk a mile in my shoes, I bet she wouldn't last a day. I bet she would be begging for mercy for her son. I bet she would be begging for empathy and compassion. I could only hope that one day, people like her will find a way to have some compassion and stop judging people because of what they THINK someone has done. Maybe one day, people like her can stop thinking that all black people are criminals.

"Umph." The woman in the first row, glances across the room and stares at Emani. This was not the first time their eyes met. Ever since this trial began, Emani catches the lady glaring at her from time to time.

What the heck is she looking at? The next time I catch her looking over here at me, I swear I'm going to tell her to go straight to hell. She can sit over there on her side of the court room and keep her eyes off me…

"I love you," Emani mouths silently to her son as she finally catches his glance. "I love you so much son, and I got you." She places her hand over her heart and smiles.

"I love you too, mom," Devin responds as he places his hand over his heart too.

Carol mouths the word, "I love you baby D," just before he turns back around to respond to whatever his lawyer just leaned over and said to him.

Mr. McCall was a middle-aged white man with a small gut that made his suit fit just a little too snug around his midsection.

He's Devin's court appointed lawyer with about four and a half years of experience. A newbie is what Emani and Carol always calls him.

"I wonder what he's saying to him," Emani whispers to Ryan.

"Maybe something that has to do with today's trial," he responds. "I really hope that Devin's attorney work harder on his defense today. Cause last time I wanted to go up there myself and defend him. Heck, I could do a better job than that."

"I know babe," Emani responds. "Me too." She drops her head and clasps her hands together. Emani would give anything to have her son home with her again. To have him free again. Many days she's prayed and asked the powers that be, to release her son. Dear heavenly father, she would begin. But other times, when everything seemed to be crumbling and freedom seemed to be slipping through her sons fingers, she wondered if there was anyone up there listening to her. She wondered had she done something wrong and this was her punishment. She put on a strong face in front of everyone, but truth is, she was crumbling, faith and all, on the inside…

The chamber doors open, "All rise! The honorable judge Kevin Watson presiding…"

Made in the USA
Monee, IL
18 March 2021